TWISTED LIES 4

SEDONA VENEZ

"Some of us think holding on makes us strong, but sometimes, it
is letting go."
—**Hermann Hesse**

❦   I   ❦

SINTHIA

I JOLTED AWAKE, rolling onto the other side of the bed, flipping over onto my stomach, and pressing my face into the pillow. I inhaled Core's scent—amber and sandalwood.

When we'd woken up early this morning, he'd taken me in every part of his master suite and bathroom. And when I'd thought my pussy couldn't take another round of pounding, he'd taken me again while we showered together—me with my legs around his waist, water raining down on us, and him fucking the hell out of me.

Hell... he fucks like a damn stallion.

Granted, I was no stranger to freaking fantastic sex, but this thing with Core felt... different... in ways I didn't understand.

From the first day I'd met him, there had been an instant connection, a spark that tethered me to him. And for weeks, almost every night, I'd crawl into bed with his name on my lips and my trusty and reliable vibrator, Beast, between my thighs. And I'd find myself waking from dreams of Core with needs Beast couldn't fully satisfy. It was embarrassing and problematic because wanting a man who was within my reach that I couldn't have was fucking with my head—big time—until I finally gave myself to him at the McKay Club. Well, technically, I'd had sex with him in his Noire lounge—his private, members-only playground, where the rich and famous indulged in discreet sexual fantasies.

Rolling over onto my back, I kicked off the blanket that had been tangled around my body before swinging my legs off the side of the bed. Trying to clear my sleep-fogged brain, I leaned forward, putting my elbows on my knees and clutching my head. I was exhausted from the last round of sex with Core.

This was way too much. I needed to take a moment to focus on something else besides fucking Core.

Sighing, I sat up before scrubbing my hands over my face.

I stood, deciding to take a hot shower to loosen up my muscles. Walking over to the chair with his black T-shirt draped across it, I picked it up, tugging it over my head. Instantly, I was engulfed in his very virile and masculine scent.

The image of his sexy eyes flashed through my mind.

Yep... he's destroyed me. The cocky but well-hung fucker.

I padded into his impressive master bathroom and spotted all of Core's toiletries lined up and perfectly organized on his marble countertops, as opposed to my stuff that was scattered about, creating a hot, disorganized mess.

He was the poster child for a man who demanded control and dominance, which was everything I deplored in a man... or at least I'd thought I did. But the more time I spent with him, the more confused I became about what I really wanted from our relationship and from him.

Do I want just sex or more?

He was complicated and dangerous with a whole lot of crazy mixed in. Plus, there was something about him that I couldn't quite figure out.

He was like that box of chocolates from *Forrest Gump*. I never quite knew what I was going to get next.

Dominant Core.

Asshole Core.

Caring Core.

Sensual Core.

Or take-no-shit Core...

On the flip side, he was constantly shattering everything I'd expected him to be—cold, narcissistic, and uncaring.

My thoughts drifted to last night when he'd shocked the shit out of me by taking care of me and protecting me when I felt exhausted, mentally and physically, after my townhouse had been broken into. Smoothly, Core had stepped in, taking charge of everything, including calling the police and fielding the barrage of questions from the officers, while I numbly rode a roller coaster of emotions—shock, fear, denial, and anger.

Damn. This shit with Core is uncharted territory for me.

My mind went back to the incident between us this morning when he'd gotten out of bed, tucked the sheets tightly around my body, and then kissed my forehead.

Before he'd walked out of the room, I'd heard him mumble, "Damn. What am I doing? I could get used to this..."

And, silently, I'd agreed.

With feet slapping against the marble floor, I turned on the rain shower, adjusting the temperature to hot.

Am I really thinking about trying to have a... relationship with Core?

My gut started churning with fear.

Breathe, Sin.

Take control of yourself.

There will be no attachments and absolutely no relationship.

Nope. Hard pass on that shit.

I stripped off Core's T-shirt before stepping beneath the showerhead and scrubbing at my skin as the jets beat against my body.

My heart was permanently closed off, and I planned on keeping it that way. Many had tried, and all had failed. Besides, there were just too many sides to Core. Some I knew, and some I suspected he deliberately hid from me. But what I did know was he was smart, savvy, and calculating in everything he did. And when it came down to it, I was his business asset.

And if there was one thing I knew without a doubt, it was that business and sex did not mix. Yet here I was, allowing Core to disassemble me like a fucking toy and remake me into a woman I didn't know. Now I felt exposed in a way that scared the living shit out of me. I hadn't spent the night in a man's bed in forever... yet I had with Core.

Stupid, stupid, stupid. I'm doing everything I swore I'd never do... Get attached.

SINTHIA

INTERNALLY, I was screaming while I quickly washed my body and hair, rinsing away the shampoo and soap. Snatching one of Core's luxurious towels, I dried myself off before leaving the bathroom. After getting dressed, I clasped the silver bracelet Dad had given me for my seventeenth birthday around my wrist before gathering all of my stuff.

When I bolted for the bedroom door, I felt like I was in a burning building and all I could see were the little lit-up red exit signs. "I'm so fucking out of here," I mumbled under my breath while walking out of Core's bedroom with my overnight bag in tow.

"All right. A cup of coffee. Okay, maybe two," I groused while padding down the stairs, "and then I'm getting the hell out of here." Unabashedly, I was never one to forgo coffee in the morning, even despite a potentially awkward situation with Core before I hit the road.

I marched through Core's palatial penthouse that was so huge that I could do cartwheels. His home was stunning, and it seemed like every detail had been considered at its conception—from the marble foyer with its discreet keyed private elevator that opened directly into his residence to the high ceilings, the marble-and-glass-enclosed fireplace in the living room, and the wide-plank, rift-sawed white oak flooring throughout.

From somewhere in the space, I heard Core's voice bark, "That's none of your fucking business, Ram!" There was a beat of silence before Core hissed, "Would you fucking stop whining like a damn girl?"

I rolled my eyes. He must be on his cell, and he sounded pissed. But that was nothing new. The fucker was always mad at something or someone. I was just happy it wasn't me... yet.

I followed the sound of his deep voice.

"Yes, Ram. I know you've had Jeff on ice for hours," he responded. "I've been busy." Silence again. "Oh, fuck off! I don't give a shit what you think." Core paused for another beat. "Yeah, real funny, fucker. Now let's get to business. Have you finished softening him up?" There was a long pause. "Good. When I get there, we'll start the real work..."

Ice for hours?

Softening him up?

What the hell?

Exactly what type of shit is Core into?

Is he a self-made billionaire, crime boss, or both?

I scowled. And what did it say about me that I was so far in with Core that I didn't give a damn either way?

I skidded to a stop when I found him standing in the kitchen, talking on his cell with his shirt off and annoyance written all over his face.

His head snapped in my direction. "Ram, I've got to go. Yes. I'll be right there," he roared before ending the call and sliding the cell across the countertop.

"Business deal gone south?" I inquired.

His face twitched. "Something like that." He flicked his eyes to the overnight bag I'd dropped by my feet. He rasped, "You going somewhere, Sin?"

There was no smile. When he crossed his muscular arms, my eyes traveled up his tall, well-built body that was pure, rippling muscle. Hardened abs trailed downward to the waist of his black designer-looking jeans.

Damn, no man should look this fucking good all the time.

And why the hell wasn't he wearing a damn shirt? His body, from chest to wrist, was a beautiful composition of Japanese tattoos and other beast-themed ink.

"Yep," I replied. "I've got shit to do."

He arched a brow. "Like?"

"Like it's none of your business," I replied while slowly plodding toward him, stepping into his massive kitchen.

We stood face to face as I leaned my hip against the granite kitchen counter.

He made a face. "That's where you're wrong. Everything about you is my business." He was studying me too closely, his expression brooding.

Keeping my gazed fixed on him, I replied, "The only thing that's officially your business is my company. Well, ninety-seven percent of it anyway." My statement was a deliberate jab. A reminder that he didn't own me and that I was still in control.

"You're the most infuriating woman I know." His calm response ignited my frustration.

I wanted to piss him off.

I needed his anger to fuel my will to hightail it away from him and away from this suffocating intimacy.

I needed him to save me from myself.

"I'll take that as a compliment, McKay."

"It wasn't." His lips curled into the faintest of ironic smiles.

"Why, sure it is. Besides, you love my sassiness and my sexy ass, which I'll be hustling on out of here once I have my coffee." I leaned in and tapped his cheek before allowing my hand to drop away. "Okay, enough of this morning chitchat. Coffee, McKay."

"What's the magic word?" He countered.

"Now," I chirped.

He growled.

"Please." I comically batted my eyes.

In answer, he reached out, grazing the side of my cheek, leaving a tingle in his wake before abruptly walking away from me and toward his espresso machine.

Holy shit! Core McKay is actually going to make me coffee.

I wasn't used to a man doing something remotely nice for me because I was so used to doing things alone.

I drew my lower lip between my teeth while staring at him.

He pressed the button on the gadget and placed a cup beneath the brew head to capture the wonderful stream of black liquid gold. When a sufficient amount of coffee had flowed into the cup, he filled another one and brought them over.

He pushed a cup into my hand. "So?" He started in his quiet, rough voice.

"So what?" I grumbled, lifting the cup to my lips and taking a small sip, savoring a much-needed awakening.

Glancing around, I took in his kitchen, which was a chef's dream—with top-of-the-line stainless steel appliances, including a wall oven and cooktop with a concealed range hood, a subzero refrigerator, and wine storage. Everything in the space gleamed —from the lacquer and glass cabinetry to the granite countertops and backsplash as well as a dishwasher with a built-in lacquer panel.

"What are your plans for today?" Core asked.

I choked on a mouthful of coffee.

Idle morning chitchat?

Is this what normal people do?

I shifted uncomfortably, feeling out of my depth as I tried to recall the number of times I'd engaged in casual banter the morning after having sex with a man. The number was zero.

With most of my previous sexual encounters, I'd actually had an exit strategy before having sex. My solution was to keep one high-heeled boot dangling just outside the door at all times. I would time it perfectly. After we both climaxed, I would simply follow the evacuation instructions I had practiced over and over in my head, and—*poof*—crisis averted. I was out of my hookup's bed before he could even pull out of me.

Ignoring Core's question, I took another sip, eyeing the cup sitting on the counter. "Why aren't you drinking your coffee?"

"It's for you."

I frowned. His sweet gesture instantly raised my guard. I waited for the other shoe to drop. *Is he fucking serious?*

This shit is too good to be true.

What is he after?

"So that's your evil plan? Ply me with coffee, hoping to get my agenda?"

"Yep. Is it working?" He winked at me.

"No," I mumbled before draining the cup and placing it on the counter. "But I know you're like a dog with a bone, and you won't let this shit go until I tell you." I pursed my lips. "I'm going home to assess the damage that bastard did to my townhouse." Something I really wasn't looking forward to.

My mind spun just remembering the chaos waiting for me in my home. The image from last night's mayhem was burned in my mind.

An intruder had violated my personal space, my home and sanctuary, and then destroyed all my shit. It was like a tornado had ripped through my home. Furniture had been slashed and thrown about. Kitchen drawers were pulled out. Broken glass and dishes littered the floor. Throw pillows had been cut, and down feathers were scattered everywhere. Nothing had been left untouched. And all I could think about was...

What if I had been home?

Would I be dead right now?

And who the fuck would have done some vile shit like that?

"Sin," Core started, "there's no need for you to run home. In fact, I'd rather you didn't until I can sort out who broke into your house."

"Hell no!" I snapped. "I'm not going to cower in your penthouse, waiting for your ass to figure this out." I clenched and unclenched my hands at my sides.

I refused to let terror control my life. By facing my fears head on, I not only was confronting what was making me so afraid—seeing months of hard work on my collection ruined and coming to terms with the daunting task of starting over—but I was also taking back control and choosing not to let the break-in dictate what I could and could not do. No one had the right to stop me from achieving my dreams.

"Core, I'm not running away from this. I'm going home."

Rage coursed through my veins when I thought about the worst part of the destruction—the remnants of my couture collection ripped into pieces and thrown around like confetti.

"And you will. But not now." He kept his voice low and soft but left no room for doubt that he'd issued a command.

"What?" I spluttered. I was the damn girl boss here. "Don't tell me what to do, Core. I'm a grown-ass woman."

His taking sexual control in the bedroom, bathroom, and any other available surface we'd fucked on was one thing, but telling me what I could and could not do outside of those circumstances was another damn thing.

"Yes, you are. All I'm saying is at least let me lessen the stress of you starting over."

My temper eased a bit when I realized he wasn't trying to control me. He was trying to help. I just wasn't used to accepting assistance. I was a go-it-alone and fix-it-myself type of chick.

"Core, I appreciate everything you're doing for me. I really do. But I'm really angry right now... well, angry and creeped the hell out." I studied him. "Someone broke into my townhouse and destroyed my collection. And if that isn't fucked up enough, the only thing they stole was my dad's ledger. Don't you think that shit is strange?" I took a deep breath before slowly letting it out.

Frustration was clouding my mind over the whole break-in situation, but the fact that the old ledger was now gone had been nagging at me with an incessant sense that I was missing something important. I just couldn't figure out what it was.

A couple weeks ago, when I'd found the ledger stashed under a secret compartment of Dad's ratty trunk, it had been puzzling to say the least.

Why did Dad take the time to hide the damn thing in the first place?

When I'd opened the book to check it out, nothing in the damn thing had made a bit of sense. It was only names, random handwritten codes, and numbers—essentially gibberish. There were too many pieces to the puzzle, and none of them fit together perfectly. But now I couldn't shake the feeling that I was overlooking a key connection between Dad, the break-in, and the ledger.

"Sin, yes, I do think it's bizarre the ledger was stolen. I already have my team working on getting to the bottom of the break-in. I've also arranged for a housecleaning service to stop by and clean up your place."

"That was fast."

The man was efficient.

How did he manage to get them to come out at the last minute and on a Saturday?

"And as far as your collection," he declared, "just tell me what you need to make you whole, and I'll take care of that, too."

Holy hell. He did all that shit for me? Without me even asking?

Core's demonstrated ability to be selfless and take care of me without my asking was a refreshing change of pace. His actions brought me peace of mind. I relaxed, deciding not to push him so hard. Besides, it was Saturday, and I didn't have any client dress fittings until tomorrow. Maybe it was best to spend a stress-free day—away from the scene of the crime—going through images of my designs stored on my Mac and coming up with a logical game plan for tackling the re-creation of my collection.

"You've thought of everything, huh?" I countered.

"No." He scowled. "Not everything. I didn't think someone

would destroy all of your hard work. That shit was totally fucked up and damn unexpected. But whoever did it... I'll make them pay for that." His jaw tightened. "Does anyone have an ax to grind with you?"

I widened my eyes. "With me? Fuck no. I keep my life drama-free. I don't have any enemies." I frowned. I couldn't think of one competitor who hated me this much. My life was uncomplicated. There was no drama, no rivals. "Except..."

My heart thumped hard in my chest.

Is Jaxon back to claim what he thinks is his—me?

My mind rejected the possibility, but the scary memory of the utter rage that had clouded Jaxon's eyes before he sliced my shoulder made me shudder. It was Core who brought me back to the here and now.

He caught my chin, and his gaze bored into mine. "Except what?"

My pulse accelerated at his question. "Nothing." I shook my head. I couldn't tell him the truth because it was ugly. I felt like a fool for lowering my guard and allowing an unstable asshole like Jaxon into my life.

He stroked my cheek. "Tell me." His eyes never left mine as he waited for my response.

It felt like being dissected, and no matter how hard I tried, I just couldn't hold up under the scrutiny.

"Years ago, there was this guy named Jaxon who started stalking me," I said softly, my throat tightening. "He became obsessed with me after just one night of sex."

"And?" His fingers stilled.

I shrugged. "And nothing. He's gone. I haven't seen him in years. Thank God."

"So you're telling me he just up and disappeared?"

I nodded.

He dropped his hand away from me and narrowed his eyes. "Sin, that's bullshit. Stalkers don't just walk away from their prey. They get what they want—their ultimate prizes and their victims. They're obsessive, sick fuckers who get off on harassing, terrorizing, and in some fucked-up cases, killing their victims or anyone else they think is in the way of their desired goal."

The truth of Core's words terrified me. The idea that Jaxon was indeed skulking around in the shadows, waiting to attack me, was way too much for me to stomach.

I shivered with disgust, remembering how the utter madness years ago had spiraled out of control after Jaxon broke into Jade's apartment and left the rose and my underwear on my bed.

"White roses," I blurted out. "I fucking hate the smell and the sight of them." I'd lived through agonizing months of huge, elaborate vases filled with white roses being delivered to me every day with one creepy message scribbled on each card.

Love you.

—J.

"Then one day, the roses mysteriously stopped showing up. I thought the madness and his obsession with me were over." I laughed cynically. "But, of course, I was fucking wrong. My Jaxon nightmare was just beginning. The bastard started showing up at every party I attended, and he chased away any guy who attempted to talk to me. When I confronted him, telling him to leave me the hell alone, that only seemed to enrage him."

Just thinking about the months of torture and fear he'd put me through, my heart raced. "Paranoid that he was lurking in the shadows, waiting to hurt me, I locked myself away in my house, only venturing out for work. After weeks and months passed without incident, I thought my world was safe again—until it all came crashing down."

His stoic expression turned grim. "What did that fucker do to you?"

The vehemence of his response surprised me. Core sounded like he would destroy anything and everything that dared to hurt me.

"He grabbed me, dragged me into a dark alleyway, and pressed a knife to my throat." I shuddered, fighting the familiar dread that seeped into my bones when I thought about that day. The memories lingered. The fear remained.

Tone as flat as ever, Core replied, "That fucker did what?"

Nothing could erase that day from my mind. The insane words of love Jaxon had babbled over and over as he brutally ripped off my clothes with sick lust in his eyes. The moment of total hopelessness I'd felt. I could still remember the bitterness that had coated my tongue when I realized I was nothing but a piece of property to him, his possession that he had every intention of claiming over and over again until I broke.

The tears had streamed down my face as I braced for the impending savage violation. Then my resignation to my fate as I lay shivering on the cold ground and letting my mind go blank. Like a petulant child, Jaxon had tried to steal what I refused to give him—illicit permission to be his. Unlike Core, who only took what I'd freely given him... me.

I recalled Core's words to me last night.

"I'll have all of you or none of you," he had clipped out. "That's the only way it will be."

And I had agreed with, "Core, we have a deal."

Core softened his voice, bringing me back to the present. "Sin?"

"A homeless man stumbled upon us, saving me. But before Jaxon walked away, he sliced me across my shoulder." I rubbed the scar that was covered by my T-shirt. "Never forget..." I whispered, fighting the cold fear running down my spine. "His words were, 'Never forget you'll always belong to me.'"

Core paced back and forth before me. "Last name?" he snapped.

I arched a brow. "What?"

He stalked over to me. "Tell me his last name," he demanded.

"Why?" I raised my chin in a gesture of defiance and met his gaze. "He's gone, Core."

"Is he?" Catching my upturned chin, he bored his eyes into mine. "What are you not telling me?"

My breath hitched as a flush of adrenaline tingled through my body. It was frightening how he knew me so well. "A vase of white roses with a note with the letter *J* scribbled on it was left on my doorstep a couple weeks ago."

"Like I asked, last fucking name?" He lifted an eyebrow. And waited.

My resolve faltered beneath the steady, authoritative regard.

"Jaxon Webb," I offered tentatively. "What are you going to do, Core?"

Not that I was averse to the idea of Core finding and beating the shit out of Jaxon... but killing him? No. That line I wouldn't cross. I didn't want that type of shit on my conscience. But more importantly, I couldn't allow Core to get into trouble with the authorities for any illegal actions he'd taken to keep me safe.

"His name has just been added to my Assholes to Destroy list."

"Core." My voice croaked as I spoke. "You can't just go around New York like some vengeful Viking, destroying everyone in your path."

"I can, and I do. I seek and destroy motherfuckers every damn day. And I don't lose a fucking wink of sleep about that shit."

Core had a certain intensity about him that always made him seem intimidating, but this was different. He was fierce, dark, and unyielding. Every word rang with power and authority. Frankly, it had me feeling a little turned on, if I was being honest.

I inclined my head. "And what will you do when you find him?"

He arched a brow. "Do you really want the answer?"

"Yes."

"He won't live." His dark words rang with deadly promise.

I swallowed. Hard. The silken threat of violence in his civilized tone reminded me that, although Core was a billionaire, wore expensively tailored suits, and negotiated million-dollar deals, he was still a ruthless predator and not a man to be fucked with.

"Well... shit," I whispered. "That's badass and unnervingly savage."

"Sin, there're things I don't tolerate." He spoke with quiet menace. "And one of them is men who abuse women." He reached out and grazed the side of my cheek with the back of his hand.

"I can protect myself, Core. Shit, I've been doing a damn good job for twenty-six years."

Despite the fact that he thought he could protect me, no one could but me, and I refused to cower behind Core's back, letting him fight my battles. I was strong and in control, and I would not let Jaxon win. And if Jaxon was back to claim what he thought was his—me—then I was ready to fight as if my life depended on it—because it did.

Core kept his answer short. "I'm all yours. If you're all mine."

My breath caught in my throat as I blinked hard. His words gave me goose bumps, stirring a longing in me I hadn't known existed until now. For a moment, I wondered what it would be like to be loved, adored, and worshipped by a man like Core, but I quickly dismissed the dumb thought.

Without thinking, I blurted out, "Until?"

He eased back, eyeing me. "That's up to you, Sin."

He was right. How far this shit went between us was completely up to me. I was in control... and I planned on keeping it. That was why I had to get out of there.

"I always trust my gut." I bit my bottom lip.

My fingers itched to trail across the all-seeing eye tattoo etched into the skin of his neck, but then I caught myself. Tenderness was not something I embraced. I fucked men and then disconnected. But that was B.C.—Before Core. Now here I was breaking all the rules with the one man I shouldn't.

No. I will not give in to him.

He reached forward, threading his fingers through my hair. "And what is your gut telling you about me?"

"Run because you're nothing but trouble." It was the damn truth.

Yes, I was very attracted to him. Yes, I wanted him like no other man I'd ever met. And yes, he scared the living shit out of me because of all of the above. Core was an itch I couldn't stop scratching. No matter how much I wanted to run away from him, I just couldn't muster up the strength to do that.

His fingers dropped away, and he stepped back slightly, making no attempt to conceal the erection tenting his jeans. "And just when I thought we had an understanding..." His gravelly voice sent vibrations of lust throughout me.

Sin... eyes off his cock. Focus.

"It's complicated, Core." My voice broke. I cleared my throat.

He stepped forward, caging me, making sure my body was flush against his. I sucked in a breath when his huge, hard bulge pressed against my stomach. Warmth flooded my pussy and then coursed through my veins like fire. My nipples strained against my bra.

"This seems pretty simple to me. I made the terms of our relationship very clear last night. It's you and me, satisfying our urge to fuck each other senseless." His chiseled lips curled. "With the added bonus of spending quality time with each other, exclusively, and seeing where this goes." He tilted his head and studied me. "And you agreed to the arrangement... happily. The deal has been made, and I'm not allowing you to back out of it. You're mine," he growled.

"Yours, like an object? We went over this last night." Pursing my lips, I pushed at his chest, and he moved back a little, his gaze burning me. "See, when you say caveman shit like that, I want to Superman-punch you in the damn face. I'm not something to be owned like one of your fucking expensive sports cars, McKay."

"No, not like an object. You're so much more than an object to me, Sin. But I won't make excuses for the man I am. I'm greedy, ruthless, stubborn, and yes, an asshole... at times. But I protect and cherish what's mine. And you, Sinful, are most definitely mine." He reached up and pinched one of my nipples through my shirt and bra, and I whimpered with a combination of pleasure and pain. "And I'm not letting you go until we both are duly satisfied. Like I've already told you, I have very dark tastes when it comes to sex, and I'm planning on exploring every one of them, leaving nothing unfucked. Including your beautiful ass."

My heart thumped wildly in my chest. I'd thought after our all night and morning fuckfest, my lustful urges had disappeared, but there was nothing settled between us.

"I agreed to sex..." I placed a hand against his cheek, enjoying the prickle of his stubble against my palm. "Not... this..." I croaked, dropping my hand.

"This? You mean us?" he replied before he angled down, grabbing my face between his callused hands.

Our mouths were a breath away, the desire and tension almost more than I could take.

"Yes, us." I confirmed.

Shit... is there anything he doesn't know about me now? Just the thought made me uncomfortable and jittery. My feelings for him were so powerful that fear flowed through me.

"Yes... that's right... us," he whispered before swooping in for a tantalizing kiss.

My body betrayed all my mental defenses, and I lifted my soft lips to his hard ones. As he slipped his tongue along the seam, a low moan escaped me, and then he was inside, exploring and teasing. He gave my lower lip a nip, followed by a soothing rub from his tongue.

Shit. Core is sexy and lethal.

And when I expected him to press his advantage, he gave me one last swipe of his tongue, bit my lower lip again, and retreated.

"Are you hungry?" he asked.

Utterly mystified by the change of topic, I stared at him. "What?" I rasped, blinking in confusion.

Yes, I'm hungry... for your cock. Is this a damn trick question?

He brushed a hand against my breast, and my nipples stiffened immediately. Liquid heat poured through me, and my stomach clenched.

"Of course you are," he purred simply. A smile twitched across his lips.

"McKay"—I suspiciously eyed him—"are you fucking with me right now? Because being a cunt tease is beneath you."

"I'm not fucking with you. I need to feed you." He smiled. The man was beyond handsome when he smiled.

My heart skipped a beat because he was taking care of me in a way no man had before. Core was being unbelievably caring and kind, and that terrified me because it was easy to walk away from someone who wasn't.

"Let me see what I can scrounge up to eat." He lifted me, setting me on the countertop.

Turning, he walked over to the subzero refrigerator and pulled out items—a plate of assorted sliced cheeses and curls of thinly shaved prosciutto and a bowl of figs and strawberries.

I arched a brow. This feast felt a little highbrow for Core. "You prepared all of this?"

"Hell no." He shook his head. "Zuri did. She calls it community service by fixing my 'sad bachelor fridge.'"

Wasting no time, he placed the items on the table next to the granite counter. Then he plucked a piece of cheese from the plate and held it out before my lips. I nibbled on it while glaring at him. I waited for his next move, but Core watched me with those devastating gray eyes, his expression giving nothing away. Before long, we were eating in comfortable silence as I examined the aftermath of my passion-fueled antics on his skin.

"Jesus. You've got lots of bite and scratch marks on you."

I wouldn't admit it out loud, but there was something so damn satisfying about marking him for the world to see.

"What can I say?" He grinned. "You're a wicked sex kitten when my tongue is stroking your pussy just... right," he purred.

"Quiet, McKay. Don't be a cocky asshole." I smacked his shoulder. "Besides, I'm no quiet lady when it comes to sex."

"I can attest to that shit." He swooped down and nipped my neck. "Jesus. The filthy, naughty words and sounds that came out of that pretty mouth of yours would even make a porn star blush." He laughed huskily. "And I loved it."

"Ooh!" I dug my fingers into his hair, yanking him away. "It's not polite to fuck and tell, McKay."

"Who gives a shit about being polite?" He winked. "What happens in the bed... bathroom... and anywhere else that I decide to fuck your luscious, beautiful body is all up for discussion between us, darling."

We looked at each other and then burst out laughing.

Damn, the vibe we had was so fucking easy and natural. I hadn't realized until now that I actually liked Core—as a person.

"You know this thing between us is crazy, right?" I asked. "I don't know anything about you, except for the shit I've read about you in the gossip section of the newspaper." I gave him a quizzical glance.

Core didn't respond right away.

"Believe me," he replied. "What they write about me is bullshit. All speculation and made-up garbage just to sell more newspapers."

Before I'd met him, I'd heard all the rumors—none of them good—circulating about the ruthless but utterly handsome Core McKay, the wealthy New York City recluse, business mogul, and eccentric owner of McKay Corporation and the McKay Club— his invite-only playground for the elite, rich, and kinky, a place to indulge in discreet liaisons, allowing all your freaky fantasies to come true.

I quirked a brow. "So you're telling me the Manhattan gossip hags have it all wrong?"

"Wrong about what?" he asked in a low tone.

"That you built your billion-dollar empire using money from drug trafficking, money laundering, and prostitution."

"Prostitution?" The look on his face was something close to disgust. "I've never messed with that shit. It's not my thing. I don't believe in sexually exploiting women."

His nostrils flared. "Hard damn work. That's how I built my empire. Nothing was handed to Ram and me. We had to fight for everything we've got, and that shit wasn't easy. But I'm not going to lie. Some of the shit we did... Well, it wasn't pretty." He scoffed. "The world of organized crime is a dog-eat-dog world. We made a fucking lot of money, and life was good... for a while." He flexed his arm muscles. "Until everyone around us got nabbed by the police, ending up serving hard time in jail, or got killed by business rivals over territory, money, or just for the fuck of it. So Ram and I decided to get the fuck out while the getting was good. We had to look out for own interests, and we went legit."

"Okay... so that would be a big check in the criminal activities box."

"Does that change how you feel about me?" He compressed his mouth into a thin line.

Mystified, I stared at him. "What? Hell no. At least, not now." I shrugged.

Before I had gotten to know him, the rumors about Core had definitely affected how I felt about him. But now? I didn't care what the tabloids proclaimed.

"I'm not perfect. You're not perfect. Shit. Perfection just doesn't exist. Besides, everyone's journey in life is different. As far as I'm concerned, it's the destination that matters."

He nodded in agreement.

"Okay, so... how did you get these?" I leaned in, tracing a finger along the light scar on his cheek and then farther up onto the jagged scar running across his eyebrow. "A gang fight over territory in Brooklyn?" I finished saucily.

He frowned while a long, uncomfortable silence dragged on. I fidgeted awkwardly when I realized Core was still on the fence about just how honest he wanted to be with me. It was as if he still didn't trust me. I pushed down the emotional hurt and replaced it with my old standby... anger.

"Okay. I'm done." I threw my arms up in the air. "This is definitely not going to work between us if you refuse to open up even a little bit."

With jerky, furious movements, I attempted to hop off the counter, but he quickly stopped me.

With an aggrieved sigh, he responded, "Sin, calm the fuck down."

"Oh, fuck off, McKay! I've shared stuff with you that I haven't said aloud in years, and the minute I ask you a question, you either deflect or I get nothing but crickets. You're the most infuriating man I know."

The tension between us was almost unbearable.

His mouth flattened. "I'm an open book, Sin." He folded his arms over his chest. "It's just that you might not like the answers you get." He bit out the words. "My past is very dark and sordid. I'm just not sure you're ready to hear about that part of me... yet."

I refused to let him intimidate me. With my chin tilted at a stubborn angle, I held my ground. "I'm not afraid of knowing the truth, Core. I'm more terrified of the unknown shit."

Running his hands through his hair, he grunted, "Fuck it." He scowled. "I got the scar on my cheek from a car bomb."

My breath caught in my throat as I blinked.

He carried on, eyebrows squeezing together. "It happened years ago." His voice went flat. "One minute, I was walking away from my girlfriend, Maya, who was pregnant with my child and sitting in my parked SUV, waiting for me to get something she'd left inside our apartment. The next instant, I heard an explosion." His hands almost curled into fists, and then he straightened them. "The force of the blast threw me back, slamming me into the sidewalk." He pointed to the scar on his cheek. "That's how I got this." There was tightness in his expression. "It's a reminder of what I lost in that burning SUV—Maya and my baby." He finished with a grave expression, the loss and pain evident in his eyes.

I felt like shit for making him relive something so fucking painful. I thought the story about the scar was going to be some epic tale about how totally badass he was. But this? My mind was still reeling from his story. Core would have been a father if Maya and his baby had survived.

Core, a father?

I blinked rapidly. That was a side of him I hadn't even known existed.

Abruptly, he turned on his heel, storming over to the refrigerator and pulling out a beer. He eyed me. "You want one?"

It took several moments before I could compose myself enough to reply. Even though it was early, I nodded. "Yes."

He twisted off the caps on both bottles before walking back and handing me an icy-cold one and taking a long swig from his.

"I'm sorry for your loss, Core."

He drained his bottle before saying, "It's been fucking years, but I'd be lying if I didn't admit that thinking about Maya still hurt like a motherfucker." He spoke with quiet menace, "The irony of all this shit is that the major reason I'd decided to turn my back on my criminal empire was for fear of losing her and my unborn child. But I lost her anyway, and my world shattered. Just one tragic moment, and she was taken away, leaving me empty. When she died, I lashed out at everyone around me, including my friends." He shrugged one massive shoulder. "Without her, my life was cold, and I wasn't alive."

"And now?" I asked tentatively.

"No woman could replace Maya. That's what I believed... until now..." His voice trailed off as he brushed my cheek.

His touch and words sent a shiver through me.

Oh. My. Fucking. God.

He continued. "But I'm at a crossroad. There's so much that you still don't know about me—and me about you."

I nodded. "You're right. There is still a lot we don't really know about each other. But I'd be lying if I said that what I know about you so far doesn't make me want to run the other way." Especially not since he'd just laid his heart bare by spilling his past and about the loss of his girlfriend and unborn child.

Maybe Jade's advice was right; I needed to heal and let go of the hurt from what Grace and Kyle had done to me.

Now it was my turn to reveal a piece of me. "I've had a pretty fucked-up past with relationships. So getting close to someone again? Trusting someone? Not gonna happen overnight." I sighed heavily. "The problem got worse when my dad died."

He kissed my forehead and whispered, "I'm sorry for your loss, Sin."

I nodded in acknowledgment. "It was such a shock. A reckless driver slammed into him, sending him off a bridge." How abruptly I had lost him hurt. It had changed me, leaving me vulnerable and scared to let any new people into my life for fear of losing them.

"Shit. That must have devastated you and your mother," he said.

"I was devastated. My mother... Grace, well..." I snorted. "She didn't even shed a tear. But she did happily burn through the money from my dad's insurance settlement on a massive shopping spree."

Just thinking about how Grace had spent the settlement on extravagant purchases, including a new condo with a homeowner's association fee that was more than what most people paid for their monthly mortgage alone, my lips pursed.

Core lifted an eyebrow. "Damn. She sounds like some piece of work."

I snorted. "Yes... she's fucking special, but not in a good damn way. That's one of the many reasons I cut the heartless hag out of my life when I was eighteen."

"Doesn't sound like a great mother-daughter relationship."

I drew my lower lip between my teeth while staring at him, hesitant to unearth the bones of my past that I had buried deep. "No, it wasn't, and it's not a subject I enjoy talking about."

Core glared at me with an intensity that made me uncomfortable. "Sin, we're talking, so let's be open."

I let out a calming breath. "Grace was never... well, a mother. As long as I can remember, there was always this wall between us. Do you know I can't recall a time when she actually hugged me?"

Painful feelings—of being unworthy and unlovable—and memories I'd repressed came rushing back at the remembrance of how Grace didn't love me. For years, I'd felt defective because she never taught me the things most mothers taught their daughters—allowing them to express their emotions, their pain, and their vulnerability without repercussions.

I continued. "I remember one day I came home from school and hugged her. You know, just to see what would happen. She shook me off like I was some pervert molesting her. I knew then that there was nothing in the world I could do to make her love me." But like an abused puppy, I still tried for way too long.

I cringed inside, thinking about back then, how fucking hard I'd worked to be everything she expected me to be—flawless. I'd even dyed my long naturally auburn hair blond like hers, which looked utterly ridiculous with my olive-colored skin and exotic, dark features. What was worse had been the sheer disdain in her eyes when she saw my failed attempts to be perfect. In comparison to her ethereal, porcelain features, I wasn't pretty enough or thin enough or smart enough. I just wasn't enough. And frankly, that truth had hurt like a motherfucker.

Unwanted memories—a bitter past I'd thought I'd buried deep —surfaced, one of the many arguments between Dad and Grace...

I WAS HAPPY... FOR ONCE—AT LEAST FOR NOW—BECAUSE I WAS with Dad, and he was alive. I had just finished watching him slave over Thanksgiving dinner while I served as his little helper by setting the table that we now sat down at, still, tense, watching the clock, and letting the food get cold while we waited for Grace to come home. With every breath I took, my heart sank deeper. She should have been back by now.

6:34 p.m.

8:27 p.m.

10:05 p.m.

Then around 11:30 p.m., Grace stumbled into the house, laughing to herself as she staggered over to the table.

Dad snapped, "You've been drinking again."

"No..." Her breath reeked of alcohol. "I swear." Then she broke out in a fit of giggles.

I hated that she laughed when she lied.

Dad looked at Grace with disappointment. "Grace, it's Thanksgiving. I promised Sin we'd spend the day together for once and have a nice family dinner."

I held my breath, waiting for Grace to say something, and she did.

"You promised her? Well, you didn't ask me shit. You always do this," she slurred. "I can never have a good time. Now you've ruined my night." By now she was screaming. "You and that little brat of yours always do!" She leveled me with a disdainful glare. I squirmed under its intensity. "Besides, look at her. She could stand to miss a couple meals." She cackled.

Tears rushed to my eyes.

"Grace! Enough!" Dad shouted.

Grace wobbled. "You're always taking up for her. Well, I don't need this crap," she yelled before she opened the door to leave again.

"Grace." Dad jumped up from the table, and I followed him as he went outside where Grace stood, trying to get into her car.

"*Grace, get inside,*" *Dad demanded. "I'm not letting you drive drunk.*" *He tried to stop her from getting into the vehicle.*

She kept pushing him away like he was some sort of pest she wanted to get rid of. "Don't try to act like you give a shit if I live or die. All you care about is Sin. What about me? Don't you love me? Or am I just here to pretend that we have a happy family life?"

"Grace, how many times do I have to tell you that I love you?" He sighed. "Now get inside. You're making a scene."

The neighbors were peeking out of their windows, watching the spectacle.

"No," she hissed. "Ian, come with me. Remember how we were before her?" She pointed at me. "It was about us... about me. Now my life is a living hell with us moving around because of her."

"Shut up, Grace," Dad hissed. "She can hear you."

"I don't care because I've never wanted her. She's not mine. She's Aub—"

"Don't," Dad yelled.

I sobbed because it hurt that she'd rejected me and thought I was a burden to her. But it had always been that way, my entire life. Dad would get into trouble for being nice to me.

"Go or stay. I don't care anymore," Dad replied.

"You're such an idiot," she chided before jumping into her car and driving away.

Dad brought me back inside the house, closing the door.

"Dad, what's Aub?"

He touched my hair. "Nothing. You know how she gets when she drinks."

"But why does she hate me so much?" I asked.

"It's not about you, Sin. She's hurting inside." He sighed heavily. "Her dad was awful to her throughout her childhood. She had no attention whatsoever. And I think every time she sees what a good relationship we have, she relives her childhood all over again."

. . .

Core's voice drew me back to the present. "Shit. That's rough, but that's her fucking loss."

"Loss?"

"Missing out on the experience of loving and caring for a beautiful, smart woman like you."

My mouth parted and then closed at such an unexpected but touching compliment. Damn... he was redefining my initial perception of him in every way. He had a fucking heart under his ice-cold demeanor.

Emotions welled up within me, and I cleared my throat, deciding to change the topic before I said or did something I'd regret like throwing caution to the wind and lowering my emotional barriers, letting him in. "What about your mother? How was your relationship with her?" Last night, he had briefly mentioned his mother had died, but he had seemed hesitant to talk about the topic any further.

"The exact opposite of your mother." He paused. "And if she were alive today, the moment she met you, she would have welcomed you into her home with no reservations because that was the kind of nurturing woman she was."

Wait... met me? Core McKay would have brought me to meet his mother?

I swallowed hard. He couldn't have meant that. I was reading way too much into his words.

Get a grip, girl!

Without missing a beat, he carried on. "To the world, she was a hard, street smart, take-no-shit kind of woman. But with me, she was so much different." He smiled wryly. "She couldn't stop hugging me, even at the most inappropriate times, like when I was trying to look cool and tough in front of my friends. And even when I was being a badass, stubborn prick, she loved me unconditionally, so I felt safe enough to be myself. Most significantly, I learned the importance of honoring my word and commitments from her. Her word was her bond. And so is mine."

"Sounds like a good woman, Core." I loved seeing that happy glint in his eyes. "It must have been nice to have that kind of foundation in your life." I envied him at that moment because it reminded me of my nonexistent relationship with Grace.

Core let out a harsh breath. "It was." A brief flash of sadness glinted in his eyes before they hardened. "Before she was murdered by a cold-blooded killer."

Oh shit. I wasn't expecting this response at all.

"Murdered?" My eyes widened.

"Yes. She was killed right in front of me."

"I'm so sorry, Core." I touched his arm. "I hope the animal is in jail at least?"

"He's not. He got away with fucking murder, and my world changed forever the day she died. I've spent my entire life waiting for the day I'll finally find him and avenge my mother's death."

I heard the agony in his voice when he mentioned his mother. The rare display of his emotion made me want to know more about the man, to dig deeper under his hard facade. My wanting such intimate emotional access surprised the hell out of me, given the fact that I stubbornly refused to give Core the same access to what lay beneath my emotional mask.

"I don't blame you for feeling that way." I swallowed hard. "If you don't mind me asking... what happened?"

I grabbed his hand, weaving my fingers through his. His fingers stiffened before they relaxed.

His eyes glazed over like he was reliving the bitter memories. "I was doing my homework when I heard my mother's bloodcurdling scream. I'd never heard something like that before. The shit was terrifying. I ran into the kitchen, and this man had her pinned against the wall."

"Did you know him?" I whispered.

"No." He shook his head. "He was beating my mother's face to a bloody pulp. I didn't give a shit who he was. I jumped onto his back while trying to claw his fucking eyes out of his head. All I cared about was saving my mother."

I squeezed his fingers, imagining the horror of witnessing that shit. It'd had to be emotionally scarring.

He continued. "It's been twenty-six years, and I can still hear the thud my mother's body made when he slammed her to the floor before grabbing me off his back and throwing me clear across the kitchen. And I just fucking lay there, helpless and weak, before he shot her and then me."

"Don't you dare blame yourself for this shit. You were young, and there wasn't anything you could do."

It was painful, watching the emotions—sadness, guilt, pain, and then back to anger—flick through his eyes. Everything he was feeling resonated with me. It was exactly how I'd felt the minute I found out Dad had died because he was out driving around, looking for me when I broke curfew.

"Fuck that. It was my fault. She needed me, and I didn't do shit to help her or save her. She's dead because of me. Just like Maya and our baby." He hunched his shoulders. His eyes sparked with rage as they locked on to mine.

"Because of you? Core, no. That's not true. None of this shit is your fault."

I was so enraged. I wanted to wrap my hands around the neck of the person who had killed Maya and the man who had murdered his mother and choke them both to fucking death. The emotional damage those people had caused him was a stain he would never be able to remove.

He released my hand. His fists clenched and unclenched at his sides. "I could have done something... anything... when that bastard placed the gun to her head. But I didn't," he gritted out.

"Stop!" I couldn't stand to hear him tear himself up like that. "You're fucking ripping yourself apart for something that's not your damn fault. Blame the fucker who killed her. Be angry with him, not yourself."

"That's easier said than done. Especially when her killer is alive, and she's dead." His eyes blazed with ire. "He stole her from me. Took away the one person who meant anything to me. And I won't rest until that asshole is taking a dirt nap." He ran a hand over his head. "I was near death, and Ram saved my life. We made a pact that day that the man who had killed my mother would pay with his life."

The rage balled up in my stomach at the senseless deaths of both his mother and Maya. And fury because the person who had run Dad off the road was never punished. Lives lost and the broken children—Core and me—left behind to deal with the emotional baggage.

"I'm so sorry." I wrapped my arms around his waist, pressing my cheek against his chest.

Core mimicked my motion, tightly holding me, as if trying to anchor himself in the here and now. "There's nothing to be sorry for. I've moved on. I've survived. I always do."

Easing out of his arms, I stared up at him. I knew he hadn't moved on. There were threads of pain and fury intertwined in his voice when he retold the story. Core's hurt, guilt, and bitterness ran deeper than a river. There was no way in hell he'd find peace until he got retribution for his mother's death. And frankly, I didn't blame him. I understood the hole in the soul death left that could never be repaired. No matter how hard you tried to mend it, the loss from death lingered forever. But the truth of the matter was that revenge wouldn't bring his mother back.

"Shit happens." His nostrils flared. "The way I see it, you can't go through life untouched by suffering. But the smart ones understand that the only way to survive is to find the meaning behind the suffering." His eyes transformed; they were now cold, hard, and flinty.

The man behind the mask was starting to make more sense to me now. He'd lived a rough life and made it out alive when most of the kids he had grown up with probably didn't.

"Core, I know how much losing someone you love can hurt."

I swallowed hard. I felt Core's pain and knew it intimately. "When my dad died, I was lost for so long. He had been my life-line. I fucking miss him every damn day."

"Death is a cruel motherfucker," he grunted.

"That it is," I whispered, comforted in the knowledge that Core and I had a connection that ran deeper than sex.

We'd both lost someone we loved, and the loss had devas-tated and molded us into the people we were today... for better or worse.

But is this enough to force me to tear down the emotional walls that protect me, letting Core close to me, revealing my true self? And if I do... could he accept me... the broken woman inside?

"Core..."

"Yes."

Without thinking, I blurted out, "I have a shitload of trust issues."

"Sin, you—"

I was a tangled knot of anxiety, waging an endless battle between my head and my heart.

"Don't." I placed a finger over his lips to silence him. "If I don't say this now, I won't ever." I swallowed hard. "Grace cheated on my dad when I was a kid, and to add insult to injury, she verbally treated him like shit. It wasn't a happy household, to say the least, so I inherited a lot of relationship issues from that. It's hard for me to trust anyone."

Reaching up, I grabbed his head, yanking it down so that we were now face to face. "I'm not looking for you to define what's happening between us. In fact, I'd rather you didn't." Because if he did, it would be like a spray of insect repellent, making me want to fly as far away as possible. "But what I am demanding is that you never lie to me... because if you do, this thing between us is over. I can't be with a fucking liar. I need you always to keep it one hundred percent real with me. Are we clear, McKay?"

He narrowed his eyes. "Clear as water." He grunted before

swooping down, claiming my mouth while squeezing my ass with one hand, the other possessively wrapped around my waist.

I almost came undone when he sucked my tongue into his mouth, twining his around it. He plundered, possessed, nipped, storming through my defenses, demanding my surrender. And I did. I couldn't do anything else.

His tongue slid over mine, around, seeking every inch of me. A fist in my hair angled my head back, granting him deeper access. He growled, a sound that rumbled down in his chest as he effortlessly hoisted me up, kneading my ass with two hands. Instinctively, I wrapped my legs around his waist, completely gone... lost in the sensation of Core.

❦ 3 ❦

SINTHIA

CORE STRODE through the house and up to his bedroom. With his hand on my back, he lowered me onto the bed and gently pushed me back while his legs forced my knees apart. He yanked off my boots, jeans, and panties, tossing them aside. One hand grabbed a firm hold of my wrists, and the other slid into my pussy, two fingers pushing inside and stretching me open. I moaned as I clenched around those fingers.

He growled again. "So fucking beautiful," he murmured with approval, pressing his mouth against my stomach, nibbling and kissing until all I wanted to do was burst into flames.

My nerve endings stirred and tingled. His touch and our physical connection felt intense, like a slow, smoldering fire. It was so much different. So much more because of the way we had both just opened up, baring our souls to each other during our conversation. It was as if we both wanted to slow down, savor the moment, linger in the essence of the momentous corner we'd turned together in our relationship.

Rising on his elbows, he hungrily looked at me before pushing my legs out a little. Now I was even more exposed and vulnerable before his gaze, just as I'd opened myself up to him, telling him about my dad and my relationship issues. He pushed my knees to my stomach before pressing them outward, tipping my pussy up in the air. As he slid his fingers between the wet folds of my heat, I arched up, wiggling closer when he slipped his fingers inside. His thumb circled and played with my clit.

I was dying for more even though I was on the cusp of my first orgasm. As I stared at him, my mind went numb. I needed more, but I was helpless. He stroked my pussy. I shivered, on the verge of exploding.

"Give it to me, Sinful," he demanded huskily.

I knew exactly what *it* was from our numerous hot-and-heavy fuck sessions.

Core dominated.

I submitted.

It was Core's sensual power play, forcing me to leave all my inhibitions at the door. In exchange, he'd push my sexual boundaries.

There were no flowery bullshit words.

No complicated promises of forever.

And no judgment for the freaky things we both desired. It was beautifully uncomplicated and liberating. Finally, I'd found a highly skilled lover with whom I didn't have to orchestrate every touch and stroke. Shit, the man fucked like a tireless machine.

And the way his eyes bored into me while fucking... It was as if I were his goddess and he were worshipping me at my altar. It was humbling, sensual, exciting, and intense.

He ensured that my sexual pleasure came before his. It didn't hurt that the man was very skilled at fucking.

In the bedroom, bathroom, and anywhere else he chose to take me, I was his be-all and end-all.

"Please," I whispered. "Lick me," I finished because I knew he had no intention of pushing me over the edge until I offered what he needed to hear.

"With pleasure."

His huge hands curled around my thighs, spreading my legs wider. His tongue thrust into my heat. That one abrasive lick sent my mind and body spiraling over the edge, and I screamed his name like a prayer.

He pulled his head back, watching as his fingers continued to stretch my greedy slit. "Scream louder, darling."

I was writhing and panting as my hips bucked wildly. His fingers thrust harder. I moaned louder when his thumb found my clit again and mercilessly played with it. I screamed and came again, feeling light-headed from the passion.

He nipped my inner thigh. "I love the taste of your cunt."

His lustful words made my toes curl. I wanted Core more than my next breath.

He eased back, standing before me for a moment, and then he stripped naked.

I shivered deliciously. He was gorgeous, fit, and muscular with a thick cock jutting out in front of him.

"Fuck me," I demanded.

His face darkened. "Who's in charge, Sin?"

"Me," I answered.

My willful streak pushed to the forefront. Core had taken me several times that morning, and each and every time, I'd submitted to his demands... willingly. But the sadistic streak in me wanted to push the envelope. I wanted to know how far Core could take our sensual play.

"Tsk, tsk," he shot back before opening a condom packet and sheathing himself. "You know better, darling." He moved in front of me, stroking his length.

I inhaled sharply, loving the sensual way he touched his staff.

"I'm in charge," he insisted softly, his voice still full of authority.

Truth be told... behind closed doors, in his bed, I wanted him to be in charge. Core knew what I wanted without me even having to ask, which was scary and exciting.

Our gazes locked when he stated, "I'm going to stick my dick up your ass."

I swallowed hard. I'd never had anal sex in my entire life.

His laugh made me shiver. "Everything in you is probably saying no, that you wouldn't like it. But the spark of excitement in your eyes... it says differently."

Core was right. My body was on fire, the need unlike anything I'd ever felt.

"On your fucking knees," he demanded.

My eyes widened. Butterflies fluttered in my stomach.

Oh shit. This is really happening... ass action.

I froze with indecision.

Do I trust him enough to be that vulnerable to him?

When it came to sex, Core had not hurt me and had given me things I hadn't known I wanted—freedom to unleash my freaky dark desire with no judgment about my sensual wants and needs—until him.

"Now," he barked.

I rolled over, getting on my hands and knees. My shoulders were pressed against the soft sheets. My ass high in the air, I glanced over my shoulder at him.

"Damn. Beautiful," he whispered. "Spread your knees wider." He used his muscular thighs to spread my legs even more.

My breath caught in my throat when he reached for the lube, squirting it onto his fingers.

The realization sank in. I was excited. The need to have him take me surpassed any desire I'd ever felt. My throbbing folds felt like he'd already fucked me. The silky feel of the bedding against my nipples sent ripples of need to my center.

"Fuck me," I hissed.

He was on top of me in seconds, his body pressing against me.

"Beg me," he whispered into my ear, "and make it good, Sin."

A soft moan escaped my lips. "Fuck me, please. Put your cock inside me. Make me yours."

"I've already done that, Sin."

I shivered as the truth of his words registered.

He taunted. "Say, *Pretty please, Core, fuck me.*" He ran a hand over my ass cheek and then to the crease. His lips trailed down my back, sending a combination of heat and shivers through me.

I became consumed by the helplessness of my position as a lube-coated finger slid into my ass with no warning. My cheeks squeezed against his invasion. Automatically, I tried to move away. He applied a little more pressure at my puckered opening. The cold and unrelenting push into my anus held me captive while he pushed his lubed finger deeper and then slowly thrust in and out.

My forbidden hole relaxed around his finger and opened up. The most amazing pleasure shot through me. Arching my back, I lifted my bottom, opening myself fully to him. He added a second finger. Again, he was very slow and cautious before he thrust in and out with his two fingers. Then he tried three fingers.

I repeated, "Pretty please, Core, fuck me."

"My pleasure," he drawled, withdrawing his fingers. "Once I've fucked your ass, you'll know just who you belong to." With strong hands on my thighs, he lifted my ass high, using his muscular thighs to keep my legs spread wide.

My hips rocked, needing him to fill me, but I was not at all certain that I wanted him fucking my ass.

Will it hurt? Will I even like it?

"Core. Um... I don't know if—"

The tip of his cock touched my opening. I tugged at the covers in an attempt to move away from him while at the same time raising my butt higher.

Shit. There was something about the sting of the head of his cock pushing against my puckered hole that was simply alluring.

"Core," I whispered.

With long strokes up and down my back, he kept me bent over, my ass in the air.

"Your ass looks so beautiful in this position." He nudged his cock a little more firmly against my bottom hole.

I groaned, burying my face in the bedding as the head of his cock pressed insistently into me. "Core... Oh! It burns." I struggled to adjust to his thick heat opening me wide.

The unrelenting pressure as he forged his way deep inside me persisted, making it impossible for me to catch my breath. The raw dominance of it staggered me. Core's hands squeezed my hips, his deep growl filling the room as his cock pressed another inch deeper.

"You're fucking tight. Just a little more, darling," he whispered.

I gulped in air, fisting my hands in the sheets. "It's so fucking deep. Core..."

His balls were against my ass as he slid the rest of the way into me.

I couldn't breathe.

I couldn't think.

I felt so taken... so consumed.

He was possessing me as no man ever had, the sharp primitiveness of the act freezing me into immobility.

This act, more than any I'd ever experienced, filled me with a sense of vulnerability I'd never before imagined. I was aware of each shift of his staff, each breath he took. He stretched me wide, moving inside me as he bent over my back, pressing his lips to my neck.

"You belong to me," he hissed. "Say it."

I felt fragile.

He completely owned and controlled me with every move of his cock, each movement drawing a trembling gasp from me.

"I can't," I breathed out.

When his hand came around my waist, settling on my mound with a rough finger pressing against my clit, the sensation was so intense I drew a sharp, shaky breath. He began to stroke, slowly moving in and out of me, the friction over my inner walls robbing me of reason.

"Sin, let go. Give me everything."

Tilting my bottom upward, I cried out as the thick head of his cock pressed impossibly deeper.

"You're mine to take. Mine to fuck deep. Mine to enjoy. Mine to protect. Mine to care for. Mine to make happy."

Nothing in my life had ever felt so intimate. So all-consuming. The connection between us made tears prickle behind my eyelids.

My nipples craved his attention. My clit burned for his touch. My arousal was so intense that I couldn't think of anything else except coming. I teetered on the edge, the erotic pleasure too good to be real… but I resisted in giving him what he wanted—all of me, both emotionally and physically.

I countered. "You have no right to ask for this."

"I have every right." Wrapping his arm around me again, he leaned over my back, his fingers parting my folds. "You are mine… and every time you look at me, you're going to remember this. You're going to remember how I can make you feel… because you belong to me and I to you."

He belongs… to me?

I stiffened as his fingers started stroking my clit, inadvertently clamping down on his cock and making my anus burn.

The flash of fire hit me so hard and fast that I froze, unable to move at all as I came so hard that I saw stars. I couldn't draw a breath deep enough to cry out. The cock inside me felt even larger as I tautened on it, stretching me so intimately and making me feel even more defenseless and exposed.

I couldn't escape it any more than I could escape the insistent strokes on my throbbing clit, his hold keeping me still, forcing me to accept all he had to give me, making me give him even more than I had known I had to give.

Fuck. He's reaching in, snatching part of my damn soul.

Core lifted me, keeping me on my knees in front of him as he buried himself deep in my ass at the same time he buried his face in my hair.

"Fuck, Sin," he growled harshly, holding me, pulling me back against him, and he came deep inside my ass. "Mine."

With a shudder, he released my hands before sitting on his heels, pulling me down to sit over his thighs. His cock pulsed inside me, drawing a moan from me as my head fell back against his shoulder.

His arms wrapped around me, the muscles beneath my thighs rock hard. "I've never wanted a woman more." He cupped my breasts. "You okay, darling? Did I hurt you?"

No, I'm not okay. I was emotionally shaken and struggled to shore up defenses that had been eradicated by the intensity of his lovemaking.

Core had made me feel beautiful and desired. I loved the feel of his muscular arms around me and the way his thighs trembled beneath mine. The level of trust it had taken to allow him to do what he'd just done to me scared me.

My body stiffened when the most frightening and, frankly, disturbing thought flashed through my head. Core could easily make me break all my rules about not getting emotionally involved with a man.

And if that happens... will sex continue to be enough for me?

My heart raced as panic started to set in.

Oh God. What if I actually fall in love with him?

Heaviness settled in the pit of my stomach.

Shit. That would be a fucking disaster.

But I knew the possibility of sex morphing into something else was real and damn unnerving.

Jesus, I'm so fucked right now.

❧ 4 ❧

CORE

WEAVING in and out of Manhattan traffic in my Porsche, I reveled in the sounds of the heavy metal music I used for meditation. I needed something to distract me from the powerful arousal that coursed through my body like fire when I remembered how, mere hours ago, Sin had screamed my name over and over again as I devoured her cunt, licking from bottom to top, teasing her clit and lapping up her cream like warm honey.

Damn. And her tight ass is incredible.

The vision of Sin's eyes dilating with lust flashed in my mind. Basic, raw hunger surged through me, beating at my self-control. My cock swelled, and the wild thought of turning my car around and going back to the penthouse flittered through my mind.

Shit... the things I could do once I got there... like order her to get on her knees and suck me hard and fast. Damn. Just the thought of how her warm, pink tongue would feel against my skin while she teased my cock before taking me to the back of her throat...

I shook my head to clear my lustful, wicked thoughts.

Sin is an addictive distraction.

Even with a string of women and business successes over the years, it had been so long since I was with anyone who looked remotely like a real woman with soft curves, pretty girl-next-door looks, and a sassy, take-no-shit personality like Sin, and it was a bonus that she more than satisfied my distinct and dark tastes in sex.

Shit, my obsession with Sin was crazy and fucking reckless, but the more time I spent with her, the more I wanted her... in and out of my bed.

It wasn't just her body that captivated me, but her wit, mind, and compassion also drew me in like a moth to a flame. My thoughts drifted back to our conversation and how Sin had instantly recognized and understood the anguish and guilt I'd felt over Mom's, Maya's, and my unborn baby's deaths.

"I'm so sorry," she had whispered before wrapping her arms around me, pressing her cheek against my chest.

Her impulsive yet simple act of affection and comfort had been unnerving at first. Frankly, it had been so long since I allowed a woman to get close—the last one Maya—that I didn't even know how to react to her consoling touch. I was always fairly detached with women, and while I kept some of them around for a few months, it was only to hook up with them. I had no emotional investment whatsoever. But with Sin, it was like the emotional walls I'd worked so hard to erect were crumbling down.

Without a doubt, Sin was the full package. She was everything I wanted in a woman—strong, feisty, intelligent, and beautiful. And I wanted her more than any woman I'd been with—even Maya.

This was a real fucked-up predicament.

I had no damn business thinking about Sin that way.

She was supposed to be a woman I was using as bait.

Just a casualty in my war against Bigsby.

I pressed on the bridge of my nose and took a deep breath. "Shit."

I really didn't need this Sin complication. My life was difficult enough, and I didn't need any distractions, especially now that I'd found my mother's killer. Besides, I wasn't relationship material, and I never would be. I fucked women and then showed them the door. Well... that had been my mode of operation before Sin.

Now my plans for Sin had changed, and I'd decided once I destroyed Bigsby, I'd tell Sin the truth about everything. Not that I'd ever lied to her in the first place. I'd just omitted and dodged telling her some pertinent information so I could keep my Bigsby mission on track and her under my control. I'd already told her the truth—that I'd spent my entire life waiting for the day I'd finally find him, my mother's killer, and avenge her death.

And Sin had replied, "I don't blame you for feeling that way, Core."

So I knew she would understand my motives when I told her the truth about Bigsby.

How could she not?

We'd both lost people in our lives that we loved.

The loss had devastated and changed us forever.

Yes, there was no doubt in my mind that Sin would forgive me, especially when I revealed that the same bastard who had killed my mother also murdered her father.

My cell rang, echoing throughout the confines of my car and rousing me out of my thoughts. Glancing at the caller ID that flashed on the dashboard, I turned down the loud music before pressing the button on my steering wheel.

"What's up, Kevin?" I answered.

"My connection came through and sent me the info you asked for on Webb."

"Damn, that was fast."

As soon as I'd gotten in my car, I'd texted Kevin, instructing him to dig up everything he could find on Jaxon Webb, Sin's stalker.

"Getting this info was a piece of cake compared to the other crap you asked me to do today."

"Come on, bro. Just hit me up with the damn info already."

I was fortunate to have Kevin on my team. He was not only one of my closest friends, the equivalent of a brother, but he was also one of the smartest men I knew. He was a valuable member of my team, handling the financing and accounting for all my businesses as well as all my private intelligence-gathering efforts. If I needed answers, Kevin would reach out to his deep well of intel connections and get that shit, pronto.

My fingers tapped on the steering wheel.

"Jaxon Webb. Caucasian. Thirty-one years old. He's the only son of a filthy-rich family from Connecticut."

My lips compressed as I waited for him to get to the point.

"Mother, Claire Webb. Father, Daniel Webb." Kevin paused for a beat. "Jaxon's parents are both attorneys..."

Is he kidding me?

I frowned. "Who gives a rat's ass that they're attorneys?" I complained under my breath.

Kevin droned on. "At their prominent Manhattan family law firm—"

I cut him off. "Fuck, Kevin!" I banged the steering wheel. "I don't give a shit about his parents. Just tell me about that asshole Jaxon!"

"Shit. Calm the fuck down, Core," he replied calmly. "There's nothing about Jaxon that's any different than most trust fund babies running around Manhattan. Shit. I've lost brain cells just reading his intel report. Why are you investigating him anyway?"

"He's stalking Sin," I gritted out.

My heart jerked as I remembered the vulnerability in her eyes and the truth laid out in her words as she'd told me what that demented asshole had done to her. I had known then that I would cut off my own arm before I'd ever let anyone harm her.

I always protected what I cared for.

"Stalking her?" Kevin responded. "Shit. Well, that's not good."

"Why?" I countered.

"Because according to the police report, he has a bad track record with women, and that raises a red flag."

"Go on." I prodded, overcome by an edgy, twitchy feeling.

"He's been accused of sexually assaulting several women. But get this; he's never been arrested or charged in connection with any of these alleged incidents."

I snorted. "Let me guess; his parents intervened." It wasn't a question, but a statement.

My business dealings with blue-blooded fuckers had given me a glimpse into their world of bribes and other shady undertakings. I'd quickly learned from watching their maneuvers that if you had money and the right connections and pedigree, you could get away with anything, including murder, without any repercussions.

"Exactly." Kevin confirmed. "His parents quietly dealt with the women while Jaxon left the country."

"Where did he go?"

"He hopped around Europe for years. But it didn't take long for his same pattern with women to start. He was accused of sexually assaulting five women in Europe. But this time, two of them ended up missing and are now presumed dead."

"Shit!" I stiffened. Disgust twisted my mouth into a sneer. There was no way in hell that I was going to allow that sick fucker to hurt Sin.

She's mine to protect... to care for.

And no one...

Absolutely no one...

Messes with what's mine...

Sin.

My pulse elevated.

"Yeah, well, that's not all," Kevin replied. "Jaxon recently came back to the US, so that can't be a good thing for Sin. Once a stalker, always a damn stalker."

This confirmed Sin's theory about Jaxon leaving roses on her doorstep. I tightened my fingers around the wheel. If there was one thing I despised, it was men who got their rocks off on harassing and intimidating women. And all the signs pointed to the fact that Jaxon had picked Sin as his next victim. Not on my damn watch. That shit was not going down.

Adrenaline rushed through my body.

"Kevin, you've got twenty-four hours to get me his address." I couldn't wait to find that coward, wrap my hands around his neck, and watch the life slowly drain from his eyes. "I need to pay that fucker a little visit and permanently shut his ass down."

"Smart move. I'll get back to you ASAP."

"Next topic," I grunted. "Did you decode Bigsby's ledger?"

Once Max and Rocco had nabbed Jeff leaving Sin's house with the ledger in hand, they had taken him to our warehouse for interrogation. Kevin's role was to take the ledger and start piecing together exactly why it was so important to Bigsby that he'd ordered Jeff to break into Sin's house to steal it.

"Shit. That was easy," Kevin bragged. "Each entry in the ledger documents the client's name, their credit card number, how much they paid, the date they hired the escort, and the name of the escort they fucked."

"Escort? How the hell did you jump to that conclusion?"

"Jemma Kane," he disclosed dryly. "She's a Manhattan madam who got busted about twenty-seven years ago because of a sting that had targeted her massage parlor. Her establishment was really a cover for her high-end escort service, and all her clients were the who's who of New York. I'm talking about politicians, judges, and Wall Street executives."

"So what's her connection to Bigsby?"

Kevin replied, "It was a painstaking process, but for each ledger entry, I ran a check on the credit card number associated with it. And every single credit card number came back to black cards issued by various financial firms and services. The charges were expensed on corporate accounts, disguised as computer repair, trading research, or consulting for market compliance. And every client credit card charge listed in that damn ledger links right back to Jemma's escort service, which funneled money to several offshore accounts listed in the ledger. Now here's the smoking gun. Every single one of those offshore accounts is closed, except one. And that active account connects to a shell company called Pomtonic International, which I confirmed is owned by Bigsby."

"Holy shit," I answered. "Is she still serving time? Because if we can get to her and offer her some cash, I'm sure she'd be willing to implicate Bigsby as part of her escort business, and then—"

"Great idea, Core. I like where you're heading, but that shit is not going to happen."

"Money talks—"

Kevin cut me off. "Jemma never served time."

"Did she make a deal with the prosecution?" I inquired.

"Don't know. She went missing without a trace while she was out on bail."

"So when you say Jemma's missing, you really mean she's presumed dead," I returned.

"Officially, according to the police, she's missing. Unofficially, she's presumed dead. It's speculated that she either jumped bail and fled to Mexico or she was killed by one of her rich clients when she threatened to reveal the names in her black book, which I think is the fucking ledger we now have in our possession."

"This shit is getting deep," I mumbled as my mind raced with questions and theories. "But why would she have kept a ledger with all this information?"

"I'd guess it was her security, her plan B, if shit went south and she got nabbed by the police."

"Exactly," I interjected. "That's what I'm thinking. So maybe when she got busted and had her back to the wall, she threatened to out her clients as a part of her plea deal with the authorities." I frowned. "This is all speculation, but it makes sense. She probably revealed the names and then went into witness protection."

"Maybe," Kevin shot back. "This whole Jemma story is just fucking odd. I can't put my finger on it, but something is off. I couldn't find any information about her background. No birth certificate, no driver's license, no photos, not even a blip of personal information about her anywhere. That shit doesn't happen unless someone wiped her background clean."

"It doesn't matter. She's gone, and so much time has passed since she went missing that even if we wanted to find some of the escorts who had worked for her, that would be a big fucking waste of time."

I thought about my conversation with Sin this morning when we'd talked about the person who'd broken into her townhouse and destroyed her collection, but the only thing they'd stolen was her dad's ledger. A ledger that Bigsby had sent his errand boy to break into her house and steal. *But how had Bigsby even known where to search for it?*

"Did Sin tell you how she ended up with the ledger in the first place?" Kevin asked.

"Her father. And before you ask, she has no clue what the information in the ledger even means."

Kevin scoffed. "And you believe her?"

"Hell yes, I believe her."

From what I'd experienced so far, Sin didn't have a deceitful bone in her body. She pulled no punches in everything she did and said—a trait I admired and respected.

"Then how did her father end up possessing Jemma's ledger —aka little black book?" Kevin inquired.

"Bro," I barked, "if I knew the answer, we wouldn't even be having this conversation. All this shit... and the connection between Jemma, Bigsby, and Sin's father is a big damn mystery. I suspect all three have something in common." I just couldn't figure out what.

"You mean all four," Kevin stated.

"Four?"

"You forgot Sin," he informed me.

"Sin is just the unwitting owner. Well, she was the owner of the ledger. We need to focus on our target—Bigsby. It's taken us over twenty years and a fortune paid to dead-end tips to get this far."

Bigsby was unfinished business, business I'd been waiting to resolve for far too many years. I had thought of nothing but revenge. It'd consumed me. Just thinking about the night when the unknown assailant wearing a gold ruby-and-diamond-encrusted horseshoe ring had shot my mother and left me choking on my own blood fueled my hate fire. My mother had died, but I survived. I'd finally found the owner of the ring— Bigsby. I had been searching for that ring for years, and it was right under my nose.

"Yeah, but what about Jemma?" Kevin started. "And her missing background is a loose end I don't like. Until I figure this out, it's going to be like a piece of corn stuck in my teeth. Fucking annoying."

I sighed heavily. Sometimes Kevin was way too smart for his own good. He had this need to solve everything, and his need for perfection was borderline obsessive.

"Kevin, one mission at a time. Let's finish the Bigsby mission first. Then if you want to chase down the unsolved Jemma disappearance, knock yourself out. Shit, I'll even fund it. Hell, I love a good thriller and suspense story just like everyone else, so it would be nice to get to the bottom of what actually happened to Jemma. But right now, I've got the team waiting for me at the warehouse, so can we move this crap along?"

"Yes. Anyway, moving on, back to Jemma." He paused. "Here's the part I think you're going to really love. Jemma had two business partners. The first was Bigsby Calhoune. The second was Sin's father."

"Which one?" I asked.

Kevin's previous investigation into Sin's family background

had unearthed that she had two birth certificates, each one showing a different set of parents. The first birth certificate had her father listed as Ian Michaels and her mother as Grace Michaels. The second certificate had her father listed as Greer Lorne Cruickshank and her mother as Aubrey Cruickshank.

"Greer," Kevin replied.

I frowned. "It still doesn't answer how Bigsby knew Sin had the ledger."

"Or if he suspects that Greer might be Sin's real father," Kevin chimed in.

I scratched my chin. "I don't think it's a coincidence that the only two people who can tie Bigsby to his former life as a pimp are either missing or dead."

"Exactly," Kevin intoned. "A narcissistic man like Bigsby would terminate anything linking back to his seedy history."

New York City's mayoral hopeful, Bigsby Calhoune, was a dirty criminal underneath his slick, cleaned-up politician veneer. He might have a new identity and life, but he was still the power-hungry thug who had killed my mother and left me to die.

My stomach felt like a rock had taken up residence when I realized Sin could be in danger.

What if Bigsby thinks Sin is one of the loose ends from his past and decides to put her on his hit list?

Knowing what I knew so far about Bigsby, I was sure he had come too far to let his new life disintegrate, which meant Sin's safety was in serious jeopardy.

My chest tightened.

I was an all-in-or-all-out type of man, and that meant doing whatever I needed to do—no matter how dark and bloody—to reach my goal.

But how far am I willing to go now that Sin's life might be on the line?

Will I offer her up as a sacrificial lamb?

The old Core would have without hesitation, but that was before I'd really gotten to know Sin. But without me even realizing it until now, the line between what I needed—vengeance—and wanted—Sin—was thin.

When push comes to shove, will I sacrifice Sin's life to avenge my mom's death?

A couple weeks ago, the answer would have been a resounding, *Yes!*

Today? I was second-guessing every damn move and decision I made. And that shit was not how I operated... ever.

When I made a strategic decision, I stuck to that shit and didn't deviate, letting the chips fall where they may. Outside of my team, people were pawns to maneuver any way I wanted. For years, I'd built alliances while doing things like blackmail, coercion, and extortion, and that had made me one of the wealthiest and most feared men in New York City. I was the puppet master, pulling the strings and making CEOs, politicians, and the very affluent dance for my amusement. Billionaires would quake in their custom-made shoes for fear of being exposed by the cache of intelligence I had about their shady business dealings and sordid sexual tastes. Information that would ruin them if I chose to reveal it.

I'm Core McKay, a billionaire, and I'm always in control.

The vision of Sin's eyes dilated with lust flashed in my mind. Indecent hunger surged through me, beating at my self-control. Sin was everything I wanted in a woman—strong and feisty. The idea of having her in my bed every night, submitting to me, for the rest of my life had my cock throbbing and my balls aching.

Shit. How the hell did I let it go so far?

I snapped out of my reverie. "Kevin, I'm pulling up to the warehouse now. I'll give you a call later."

Finally, the time had come to get answers and put all this shit with Bigsby behind me. Of course, after I destroyed his ass.

❧ 5 ❧

CORE

I PARKED BESIDE RAM, who was leaning against his own car with his cell in hand, texting. As soon as I stepped out of my vehicle, closing the door behind me, the nauseating smells of stale food, garbage, and exhaust fumes slammed into me.

Damn. I hate Newark.

Ram pushed away from his SUV and stormed up to me. "About fucking time," he hissed. "I've been waiting hours for you to haul your ass down here."

"I was busy," I barked.

"Busy being cock deep in pussy doesn't fucking count." Ram countered.

Leave it to Ram not to beat around the damn bush.

"Fuck off, Ram," I grunted, walking away, but he easily kept pace.

"Look, bro, I'm just calling it like I see it." Ram defended. "We've had Jeff on ice for hours, and you went MIA on our ass. It's not in your fucking DNA to neglect business, especially when we're so close to bringing down the man who killed your mother."

"Sin needed me."

The man I had been before I slept with her and got to know

her better would have wondered what the hell was wrong with me. She was supposed to be a means to an end. Nothing more. No attachments.

The man I was now... I was her mercenary gladiator, ready to fight and kill anyone who dared to harm her.

I want to protect Sin from the world.

"Did she now? And since when did you start caring about her needs?"

I retorted, "It's fucking complicated."

"Did you actually just say, 'It's fucking complicated?'" He burst out laughing. "It's confirmed; you're losing your mind."

He was right.

How did casual fucking with no strings, no emotional attachments, and no expectations turn into this—me getting greedy and wanting more?

Now I never want to let her go.

"We all think this shit between you and Sin is messing with your head and making you lose focus on the business at hand."

"All?" I countered.

I knew that *all* meant the entire team—Zuri, Kevin, Rocco, Max, and him. That was one of the many downsides of working on a close-knit team. It was like a fucking high school.

"Yep." Ram nodded.

"Not that it's anyone's damn business, but in the interest of shutting down the little girl's gossip clique you're obviously the president of"—I looked at him with hard eyes—"my head is fully intact, and I'm completely focused on our mission."

"Are you sure about that? Because the Core I know wouldn't have ghosted us like you did last night. For that matter, the fucking Core I know wouldn't have brought Sin to his damn place to play house with, especially since she's a woman he's using as a pawn." He paused. "And if I didn't know better, I would think that you've claimed her ass and marked her *Property of Core McKay.*"

"I have," I confided bluntly.

Ram skidded to a stop. "What?"

I stopped, turning to face off with him. "You heard me. I've decided to keep her and see where this relationship between us goes."

Ram's mouth dropped open, and then he closed it. "Keep her?" He laughed. "She's not some damn puppy you can play around with and then give away when she stops being cute and cuddly."

The reminder that I was breaking my number one rule of never mixing business with pleasure was fucking with my mind. My obsession with Sin was crazy and fucking reckless, but I found myself shaken by how my need to possess her had quickly changed to my need to keep her as mine... forever.

"Who said anything about giving her up?" I crossed my arms.

"Hold the fuck up." Ram held up his hand. "Are you actually talking about dating her?"

"Come on, bro. You know me..."

Ram arched a brow. "Do I?"

"You do. And you know I don't date. I fuck. That means me fucking her whenever I want, wherever I want, and however I want. Exclusively."

"That means you're dating her."

I shrugged. "Whatever. I'm not trying to label what Sin and I have."

"Whatever?" He looked at me like I had two heads. "Core! Use your damn head and not your cock."

"Relax," I answered.

"I will not fucking relax. Sin makes you vulnerable."

"Ram, everything is under control. I've got this." I wrinkled my forehead.

Ram snorted. "You've got this? No, you don't. I'm not the smartest person when it comes to figuring out women, but I have enough common fucking sense to know when Sin finds out she's been used and manipulated just so you could get to Bigsby, this is not going to end well—for you." He eyed me. "Believe me.

Hell hath no fury like a woman fucked over by a man. Men have been castrated for less."

"Like I explained, I've got this shit." But the tightness in my chest bore witness to the effect Ram's words had on me.

Ram is right.

I rubbed the back of my neck.

When, not if, Sin found out the truth—that I'd manipulated her just to get to Bigsby—she was going to go ballistic on my ass.

Frankly, her anger I could deal with.

But her walking away from me? From us? Now that possibility is fucking with my head big time.

I pressed my lips together in a slight grimace.

Ram just stared at me. "Bro, just tell her the fucking truth, and if she walks... good riddance. Not that you'd care..." Ram's voice broke off with a small frown. "Wait... what the fuck? I know that look on your face. You do care."

My irritation rose. "What look?"

He shrewdly assessed me. "The look you get when we're about to take over a company—predatory, focused, and possessive."

Ram knew me well. He was right—again. I wanted Sin despite the fact that there were a million reasons I shouldn't.

Ram went on. "After all these years and so many other women, what's so special about Sin?"

Everything—from her take-no-shit attitude to her point of view about sex and me.

Sin pulled no punches and was a welcome change from the women who threw themselves at me because of my money and those I slept with to sate my sexual cravings. None of what I'd had with previous lovers was real, and all of it had been exhausting.

Sin was my kind of perfect. A woman I'd never dreamed of encountering after Maya—the first woman who had loved me for me, stood by me when I was poor, and grounded me. Maya had been my balance, my rock. The major reason I'd decided to turn my back on my criminal empire was for fear of losing her and my unborn child. But I'd lost them anyway, and my world had shattered into a million pieces. For too many years to count, without her, my life had been cold, and I hadn't been alive. Until Sin. Now I could let go of the memories of my life with Maya and move on.

"None of your damn business," I snapped.

"Seriously?"

In that moment, I realized I needed Sin because she filled an emotional gap I'd thought was buried deep and lost forever. Her taste, smell, and body were imprinted on my mind. Ingrained in my mind from the first time I'd fucked her. I couldn't remember the last time I'd wanted someone with the intensity I felt for Sin.

I sighed heavily. "Because Sin's the only woman who truly understands me. Fuck! She's the only woman I ever told about Maya or my mom. That's what she does to me. And even after I told her all that shit, she still accepts me for who I am. She doesn't want to try to change me. And that's the kind of woman I won't ever walk away from."

"If she means that much to you, then tell her the truth," Ram insisted.

"When the time is right, I'll tell her what I did and why. Sin's smart. She'll understand, and we'll move on... together."

Ram laughed. "And everyone thinks I'm the fucking crazy one." He shook his head. "She won't understand that you've used her. No woman would. And there will be no moving on *together*. Look, bro, I get it. You're the master of everything you survey. You're Core motherfucking McKay. Billionaire. Ballbuster. In control of everything you touch. But Sin is different. This whole fucked-up situation is different. She'll walk away from you once she knows the truth."

"If it happens, I'll deal with it." My stomach tightened with the knowledge that there was a big possibility of losing Sin... and frankly, I didn't know if I could deal with that shit.

Now that I'd had a taste of life with Sin in it, going back to my cold, sterile world of caring about nothing but money and my team felt empty. My muscles tensed as I just imagined a world without Sin by my side. Strangely, the thought made me feel like a man deserted on an island... alone.

Ram laughed. "Seriously, this shit is hilarious. You were the mastermind behind this whole plot to get close to her and then use her as a fucking pawn to get revenge on Bigsby, and then you lied to her—"

I cut him off. "I've never lied to her. I've omitted information and evaded talking about need-to-know information that might jeopardize our mission. But I've never fucking lied to her. Ever!"

Ram shook his head. "If that's the excuse you're going to give her, then, bro, you're in a shitload of trouble. Because if there is one thing I know, there isn't a sane woman walking this earth who's going to blindly accept the load of shit you just told me."

"When I explain everything to her, she'll understand my motives."

"Uh-huh." Ram looked at me with wide eyes. "And how do you think she'll feel when she finds out you were the puppet master behind all her deals with the retailers screeching to a halt?"

I winced when I remembered the fact that Ram and I had contacted every retailer we owned a major stake in and told them the deal to carry Sin's line was dead until we personally approved it. More importantly, how Sin had flinched as if I'd physically slapped her when I told her that my sources had informed me that her retailers were getting cold feet about the viability of her collection and were pulling out of her deals. What she didn't know was that, with just one phone call to my shadowy connections—who were wealthy, deadly, and ruthless— I had killed all her retail agreements.

"I fixed that situation," I retorted. "I called them all and approved her deal to go forward."

Ram cocked his head, looking at me like some horrible experiment gone wrong. "Um... let me get this straight. You're taking credit for fixing a situation you created? Man... this is classic Core McKay bullshit."

"Like I said, she'll understand."

"Okay, Core. If you say so..." He clapped me on the back and walked away, laughing.

I'd be damned if I'd admit it aloud, but he was on point about this, too. This situation between Sin and me was a messy, fucked-up predicament that, for the first time in my life, I had no clue how to fix without losing her in the end.

6

CORE

W HEN I OPENED the warehouse door, slipping inside the dark building, I quickly snapped my mind into business mode and to the matter at hand—interrogating Jeff. I'd planned on the process of breaking him down to take hours. So I'd told Sin I wouldn't be back home from taking care of business until tomorrow morning.

The first thing on my agenda was finding out where Jeff was holding Lexis, Ram's sister, and then getting her back... hopefully alive. The second was getting confirmation from Jeff about why the ledger was so important to his boss, Bigsby.

I glanced at Ram, who was pacing back and forth while talking on his cell.

"Kevin, are you sure?" He paused a beat. "Don't be a dick. I just want to be sure." There was another moment of silence. "Yeah. Okay. I'll tell Core. Talk to you later." He ended the call before striding up to me.

"Tell me what?" I asked.

"Kevin just got word from his sources that the Feds are mounting an investigation into the Super PAC backing Bigsby."

"Why should I give a shit if they shut UF-Star down?"

It was no secret that UF-Star was a Super PAC—an independent political action committee that had been spending a ton of money to promote Bigsby for New York City's new mayor. No one but us knew that for a huge fee, Bigsby had arranged to help a group of traffickers clean their money through his shell company, Pomtonic International. In addition, in exchange for the traffickers contributing to UF-Star, Bigsby had made a deal with them that once he got elected, he'd turn a blind eye to all their illegal activities for a percentage of their profits.

"But it's not just UF-Star," Ram interjected. "It's the sex trafficking ring Bigsby's involved in. Kevin's intel says it won't be long before the Feds arrest Bigsby."

"Shit. That's not good."

"What's the problem?" Ram asked. "That's what you wanted, right? To destroy Bigsby? Now you don't have to get your hands dirty. The Feds and prosecutors will end him."

The truth of the matter was that I wanted to get my hands dirty.

I wanted to personally destroy him. It was the only way to ensure that everything went according to plan.

I was close to finally destroying Bigsby Calhoune by stripping away everything he held dear—his wealth, freedom, political career, and trophy fiancée, Cate.

Now I had everything—Bigsby and the one woman who had unknowingly made it all happen, Sin.

But why is the taste of revenge so bittersweet on my tongue?

"I've waited too many goddamn years to destroy that fucker. I'm not going to sit back and let him slip through my fingers. He has to pay for killing my mother. Besides, I'll be damned if I trust the incompetent Feds. They could mess it up, allowing him to get off on some technicality. No. I've got to personally make sure he ends up in jail for the rest of his life or six feet under. Either way, my job will be done, and I can mark this mission complete."

"Well, we'd better wrap up this shit fast because once the Feds nab him, he'll be out of your reach."

We moved off through the space, our boots sounding like trumpets as they slapped against the hard concrete floor in the cavernous, dark space. Rats almost the size of kittens ran across the floor to hide. The air was stale and cloying.

"What's the status of Project Jeff?" I asked.

"Like we planned, Max and Rocco have been softening him up for us and keeping him awake all night with rounds of throwing ice-cold water on his ass. Max reported that it wouldn't take us long to break him."

Sometimes, it took us days to break our captive and other times, hours.

"Good," I answered. "We'll start with questions about Lexis's location, and then we'll grill him about the ledger. I need him to corroborate what Kevin found out."

We made our way down the metal stairs and through the corridor.

"You don't know how bad I wanted to storm into that room last night and wrap my hands around Jeff's neck," Ram replied.

I knew that, deep down, Ram felt guilty for Lexis's disappearance. Well, more like guilty for not pressing her for more information about Jeff Barolo—a man who had become her boyfriend after dating her for only two weeks.

Ram had grown suspicious when Lexis refused to introduce Jeff to him, so Ram had driven to her college—Massachusetts Institute of Technology—only to find out from her friends that Lexis had dropped out and vanished with Jeff.

After a background check, we'd found out Jeff was some budding yuppie pimp who had a track record for ensnaring pretty young college freshmen women into a life of sex trafficking.

It had been hell trying to find any information on the location of Lexis because the human trafficking world was dirty and secretive. One tip after another had led to dead ends, which had frustrated us and pissed us off.

Every time we'd gotten close to finding Lexis, Jeff would

transport her across state lines, leaving no trace. The last hot lead we'd gotten was that she'd been traded to a trafficker in San Diego.

After months of attempting to infiltrate the seedy traffickers' world, playing games of subterfuge while trying to find Lexis, we'd finally gotten a solid clue from Sarah, one of the girls Lexis had worked with who had escaped Jeff's clutches. She had given us one name—Ben Vargos—that ultimately led to Jeff and Bigsby.

After we'd kidnapped and interrogated Ben—who was also among the human traffickers cleaning his money through Pomtonic International and pumping a hell of a lot of money into UF-Star—he had given up information on his connection to Bigsby and who Bigsby was working with to get women... Jeff Barolo.

Ram ran his hand over his hair. "I swear, if Jeff killed my sister, I'll—"

"Don't even fucking think it," I barked.

We both knew the odds of Lexis being alive were slim, but I was still optimistic. We had done some more digging into her disappearance and unearthed info that corroborated our current belief. Lexis had not dropped out of college or run away. From all the dots we'd connected, she'd probably thought she was going on a weekend getaway with her "perfect" boyfriend, Jeff, and then got trapped in the world of sex trafficking.

"She's been missing for almost a year," Ram grumbled with bleak eyes.

It was hard as hell to watch my levelheaded friend slowly become emotionally unhinged with each passing day Lexis remained trapped in that horrid world.

"Even if she's still alive, she won't be the same Lexis she was before she got abducted by that piece of shit."

It was grim but true. We both knew that the old Lexis—who was always happy and cheery with an *I believe there are more good people than bad* perspective—would no longer exist. There was no way that she'd come back from whatever hell she was currently experiencing without some emotional and mental scars.

We'd heard all the dark things that happened to the women Jeff had lured from their normal lives and made into sex slaves. Many of the victims weren't just runaways or kids who'd been abandoned. Lots of them had come from what would be considered good families and had been coerced and trapped by clever predators like Jeff.

My eyes narrowed as I just remembered Sarah's horrific tale of her life with Jeff...

SARAH WAS NINETEEN WHEN SHE HAD BEEN APPROACHED BY AN older man—Jeff—who promised he would change her life forever. It'd started as a whirlwind romance. The pair had bumped into each other time and again around Brooklyn. She'd proclaimed that it'd felt like a series of coincidences. He'd called it fate. It was neither of the two. It was part of the game. Then things between them had progressed quickly. He'd met her family, and the two had made plans to go on a trip to California. It hadn't been until they were there that Jeff's intentions became clear.

"I met Jeff the same way all of us did, including Lexis—at a party. I didn't realize I had been marked. We all had," Sarah revealed to us. "He even met my mother."

She confided that the change had happened quickly and dramatically. "One morning after we arrived in California, Jeff shoved a pair of heels and a tiny black dress into my hands and told me to 'get to work.' I thought he was joking, but I was wrong. He took my clothes, my shoes, my keys, my phone," Sarah recounted. "He explained that he was actually a pimp, and this was how escorts were made."

His plans for her were detailed and disturbing. He took her directly to a wealthy client's house and forced her to have sex. It would not be her last client.

"Jeff kept all of us off the streets. We only had sex with people he knew. It was like all these rich, perverted men knew each other... like it was some dirty sex club."

During that time, Sarah explained she hadn't tried to escape because Jeff had threatened her and terrified her. "He swore his clients were rich and powerful and would think nothing of going after my family. I believed him because the client homes he'd brought us to were so huge and fancy. It was like shit you only saw on a reality television show."

Ram and I realized then that the fact that Sarah and all of Jeff's girls, including Lexis, were kept off the streets was what made it almost impossible for us to track Lexis down.

Sarah reported that she'd spent eight months being moved from state to state—essentially, she was on tour—servicing clients at their homes or parties to have sex. It was at one of those client parties that she'd met Lexis.

"Lexis was lucky," Sarah whispered. "She didn't have to work the parties like the rest of Jeff's girls. It was as if Jeff was showing her off to his customers like some trophy. I'd heard several clients making offers to Jeff to fuck her, but he'd just tell them that she was his. But I knew better. Jeff was trying to get the best offer he could for Lexis."

"Did you talk to her?" Ram asked.

"Yes"—Sarah fidgeted nervously—"but she was high."

Ram hissed, "Lexis doesn't do drugs."

"But Jeff does," Sarah replied. "And he would force us to take drugs all the time. He suggested it made us less uptight and more fun around the clients." For Sarah, sleeping with those men was like a death sentence, and she finally worked up the nerve to escape. "I waited until the client was almost asleep and told him I was going to go outside and smoke a cigarette. And then I ran for my life."

I SNAPPED BACK TO THE PRESENT.

"We're getting closer to finding Lexis—alive," I told Ram. "The sooner we find her, the better, bro."

"Stop bullshitting me, Core," he hissed. "I know what animals like Jeff and Bigsby are capable of doing to women they view as prey."

"Yes, but we've still got to hope for something good to come out of this clusterfuck."

Ram huffed out a breath of air. "Lexis and I had a big argument before she disappeared. I ordered her to come back to New York, and she told me that it was her life and for me to fuck off. I'm not going to lie; her defiant attitude pissed me off. So I shouted some shit to her that I'm not too proud of... but dammit, it was time for tough love."

"So now you're blaming yourself because she trusted that fucker Jeff?"

The only one responsible for this mess was Jeff. He'd manipulated Lexis into putting her trust in a man who didn't deserve it or her.

An image of Sin's smiling face flashed into my mind, and the irony and similarity of the Lexis and Jeff situation chilled me to the bone.

Didn't I do a very similar thing to Sin by making her believe she could trust me? When my intention from the very start was to use her just to get to Bigsby?

There was a heaviness in my body.

I didn't deserve Sin's trust, and I damn sure didn't deserve her. But I was a greedy man who wanted more than I was entitled to.

Ram's voice broke into my thoughts. "Yes, I spoiled her too much and sheltered her from the realities of life because I wanted to make up for the rough way we had grown up. If I'd just told her straight up that she didn't know shit about love or men, then maybe she wouldn't have hooked up with a predator. It's my fault she chose Jeff over me. I fucking pushed her too hard, and maybe she's dead because of me." His eyes took on a steely glint.

"Ram, you know I have your back, no matter what, bro."

Ram roughly blew out a breath before nodding.

I continued. "So let's not jump to any conclusions when the answers are right behind this damn door."

Adrenaline pumped through my veins as we stood before the door.

What we were about to do would be brutal, but we had to get Lexis back, and there was nothing I wasn't willing to do to accomplish that.

My mind slipped into the dark and lethal place, and the ugly monster that I kept caged came out to play. He didn't give a shit about anyone or anything but his prey—Jeff.

Grinding my teeth, I grabbed the doorknob, yanking open the door before stepping into the damp-smelling cell.

My eyes quickly adjusted to the darkness as we strode in. Ram closed the door with a decisive click.

I nodded curtly to Max and Rocco, my enforcers, before my eyes locked on the man in his early thirties—according to our intel—who was lashed to the metal chair sitting between Max and Rocco and was surrounded by buckets, a stack of towels, a bottle of pink solution, and a watering can resting on the floor.

Jeff's body was wet, stark naked, and shivering.

His eyes widened at the sight of Ram and me. "What the hell is going on now?" he squawked and then warily eyed me.

My nostrils flared slightly before I responded, "Hello, Jeff."

"Who are you?" he furtively glanced around.

"I'm your worst fucking nightmare." I fixed him with a cold stare.

"Do you know who I am?" Jeff stuttered while trying unsuccessfully to move his legs that were spread eagle and bound to the chair

"Dead," I replied, "if you say another damn word without my say-so. I'll kill you right here."

Jeff glanced around, and I could see the sheer fear in his eyes.

The room was silent, except for the low whir of the air conditioner. Ram moved toward the table smack dab in the middle of the room.

"Meet Ram." I jabbed a finger in Ram's direction. "Lexis's brother."

Jeff's face turned ashen.

"And I'm going to break you in half," Ram hissed while snatching up a pair of black latex gloves and impatiently snapping them on. "If I don't get my baby sister back... alive."

Jeff bucked against the rope binding him to the chair. "Untie me!" he shrilled.

Max growled, slapping him on the back of his head. "I will snap your damn neck. Shut the fuck up."

Ram sneered but remained eerily silent as he moved to sit on the edge of the table.

Jeff's face contorted with pain. "What the fuck is this shit about?" he squeaked while watching me move unhurriedly toward the narrow table.

I ignored him while taking off my leather jacket, folding it, and then laying it over the table ever so carefully. I cracked my knuckles before slipping on a pair of black latex gloves.

"All I was doing was visiting a friend when these two men"—his eyes darted toward Max and Rocco—"kidnapped me, brought me here, stripped me naked, and started torturing the shit out of me."

My eyes were cold, my voice flat. "And they're the nice ones. Me?" I shrugged. "Not so much."

"Come on, man. This is totally fucked up," Jeff screamed. "And illegal." He struggled uselessly against the rope.

Rocco snorted. "Ain't this some crazy shit? You're a sex trafficker complaining about us doing something illegal. Men like you should be buried alive."

"So Sinthia Michaels is your friend?" I asked with a sharp tone.

"Yes." Beads of sweat dripped down his forehead.

I arched a brow. "Do you really want to lie to me?"

"She's a friend of a friend," Jeff stuttered. "And I was picking up something from her house."

I cracked my knuckles. "Now we can do this the hard way or—"

"The easy way?" Jeff croaked.

"No." I shook my head. "I was going to say the harder way. And if you interrupt me again, I'm going to knock out your damn teeth."

Jeff gulped.

I smiled coldly as I rolled up my sleeves, displaying my tattooed forearms. "I'm not going to lie to you. There's no way you're going to get through my interrogation without a lot of blood spilled—yours—because I happen to hate lowlife mother-fuckers who deal in human trafficking."

"This is bullshit!" Jeff's panic was distinct. "I don't do that shit. I swear."

"You lying fuck." Ram stormed up to Jeff and punched him in the face. He grunted in pain. "You pimped out my sister."

Jeff spit out blood along with a couple of teeth before screaming, "I didn't. Not Lexis. She's mine. Bigsby wanted me to, but I didn't. I swear."

"She's yours?" Ram roared. "My sister is not your damn prop-erty. She fucking trusted your ass, and you treated her like a whore."

Jeff's lips and chin wobbled before he mumbled, "I'm sorry."

I eyed Jeff. "This is how it's going down. I'm going to ask you some questions, and I want straight answers." My voice was harsh. "Where's Lexis?"

"If I tell you, Bigsby will kill me." Jeff's body trembled.

"And if you don't tell me, I'll kill you. So it sounds like you're in a real fucked-up predicament. But the difference between Bigsby and me is I'll make sure you stay alive for five long, agonizing days until you beg me to end your life." I smiled coldly. "Your choice."

"Fuck you," he spit.

My voice dropped to a lethal, low whisper. "No. Fuck you."

I nodded to Rocco and Max. They yanked the chair Jeff was sitting on all the way back so it dangled precariously on its back legs. Picking up the damp towels from the floor, I slapped them onto Jeff's inclined head before pouring water over his scalp. The damp cloth was not essential but was a bonus multiplier of the torture. I continued pouring water over his face, and Jeff struggled and inhaled. In turn, the inhalation brought the damp towels tight against his nostrils as if a huge, wet paw had clamped over his face. His legs, chest, and arms twitched involuntarily. The inhaled water was an instant, life-threatening situation; even the smallest amount of liquid in the larynx and trachea was an immediate, hardwired hotline directly to the panic portion of the brain that death was imminent.

He struggled, but not as much as before. I nodded to Max and Rocco, and they righted Jeff's chair. I yanked off the soaking, stifling layers. His head lolled back, and he was barely coherent.

"I know your lungs are burning." I stepped back, drying my hand on a clean black towel. "I can see the panic in your eyes. You want this to end, and I promise I will end it. Just tell me what I want to know. Where's Lexis?"

He coughed. "She's in Connecticut with the other girls. And if you keep me alive, I'll take you to her." He looked around with uneasy eyes.

Ram snapped, "Either tell us where she's at or we'll do to you like they castrate the bulls." He held up the metal forceps. "We'll put a rubber band around your balls, cutting off the blood circulation until they fall off like rotten grapes. Your choice, Jeff."

Ram squeezed the castrater as if testing out the device. Jeff looked on with disbelief.

"Okay, okay." He stammered out a Greenwich, Connecticut, street address.

Ram quickly entered the information into his cell and then glanced over at me. "I just sent Kevin the info to check it out." He then stared at Jeff. "And if it isn't correct, this shit is going to get real nasty."

It didn't take long for Ram's cell to beep with an incoming text. He tapped the screen and reported, "He's heading over to the address right now. He'll brief us once he gets there."

I twirled a chair around, and I sat in front of Jeff. "See how easy this shit can be? Now let's move on, shall we?" I leaned forward. "Let's talk about Sinthia Michaels. Why did Bigsby send you to break into her house to steal the ledger?"

"I don't know what you're talking about," Jeff stuttered.

"You don't?" My voice dropped to a threatening whisper.

I nodded. Rocco yanked the chair back. Max slapped the damp towels over Jeff's face and then started pouring water over him. Jeff struggled, but Max didn't relent. Jeff thrashed more frantically until Rocco righted the chair. Max whipped off the towels, and Jeff gasped for air.

"Why does Bigsby want the ledger?" I yelled.

"I don't know anything!" Jeff screamed.

Ram walked over to him and punched him in the face. Jeff whimpered as blood trickled down his cheek.

"Jeff," I started, "come on, man. I thought we had an understanding that you were going to tell the truth."

Jeff silently looked at me.

I continued. "How about this? I'll tell you what we know, and we'll start all over again."

Jeff nodded while nervously licking his lips.

"Good," I grunted and fixed him with a cold stare. "How we hear it, the reason we had such a hard time finding you is because you're being protected by Bigsby. We know you're now his errand boy. You recruit the women for him, and he pimps them out to his rich friends. We hear there's a huge demand from his rolling-in-it friends to fuck fresh, untrained women any way and anywhere they want."

Jeff nodded. "Yes... to everything."

"See how easy that was?" I replied. "Moving on... Bigsby sent you to Sin's house to break in and get the ledger, which you did. But you also did a little more than that, didn't you? You trashed her house."

"What?" Jeff squeaked. "No." He shook his head in denial. "Don't know what you're talking about, man. Yes, I broke in and stole the ledger, but I left the house exactly how I found it. Trashed." His Adam's apple bobbed.

Max's body tensed. "You lying piece of shit!"

He stalked toward Jeff before hitting him hard across the head. I watched with disinterest.

"I'm telling the truth," Jeff replied. "I took the ledger for Bigsby, but I didn't trash the fucking house. I swear." He paused. "I'm not dying for Bigsby. He ordered me to do a job, and I did it. If you just let me—"

"Max," I hissed, "go find out who trashed Sin's place."

"You actually believe that piece of shit?" Max asked.

I glanced over at Jeff, who stammered, "I swear. It's the truth."

He looked like a desperate man with nothing to lose who was fighting for his life, which he was.

"Yes, I do," I gritted out to Max. "Get on this now!"

Max nodded before walking out of the room with his cell in hand.

I eyed Jeff. "What were you told about the ledger?"

"I'm not saying anything more until you release me," Jeff demanded.

"You will talk," I replied and then eyed Ram. "Let's try the castrater, shall we?"

"My pleasure," he answered with a wicked gleam in his eyes.

"It might take him a couple tries to lock on to your shriveled-up balls," I informed Jeff. "But practice makes perfect."

"I'm not talking, you sadistic bastard!" Jeff yelled.

"Well, that's the spirit. How about we kick this party up a notch?" I countered before nodding at Rocco, who brought me the small machine with two metal pads attached to it. He placed the device on the floor by my feet.

"Let's play." I flipped on the machine. I picked up the two metal paddles attached to the device and asked him, "Have you ever watched the show *Naked and Afraid?*" I slowly touched the paddles together, causing sparks to fly into the air.

The color drained from Jeff's face.

"Rocco, let's proceed," I ordered.

Rocco pushed the button on the machine, causing the electricity to pulsate harder through the paddles.

"Time for the fireworks to begin." I pressed both pads to Jeff's scrotum.

His face contorted as he howled with pain.

7

SINTHIA

The doorman grandly opened the door for me before I stepped out of Core's building after he left for his urgent business meeting. Hurriedly, I zipped up my leather motorcycle jacket as the cool, crisp air engulfed me.

I loved October; it was the best time of the year to walk around New York City because all the touristy summer crowds had disappeared. It was a beautiful Sunday, but I had to forgo my leisurely walk through Manhattan.

Yesterday, I'd worked until late night on my designs and then eaten a quick meal before falling into a deep sleep. When I'd woken up this morning, I'd felt pleasantly refreshed but missed Core's warm body. He'd given me the heads-up yesterday that his business deal would take a while to negotiate, so he wouldn't be back until today. But before leaving, he had insisted that someone from his team drive me around today. At first, I'd resisted, not liking the idea of being followed around the city like I needed a babysitter, and we'd passionately argued back and forth about the topic. But eventually, his logic and concern for my safety due to the break-in at my townhouse had finally won.

Truth be told, the idea that the person who had caused such destruction of my property, including my collection, had not yet been caught caused me unease. Now that I'd left the cocoon and safety of Core's penthouse, a sense of dread and paranoia seeped into my bones, and I was glad Core had been so insistent.

I inhaled deeply, taking in a lungful of the fresh air, and mentally shook myself. I had to stay on my game.

Buck up, Sin. Put on your big-girl panties.

I straightened my back and slung my leather handbag over my shoulder before walking toward Zuri. She was Core's well-paid minion—her words, not mine—whom I'd met for the first time on Friday when she dropped off Core's invitation to the McKay Club along with an expensive, beautiful dress he'd purchased for me to wear that night. Frankly, when Zuri had strode into my townhouse, I hadn't known what to make of her due to the fact that things were a little tense between Core and me, and anyone linked to him had been on my shit list just from their mere association. But after Zuri and our mutual on-the-spot should-I-like-you analysis of each other, we'd concluded that we liked each other so far.

I waved at Zuri, who was leaning against her expensive black SUV. She looked like she'd just stepped off the fashion runway. Her dark autumn skin tone along with her sleek flaming-red tresses, pulled up into a high ponytail, gave her an exotic look. Her eyes, as usual, were shielded by aviators.

She pushed away from her car, stepping forward and then hugging me. I returned the embrace before pulling back.

"Well, don't you look absolutely hot in that outfit?" Zuri complimented me. "Damn. You're giving me a lady boner."

I laughed. "I aim to please."

Today I was rocking a cool graphic tee and cuffed skinny jeans that I'd amped up with statement accessories. A pair of gold hoop earrings, a logo handbag, and red-bottomed shoes.

"So you drew the short straw today and got assigned to be my driver, huh?" I gave her a mock frown, but frankly, I wasn't put out by Core assigning Zuri to be my babysitter. I liked her, and that was saying a lot for a person like me who didn't easily click with people and therefore kept her circle of friends really small.

"Assigned?" Zuri whipped off her sunglasses. "Hell no. I volunteered." She smiled impishly. "I wanted to hang out with you today. Believe me. The alternative of having the other guys on the team drive you around would make you pull your hair out. I love them and all, but they can be a bit abrasive. Just way too much grunting and knocking stones together like cavemen if you ask me."

"So basically what you're saying is they're assholes, just like their boss?" I grinned sassily.

"Exactly." Her eyes lit with a twinkle of mischief.

I opened the passenger door and slid in, watching as she sauntered around to the driver's side. Zuri got into the car, fastening her seat belt.

"So where are we heading today?" She turned on her vehicle and revved the engine.

"To my friend Cisco's boutique." I rattled off the address while fastening my seat belt. "Today is the last dress fitting for my two best clients." I sighed heavily. "Luckily, I sent their gowns to the boutique days ago for alterations. It would have been a mega clusterfuck if the dresses had gotten destroyed last night along with the rest of my collection."

I'd already designed the gowns for Ariana Bellisario—the mother of my bestie, Jade—and Erika Watson—Ariana's best friend and Jade's television executive boss—to wear at an upcoming fundraising gala. And I needed to make sure their gowns were perfect. So I'd sent their gowns to Cisco's—the boutique where all of my clients' fittings were done—so my friend Summer, who was a top-notch seamstress and the only one I trusted to work on my designs, could put the last-minute touches on the gowns.

My mind drifted to Jade. I missed her. There were so many times yesterday and today when I had been so tempted to call her, telling her everything that had happened since she left for

New Zealand to start production on her first directorial feature. But I didn't want Jade to worry about me or feel compelled to hightail her ass back to New York, ruining her movie shoot. Just because my dreams were on hiatus didn't mean Jade's had to be destroyed over my drama.

Zuri pulled out of the parking space. "Core told me about your break-in." She ripped her gaze away from the road long enough to give me a sympathetic look before turning back to concentrate on weaving through Manhattan traffic.

"I'm kind of numb about it, frankly." I stared out the window, looking at everything but processing nothing. "The funny thing is I couldn't give a shit about all of my personal possessions that were destroyed. Those things I can buy back, but it's all the damn work I put into finishing my collection. That's the part that hurts like a fucker."

I bit my bottom lip, staring at the bumper-to-bumper gridlock.

I'd had only five more over-the-top pieces to complete before I sat down with the buying and marketing teams to decide which designs would make the final cut, essentially eliminating designs to be made and sold via the retailers. And I'd excitedly anticipated the final stage—when my collection would go on sale.

Damn! My collection was almost complete. Now I have to start all over again.

The thought was frustrating and daunting.

Horns honked loudly, mercifully jolting my thoughts back from an impending descent into depression.

"Sin, I'm really sorry about your collection," Zuri replied while zipping in and out of the snarl of taxicabs and buses. "The pieces that I saw when I was at your house were so beautiful. It's going to take a lot of work, but you can rebuild the collection. And whatever you need, you can count on me to help you."

"Thank you, Zuri." I smiled at her while fiddling with my seat belt.

"And I just heard from the cleaning company. There was more

work than they had originally estimated, but they'll have your townhouse finished today." Zuri cursed and hit her horn. She mumbled under her breath about terrible New York drivers while tapping the steering wheel as we sat in heavy Manhattan traffic.

"I appreciate it, but no amount of cleaning is going to make me feel comfortable in my house again," I returned. "Whoever broke in violated my space... my home. Honestly, I'll feel better once the police find out who did it."

The gridlock eased, allowing Zuri to smoothly drive ahead. "Unfortunately, the police probably moved on to another case. But I wouldn't worry about it. Core will find the person who did it and make them pay."

I clenched my fingers around my leather handbag. "You have a hell of a lot of faith in him."

"Don't you?" Zuri shot back.

I contemplated my response before uttering a word. Zuri was employed by Core. More importantly, she was his friend, so I knew where her loyalty lay. However, I wouldn't be me if I didn't keep it real with her.

"I have faith in myself." I shrugged. "I've learned the hard way that people tend to have their own agendas. It's just second nature for me to question people's intentions."

My past experience with toxic relationships, with Grace and men, made me so conscious of people—what they said and why they wanted to be with me.

"Sin, no one is perfect, especially not Core. It's just..." She shook her head. "Never mind."

"Zuri, spit it out."

"I just assumed that after spending time with Core, you saw that little bit of potential of sticking it out with him."

"Look, Zuri, I like Core... a lot. Probably more than I should, especially given the fact that our business relationship didn't start out on the best foot." Not with him swooping in out of nowhere and taking control of ninety-seven percent of my business. "Yes, our relationship has changed for the better, but how I feel about Core is complicated."

My mind was telling me one thing—not to get too attached—but I felt like I already was.

"Hmm... complicated. That's code for: *He scares the shit out of me—emotionally.*"

I blinked, startled that she'd read me so fast. "Hell yes, he does," I answered. There was no need to lie about it. "I've moved from wanting to shank him to wanting..."

"More than just sex," Zuri finished.

"Yes," I replied. My throat instantly went dry as I just felt the emotions stirring inside me while I tried to wrap my mind around the concept of Core and me together... like in a real relationship.

"Trust me on this," Zuri confided. "This is new territory for Core, too." She paused. "Zero. That's the number of women he's brought to his penthouse."

My mouth dropped open with shock before I shut it. "I don't understand..."

"You don't know much about the man, do you?" Zuri asked.

"Apparently not." I nibbled on my bottom lip.

Abruptly, Zuri pulled over to the farthest lane and out of traffic. She double parked and then put on her hazard lights. "Do you want to?" she asked before unsnapping her seat belt and turning to squarely look me in the face.

"Want to what?" I asked.

"Know about him?" She pursed her lips.

I ran my fingers through my hair. "You work for him, and you're his friend. So why would you tell me anything about him?" I unfastened my seat belt to get more comfortable.

"Core is not just my friend. He's the big brother I never had. He has my back, and I have his. And I would never tell you anything that would betray the trust and bond Core and I share." She blew a strand of hair that had fallen across her eye.

"All I'm saying is I don't give a shit about the who, what, and why he came into your life. That's the past. This is the now."

She jabbed her finger in the air. "He has everything a man could ever want—money, friends who love him, freedom, and power—but he doesn't have that one person. I want that so much for him because he fucking deserves a chance at something real. You are that real. A chance for happiness." She scowled. "But you two are the most stubborn people I know. You're scared of being hurt. Core wants to stick his head in the sand and pretend he won't be fucked up emotionally if you walk out of his life for good. This shit is not rocket science. Will you both just lay your damn cards on the table with each other and see what happens?"

"I wish it were that simple, Zuri. I've been through some things in my life that I haven't quite healed from."

"Sin, so has Core. Growing up, he went through some crazy shit that would have broken a lesser man."

"Don't you think I know that? Shit. I thought my life was fucked up, losing my dad the way I did, but damn... with Core's mother being killed so brutally and in front of him..." I swallowed hard. "I'm not going to lie; I think that would have broken me."

Zuri's mouth parted and then snapped shut.

"What?" I asked.

"Wow." She shook her head. "I can't believe he told you about his mother. Talking about her is pretty much taboo for him, even with us—me, Ram, Kevin, Max, and Rocco—and we're family."

I silently digested what she'd revealed. Core had shared this deeply personal experience... with me.

Any traces of doubt that he cared about me disappeared along with the little nagging voice in my head that berated me for trusting him, for agreeing to give our relationship a chance to grow.

I guess I should listen to my heart... right?

8

SINTHIA

"Zuri," I said while stepping off the elevator with her by my side, "you know you don't have to hang around for this."

"Wait." She skidded to a stop, giving me a mock glare. "Are you trying to get rid of me already?" She pouted playfully. "And just when I thought we had this bestie vibe happening. Don't you like me?" She dramatically fluttered her eyelashes.

I rolled my eyes. "No."

Zuri cocked her head to the side.

"Maybe," I replied before my lips curled up into a smile.

Zuri fist-pumped. "Yes! I knew it."

"Okay, okay. Now move your needy ass on," I demanded before swaying away from her. It didn't take her long to catch up with me. "Are you sure you won't be bored? Watching client fittings is not exactly exciting, and they tend to be long." But for me, it was the exact opposite. I loved everything about my design process—from creation to seeing my clothing on my clients—but I was a fashionista and loved all things clothes.

"Bored? Are you crazy?" Zuri countered. "Jesus. My heart is pounding like a high school virgin about to get her cherry popped." She winked at me. "I mean look at this place. It's a paradise for a clotheshorse like me." She gestured widely to Cisco's boutique.

The space was sleek, modern, and very glam. The walls were painted black, which allowed the rich colors of my designs on display to pop against the beautiful darkness. It contrasted against the plush velvet furniture and natural light in the space that had been designed with a contemporary look in mind.

I smiled at her. "I knew there was a reason I liked you so much."

I scanned the studio. I loved the ambiance at my friend Francisco "Cisco" Rodriguez's upscale boutique and that it was blissfully quiet. Unlike other boutiques in this neighborhood, Cisco's place was by appointment only, which his rich and discerning patrons loved.

"Those are your designs, right?" Zuri gestured to my pieces that were displayed like eye candy in the middle of the space.

"Yes." I confirmed proudly. "They're some of my pretties."

"Damn. Your designs are badass."

"Okay. So now you're just bucking for a discount," I groused good-naturedly. "But that shit isn't happening. I have damn bills to pay."

Zuri laughed. "Jesus. You're funny and straightforward, and you live your life unapologetically. I really like that about you. Core's lucky I'm not into chicks, because I'd shank him for you."

"Girl, you're cray-cray. I love it," I replied with a wink. "Follow me," I ordered, dropping my leather handbag onto a plush ottoman. "Let me give you the tour," I instructed, looping an arm through hers, ushering her across the space. "Okay, these are all my designs." With one hand, I gestured to the wall-to-wall racks.

Zuri fanned herself while gawking at the clothes. "Oh Lord. There's movement in my vajayjay, an honest-to-goodness tingly fucking sensation. I want one of everything."

I gave her an impish smile. "Aren't you even going to look at the price tags?"

"Nope." Zuri lovingly stroked a dress. "It's all going on my McKay black charge card. These outfits are my bonus for having to put up with a bunch of cavemen assholes."

"Shit. Why didn't you say that from the get-go? I'm more than happy to help you spend Core's money on my clothing." I stepped forward, pulling out a bright, sparkling orange halter top and a full, ruffled black silk organza skirt. "This is new and would look fab on you."

Zuri squealed like a schoolgirl. "Love it."

"Pick whatever you want and put it on the empty rack. Cisco will bring everything upstairs and set up a fitting room for you."

I dug into my pocket, pulling out my cell and aiming it at her. "Zuri, smile and hold up the dress. I'm sending Core a photo of what his money is buying."

Zuri struck a vixen pose. "Cha-ching!" she chirped as I took the photo and then hit send.

"I can't wait to see Core's face when he gets his charge card statement," I crowed before shoving my cell back into my pocket.

Zuri started putting clothes on the empty rack. "Nothing fazes him. Believe me," she answered while looking through the other outfits on display.

"Fill the rack up, sweetie." I urged. "You deserve it." I winked at her.

"Sin!" Cisco exclaimed, rushing over to me.

Dressed in black jeans, a crisp blue shirt, and his signature old Rolex, he barely paused before closing the space between us and then yanking me into his arms. I hugged him back without any hesitation.

"Sin, don't be angry," Cisco muttered into my ear before pulling away and clasping my hands. "This is not my fault," he finished as his eyes swept over me from head to toe. At thirty-six, he still looked boyish, but he had intense dark eyebrows that conveyed his seriousness. He released my hands, dramatically fanning himself with his hand. "*Ay, Dios mío!* I really don't need all this drama today."

I knew from experience that when Cisco started spouting Spanish, shit in his world had hit the damn fan.

I arched a brow. "What the hell are you talking about?"

"Sin!" a woman's voice exclaimed. "Jesus. I'm so happy to see you. Listen, I need—"

"Tabitha?" I cut her off.

What. The. Fuck?

Just a couple weeks ago, we had been at the McKay Club, laughing and drinking. Gone was the polished veneer of Tabitha Thorp, celebrity designer. Now she looked haggard. Her face was gaunt. The head-to-toe black ensemble she wore looked at least two sizes too big and accented her now-unattractive, rail-thin body. Her hair appeared frizzy and unwashed. Essentially, she was a hot mess.

I watched in disbelief as she swayed toward me with a huge grin on her face like we were besties, when all I wanted to do was cunt-punt her ass across the damn room. I was so glad Cisco's was an appointment-only boutique, which was now empty except for the four of us, because I was about to go Brooklyn on Tabitha's scheming, conniving ass.

Tabitha grinned. "Yes, it's me, darling. In the flesh."

Cisco had told me about the Manhattan gossip mill running rampant with news that Tabitha, my former mentor and long-time friend, was back in town and frantically calling around, begging friends for money. The last place I'd expected to see her was here. Well, not after she'd abruptly shut down her boutique, disconnected her cell, and left New York without a trace.

"So the rumors are true. You're back in town and begging for money?" I directed at Tabitha.

"Begging?" Tabitha scoffed. "Hardly. I'm asking for generous donations just to tide me over." Tabitha sniffed disdainfully. "You see, I've run into a bit of trouble. And I'm reaching out to good friends like you and Cisco in my time of need."

With every haughty syllable she'd uttered, rage raced through my veins at her gall to act like everything between us was the same. It wasn't and never would be again.

All I saw was red.

"Trouble?" I hissed at Tabitha while steadying myself, using Zuri's frame as I hopped from one foot to the other, pulling off my red-bottomed shoes and tossing them aside. "You don't know what trouble is, you backstabbing bitch!" I lurched for Tabitha as I demanded, "Cisco. Move."

"Ay, Dios mío!" he whispered. "No!"

Zuri quickly wrapped her arms around me, restraining me.

"Zuri! Let me go," I commanded.

"No," Zuri answered while turning me around to face her. "Lord knows I like a good catfight, but this bitch is not worth your time."

"Bitch?" Tabitha screeched.

"You heard me." Zuri taunted Tabitha, still eyeing me. "Sin, don't do this. Take a deep breath. Walk away from this shit."

She was right. Tabitha wasn't worth the effort or the scene I would be making by beating her ass. But there was no way I was leaving that room without a fucking explanation from Tabitha.

Nope. I want—no, need—damn answers.

Zuri stared at me. "I need to make a call. So are you calm and collected now?"

I nodded.

Cisco's face was flustered when he asked, "You okay?"

I nodded.

He slowly stepped aside, giving Tabitha the evil eye. Zuri pulled out her cell and started texting rapidly but still kept an eye on Tabitha and me.

I squared off with Tabitha. "Okay, Tabitha, let's get this ugliness over with. Why didn't you tell me that my investor was McKay?"

When Tabitha had called me out of the blue, all excited about one of her business connections being willing to provide financing in exchange for a small percentage of my future profits, I had been skeptical but desperate for funding to expand my business and start my new clothing line. So I'd just blissfully signed the contract. The ink hadn't even dried on the document when two million dollars was deposited into my business account with the promise of another million in six months. Little had I known that the investor was Core McKay or that I had stupidly given away ninety-seven percent of my business.

"What difference did it make who he was?"

"You know why. And you know me. I would never have gone into business with a man like Core."

"Hey!" Zuri protested. "What the hell is that supposed to mean?" she asked with narrowed eyes.

"Oh, don't get all snippy," I responded. "You and I know that I've changed my original viewpoint about him. But I'm keeping it real."

Given what I'd heard about Core through the grapevine before I met him—that he'd built his billion-dollar empire from illegal activities—I never would've been desperate or stupid enough to pick him as my investor.

I eyed Tabitha. "Now, back to our conversation. Why did you hide the truth that my secret investor was Core McKay?"

"It's complicated," Tabitha replied sharply.

Heat flushed through my body. "Complicated?" A bitter tang coated my mouth. "It seems pretty straightforward to me. You steered me into a deal you knew I wouldn't have taken if I had known it involved Core. And given our former long-standing friendship, in my eyes, that was a really fucked-up thing to do."

For fuck's sake, she had been my trusted mentor, and I'd thought she was my friend. That type of betrayal was not something I could just sweep under the rug and walk away from without finding out why.

"I didn't make you do anything, Sin." Tabitha snarled. "I made a business introduction; that's all. You signed the deal."

I blew out a noisy breath. "Let's be clear. I'm not blaming you for my stupidity in signing the damn contract without looking at the fine print." I pointed to myself. "That fucked-up move is all me. But damn, I trusted you as my friend. You could have been straight with me and told me Core McKay was the secret investor. You owed me that much."

"I don't owe you shit." Tabitha jutted out her chin.

I tilted my head. "Don't make me hurt you, Tabitha." I countered. "Answer the fucking question. Why didn't you tell me the truth about McKay?"

I was like a dog with a bone, and there was no way in hell I was going to stop until I had the answers I'd waited so long to hear from her.

Tabitha's eyes darted around. "I can't talk about this," she whispered. "You don't know him like I do. He'll..." She swallowed hard.

I arched a brow. "He'll what?"

Is she actually scared of Core? No. That's bullshit. She was stalling. Playing games with my head by trying to avoid telling me the truth.

Tabitha's mouth formed a thin line. I knew she wasn't going to budge on her stance. So I decided to come at her from another angle.

"What's your relationship with Core? Are you friends?" I demanded.

I suspected the answer was no because they just didn't seem like the type of people to run in the same social circles. Plus, there was something about how Tabitha had reacted when she mentioned that she couldn't talk about Core; she looked terrified.

"Sin!" Zuri interjected.

I threw up a not-now hand. "Mind your damn business, Zuri," I retorted.

"No," Tabitha drawled. "Core and I are not friends."

Warning bells started ringing in my head.

I pushed on with my inquisition. "Let me get this straight.

Everything you told me about your business connection, Core, was a lie?"

"Not exactly," Tabitha said.

What the fuck is going on?

"Not exactly? What the hell does that mean?" I was pissed at the fucking trust and friendship violation. "Did you even know Core?"

"I knew him, but we're not friends." She paused. "We grew up in the same neighborhood."

Okay. That I believe.

From what Core had told me about his difficult childhood and what I knew about Tabitha—that she had grown up in the rough streets of Brooklyn, doing things she wasn't really proud of—her words, not mine—it made sense that they knew each other from years ago. But what didn't make sense was how or why they'd reconnected over my business.

"And?" I prompted.

"And what, Sin?"

I huffed with exasperation. "You would have me believe that you just happened to reconnect with Core—a man you weren't even friends with? And he just happened to be interested in going into business with me?"

She threw her hands up in the air. "I don't have time for this fucking interrogation. I have shit to do, so let's get to the damn point. Core approached me about meeting you. He had money. You needed money. Problem fucking solved."

My body stiffened. "Wait. Core approached you? Why?"

"Ask him. Now, are we fucking done?"

"Tabitha, you're such a bitch to everyone!" Cisco snapped.

"Oh, shut up, Cisco," Tabitha replied.

I glanced over at Zuri. She was still tapping furiously on her cell.

Who the hell is she texting while this reality show is in midswing?

"Look, Sin," Tabitha retorted, pressing her hand into my arm.

"Don't touch me," I roughly shot back.

Her fingers dropped away from me.

Tabitha stepped closer, whispering in my ear, "I'm not who you need answers from. You need them from Core."

I frowned at her words even though I knew she was right. There was no way he was going to squirm away from my questions tonight.

Tabitha carried on. "All I'm asking for is some money to tide me over until I can get myself together."

"You're really a piece of work, Tabitha." I looked her up and down. "After what you did to me, you actually think I'm going to give you money?" I snorted.

"Why not?" Tabitha whined with a sullen look on her face.

"Because you probably sold me out to the first bidder—Core." I jammed my hands on my hips. "You already got your penny out of this pound of flesh. Now get the hell out of my damn face."

Tabitha twisted her expression into an ugly mask of hate. "I mentored you. You were my protégé. I showed you the fucking ropes."

"That makes what you did to me even more tragic," I pointed out.

"I was the one who took you under my wing and helped you make all the right connections!" Tabitha screamed.

"Like Core?" I sneered.

"I made you."

I felt nauseous from the way Tabitha was looking at me. It was *The Silence of the Lambs* creepy. Like she wanted to rip off my skin and wear it like a fucking fur coat. Tabitha was a selfish, self-serving cunt who only cared about herself and money.

Fuck! Jade was right all along. Tabitha is jealous of my success.

"You made me?" I arched a brow. "What the fuck are you smoking?" My nostrils flared with anger. "I worked hard to get to where I am today. It was my blood, sweat, and tears."

"You fucking owe me, Sin!"

"I don't owe you shit. And anything you've done for me, I've paid back threefold by allowing your lazy, washed-up designing ass to sell my clothing at your bargain basement boutique."

"You little..." Tabitha sputtered.

I backed her into a clothing rack. "I dare you to say it."

She swallowed hard.

"Give me a reason to go Brooklyn on your ass," I hissed, shoving her head back. "And just so we're perfectly clear, you are officially on my *To Be Shanked with a Dull, Rusty Knife* list. So stay clear of me from this point forward."

Someone cleared their throat loudly. "Are we interrupting something?"

My head snapped around to see my clients and friends, Ariana and Erika, looking on with wide eyes.

"Nope," I answered. "Nothing to see here."

I snidely looked at Tabitha before stomping over to my handbag and then shoes, picking them up before walking away toward the stairs, which led to the dressing lounge.

Tabitha had destroyed years of friendship, and I was pissed and damn hurt. But I was also grateful that the truth about her loyalty to me had finally been revealed. Now my blinders had been yanked off. Now my eyes were wide open. And even though she had answered some questions, there were still so many left unanswered. But there was one thing that was apparent; Core had actively sought me out via Tabitha. But why? It didn't make any sense.

Why would a billionaire want to buy my fledgling fashion business?

It was as if he'd used Tabitha just to get to me.

No. That couldn't be right. My conclusion made no sense.

Before meeting Core, I had been in debt and hadn't even had a mainstream clothing line. Yes, I'd had a strong cult following, but in order to take my business to the next level—fashion mainstream status—I'd needed money and an investor to get my clothing line into all major retailers. Frankly, from a financial perspective, I'd needed Core more than he could ever need me.

I bit my bottom lip. Still... there was something that needled me about the fact that Core had asked Tabitha to vouch for him.

I pulled out my cell and tapped his name on my contacts list, instantly calling him. My eyes narrowed when it went to voicemail.

Why is his phone off?

"Core, call me now," I instructed before ending the call and marching up the stairs.

I didn't like secrets... especially potentially dirty ones.

No. I have to address this shit straight on.

My chest tightened.

But am I making a big deal out of nothing? Maybe Core's rationale will be simple and straightforward...

But, if it is... then why was Tabitha petrified to talk about the subject?

❦ *9* ❧

CORE

IT WAS SUNDAY MORNING, and I was still in the cell with my team, Ram and Rocco, and our prisoner, Jeff.

I had all the information I needed from Jeff Barolo, who was tied to the chair, his body slumped against the bindings that tethered him to the seat. His muscles were still twitching from the electrical current I'd tortured him with. And I felt no guilt about Jeff's predicament.

Jeff was a bottom-feeder and Bigsby's errand boy, and they both dealt in human trafficking. The brutal realities of human trafficking were deplorable and destroyed the lives of tens of thousands of women like Lexis every day.

Pulling off my black latex gloves, I tossed them into a black garbage bag. Now that Lexis and the women had been saved today when Kevin arrived at the Greenwich address Jeff had given us, we could move on with our Bigsby mission.

Damn. I still can't believe it. After all these years, I might finally have the ammunition to take down Bigsby. Shit.

The ledger combined with an actual recording of Bigsby bragging about his kills would be ironclad evidence.

Impatiently, I was waiting for Kevin to get back to us, confirming the existence of Jeff's evidence—a secret recording of

Bigsby bragging about killing several people—that he'd stored in the cloud.

My cell rang; I put it on speaker so Ram and Rocco could hear, too. "Did you get it?"

"Yes. Just like Jeff insisted, there was a password-protected audio file. After unlocking it, I cleaned it up a bit."

"But it's legit?" I asked. "Nobody's tampered with it?"

"Yes," Kevin replied. "I checked. It's authentic. I had my computer program compare Jeff's file against a recording of Bigsby's mayoral debate. No anomalies between the two were found. You ready to hear the shit or what?"

"Go," I snapped, sitting down on a chair.

The recording that Jeff had made started...

"I'm not fucking around with you, Jeff," Bigsby shouted.

The recording was peppered with the sounds of scuffling and grunts of Jeff being roughed up by him.

Bigsby demanded, "Where the hell is Ben Vargos?"

I snorted. *Dead... by my orders.* There was no way in hell I could let a piece of shit like Ben back on the street after we'd interrogated him for intel that pointed us right back to Bigsby and Jeff.

Jeff's high-pitched voice screamed in the recording, "I told you I don't know. I swear."

Bigsby barked, "If I find out you're lying to me..."

"I swear. I'm not." Jeff huffed and puffed as if Bigsby was choking him. "Just like you asked, I tried to find him, but he's disappeared. No one knows where he is."

I nodded. *Truth... Max and Rocco buried him somewhere he won't be found.*

Bigsby bellowed, "You think he's the one talking to the Feds about me?"

"Probably," Jeff stammered. "How else would they know you're laundering money through Pomtonic? Someone is talking."

"Yeah! Someone's snitching all right," Bigsby snarled. "It could be Vargos or... you, asshole!"

I arched a brow. Bigsby was right. Someone was dropping a dime on him. But it wasn't Ben; he was dead. And it couldn't be Jeff; that fucker was terrified of Bigsby.

So who's talking to the Feds?

I made a mental note to have Kevin find out.

"Bigsby, I swear," Jeff blubbered on the recording. "It's not me. I would never betray you."

Bigsby growled, "It'd better not be you because that shit will earn you a damn dirt nap."

There was utter silence and then the sound of something creaking open.

"What's in the safe?" Jeff asked with a nervous voice. "Bigsby? What the fuck?" There were sounds of objects dropping. "Come on, Bigsby," he yelled. "Why are you pointing that gun at me?"

"You scared?" Bigsby taunted.

"Yes!" Jeff squeaked.

"You should be."

"Be careful with that gun, Bigsby." Jeff's voice trembled.

"What did I tell you that I do to people who betray me?" Bigsby asked in a menacing tone.

"You. Kill. Them!" Jeff yelled.

"Exactly," Bigsby growled. "See this gun? It reminds me of what I'm willing to do to get what I want. More money. More power. More pussy. And I'll crush anyone who even thinks about getting in my fucking way."

Jeff blubbered, "Listen to yourself, Bigsby. Why would I want to stop you? I want what you want. I stopped recruiting women for Ben and came to work for you. I didn't have to. I could have let Ben be the middleman between us, but I didn't because I knew you were the man with the master plan. You and me... we're partners."

"We're not damn partners," Bigsby snapped. "You work for me, asshole."

"I thought…" Jeff's voice trailed off.

"Leave the thinking to me, idiot." Bigsby laughed coldly. "I'm the brains. You're the help who gets the girls. That's where our business arrangement starts and ends."

"But I thought if I bagged more bitches, you'd think about—"

"Making you partner?" Bigsby asked. "Hell no." He chortled. "The last business partner I had was Greer Cruickshank, and he was a hell of a lot smarter than your dumb ass."

My shoulders bunched, but I kept my face expressionless. Cruickshank was the person Bigsby had bragged about to Mom before killing her.

Bigsby carried on. "In fact, Greer was too damn smart for his own good. That's why I had to burn his ass alive." He chuckled. "The idiot wanted out of our business arrangement because he had fallen in love with that Jemma Kane bitch. She'd pussy-whipped the chump." He snorted. "No one leaves me… ever. Not unless it's in a damn body bag." He paused. "My only regret is that I put too much trust in our friendship by letting him bring Jemma into the business—especially when I didn't know that bitch at all. Shit. By the time I realized they were fucking each other and she was pushing him to get out of the business, it was too late. She'd already sunk her greedy little claws into his ass." There was a beat of silence. "But I got even with that conniving wench by snitching her out to the Feds. I just never knew she and Greer had a baby together—that Sin Michaels chick—until years later. Shit. If I'd known about their child, I would have cut that baby right out of that backstabbing whore's belly."

What. The. Fuck?

I stood up and started pacing across the cement floor.

Sin's parents are Greer Cruickshank and Jemma Kane?

"Holy hell!" Ram hissed, running a hand through his hair. "This shit has officially crossed into high-drama, reality show territory," he yelled.

Startled awake by the sound of Ram's voice, Jeff bucked

against the rope binding him to the chair. "Untie me!" he screamed in a high-pitched tone.

Rocco growled, "Shut the fuck up!" before punching him so hard in the head that the chair rocked onto its back legs from the weight of Jeff's naked body tethered by the rope. Rocco's hand snapped out, righting it.

Jeff blacked out again.

I stopped midstride. "Not another word from anyone," I ordered.

The room went silent, except for the low whir of the air conditioner and the sounds from the recording.

"What's happening?" Kevin's voice inquired through my cell's speakerphone.

"Press pause," I instructed Kevin.

"Done." Kevin confirmed.

I needed a minute to process the information from the recording plus everything that I knew. Kevin's investigation into Sin's family background had unearthed that she had two birth certificates, each one showing a different set of parents—the first, Ian Michaels and Grace Michaels, and the second, Greer Lorne Cruickshank and Aubrey Cruickshank.

My mind raced to connect the dots.

Is Jemma an alias for Aubrey?

I made another mental note to have Kevin find out if my assumption was correct.

"Kevin, go back a couple seconds in the recording," I demanded. "And then resume playing."

Kevin did just that, and the recording started playing again.

Jeff asked over the recording, "Damn. You would have killed their baby?"

"Shit, I've done worse," Bigsby confided in a chilling voice. "Like that stripper Stella who tried to blackmail me after she overheard me talking about killing Greer. She had the nerve to threaten me by saying she'd keep her mouth shut for a price."

My fists tightened. Stella was my mother. The woman he'd killed without a damn thought.

My mind snapped back to the present when I heard Jeff's voice on the recording. "Did you give it to her?"

"Yeah, she got it all right." Bigsby laughed. "Right in the fucking head with this .357 Magnum."

Fucker.

I clenched and unclenched my fingers.

Then there was the sound of a phone ringing on the recording.

"Shit," Bigsby exclaimed. "It's that nagging bitch Cate calling me again."

I tilted my head to the side at the mention of Cate Bellisario —Bigsby's socialite fiancée.

Bigsby continued. "If I have to hear her ass whining again about some fucking detective her sister hired to dig into my background, I'm going to wrap my hands around her scrawny neck and choke her to death." He mocked Cate's voice. "Bigsby, Irvin is an excellent detective. Are you sure there's nothing he'll find?" He paused again. "Fuck Cate and her uptight bitch of a sister, Ariana. Shit. Once I become mayor, I won't need her or the Bellisario family name anymore."

Jeff inquired, "Will Irvin find anything on you?"

"Fuck no," Bigsby spit. "I paid a lot of money to make sure my past was buried. There's nothing linking me to that time in my life, except that fucking ledger."

"What ledger?"

There was a long pause before I heard a heavy sigh.

"When I was running girls with Greer and Jemma, we kept records of our business. It was like our little black book. I thought the ledger burned up along with Greer... until Grace contacted me."

"Grace?" Jeff asked.

"She's the wife of Ian Michaels—Greer's brother. Her greedy

little ass wanted money in exchange for giving me back the incriminating ledger. Little did she know that book was both a curse and a blessing. Yeah, it links me back to my past, but it's also the only leverage I still have on rich and powerful fuckers in this city."

"But how the hell did she know about you and the ledger?" Jeff jabbered.

Bigsby replied, "She told me when Ian heard I was sanitizing my past and starting to go legit, he got nervous and told her if anything happened to him, he needed her to protect Sin because he had incriminating evidence against me that could get them all killed. Apparently, Grace saw dollar signs and went behind his back, trying to extort money from me."

"So why didn't you kill her?"

"She gives good head." There was loud laughter. "I was going to kill her after she gave me back the ledger... Well, I was going to kill them all."

"All?"

"Grace, Ian, and Sin. But Ian found out his wife was trying to make a deal with me, and he threatened to expose me with the ledger if I didn't leave him and his family alone."

"Stupid bastard." Jeff snorted.

"Yeah... no one threatens me. So I hired someone to run him off the road, killing him. And that's when shit went left. Grace couldn't find the ledger in any of Ian's stuff. She was drunk most of the time, and it was years before she remembered some old trunk that used to belong to Ian that she'd allowed Sin to take. Grace swore up and down that was the only place the ledger could be—in that trunk."

The playback of the recording stopped, and Kevin relayed, "Core, that's all there is."

"Shit. That's more than enough." Rocco grunted.

"That's for sure," Ram remarked while looking over at me. "Now we have everything we need to destroy Bigsby. The ledger and this secret recording. We can call this mission a success once we leak this information to the media, and Bigsby's life as he knows it will be over."

My jaw tightened. "The plan has changed."

The original plan to strip away everything Bigsby held dear—his wealth, freedom, political career, and trophy fiancée, Cate—had been scrapped the minute Jeff exposed just how ugly a monster Bigsby was—a psychopath that had gotten away with a shitload of murders.

Rocco sighed heavily. "That's what I thought you'd say. I knew there was no way you'd let that fucker live now that we've gotten solid confirmation about all the people he's killed."

I narrowed my eyes. "Once I'm done with Bigsby, no one will ever know he existed," I answered. "And I can finally move on with my life."

"So what's the new game plan?" Ram asked.

I cracked my knuckles. "We need to draw Bigsby out and then kill him, putting an end to this crap once and for all."

"Agreed," Ram and Rocco roared in unison.

"Damn." Rocco shook his head. "I can't believe that fucker put a hit on Ian Michaels."

"Or the fact that Ian is Sin's uncle and not her father, like she thinks." Ram chimed in. "Shit. Her whole world is going to be blown apart when she finds out the truth."

I bit back the expletive hovering on my tongue. Sin had told me that her father—or rather, the man she thought was her father, Ian Michaels—was killed in a freak car accident.

How is she going to handle the truth? That it was a damn hit by Bigsby?

"Well, this confirms Kevin's intel," Ram declared. "The apartment fire that killed Greer was arson. And now we know why Bigsby did it; he was pissed that Greer wanted out of their business partnership." He frowned. "The fucked-up part is that Bigsby thought the ledger was burned in the fire"—he shook his head—"and if Ian had just kept his mouth shut, he would still be alive today."

"Probably," I muttered. "Damn! This Bigsby shit is one big clusterfuck." Adrenaline rushed through me as I just thought about all the lives Bigsby had destroyed. "But at least after all these years of wondering why that sick fuck killed my mother, now I know why." It didn't make losing her any easier, but I had answers now.

"And we got Lexis, and she's safe," Ram disclosed.

I nodded. We were all grateful that Lexis and the women were now under the protection of the authorities. But with Lexis, we had a whole other bag of issues. Even though she was happy to be rescued from her nightmare with Jeff, she was emotionally traumatized and embarrassed by the whole incident, and she refused to come back to Manhattan with Kevin. She tearfully offered that she wasn't ready to face Ram or my team or her old life. It wasn't the happy reunion Ram and the team had been anticipating, but we knew she needed time to heal. So Kevin had called one of his trusted contacts who could spirit her away to a highly secured facility that specialized in rehabilitating victims of domestic sex trafficking.

"But doesn't anyone think it's a bit strange that Bigsby didn't mention anything about killing Jemma or Aubrey?" Rocco asked.

"Exactly," Ram answered. "Plus, I bet you right now Jemma and Aubrey are the same person."

"I wouldn't take that bet because I was thinking the same thing," I gritted out. "Kevin, I need you to check out a couple things. One, who's talking to the Feds about Bigsby? And two, is Jemma an alias for Aubrey?"

"Okay," Kevin responded. "I'm out. I'll see you all back at the compound." He ended the call.

"So we know that Bigsby's a psychopath," Rocco hissed. "Do you think Sin's safe?"

"Hell no," I replied. "Bigsby's a loose cannon, and he wants the ledger back. So who knows what he'll do to get it?" And I wasn't about to find out. I would protect Sin with my last breath.

"Time to wrap this shit up," Ram suggested, looking at the unconscious Jeff.

"Shit!" Rocco barked. "I missed a 9-1-1 text from Zuri."

My eyes narrowed. "What's going on?"

Rocco read the text aloud. "*Tabitha's here. Asking Sin for money.*"

Tabitha Thorp was a disposable piece of trash who had served her purpose when I recruited her to help me get close to Sin.

Rocco continued to read. "*Catfight going down. Get your ass over here now!*"

I hurried over to my cell. "Zuri," I voice-dialed with the phone on speaker.

"About damn time!" Zuri whispered urgently.

"Can you talk in private?" I asked.

"Hold on." There was a pause. "Okay, I can talk now."

"Where's Sin?" I questioned.

"She stormed upstairs... pissed. Look, I can't talk long. I need to make sure Tabitha doesn't dash after Sin and cause more trouble."

"What did Tabitha tell her?" I demanded.

"Enough."

"Shit." I flattened my lips.

Weeks ago, when I'd gotten the call from Kevin about Bigsby's interest in Sinthia, my first question had been, *Who the fuck is Sinthia Michaels?*

It hadn't taken Kevin long to do a thorough investigation, but he hadn't found anything linking Bigsby to her. I had known though that if Bigsby was interested in Sin, there had to be a sinister motive, which was why I had to acquire Sinthia Michaels's business fast. I'd had Kevin search through her background again, looking for anything that could be used as leverage. Surprisingly, Sin was squeaky clean and free of scandal. Frustrated and running out of time and options, I'd found a chink in her armor—money.

She'd needed money, and I had lots of it. But to my frustration, I couldn't find a way into Sin's small inner circle without raising suspicion or scaring her off.

That was when Kevin had found the game changer—Tabitha Thorp. I had known Tabitha from the old neighborhood. When we were young, we had hung out in the same criminal circles. The only difference was back then, the now-famous Tabitha had run drugs for her boyfriend, Ben Vargos. I'd even fucked her several times behind Ben's back. She was a money-hungry whore who could be easily manipulated.

So when I'd found out the currently successful Tabitha Thorp owed a shitload of money to her unsavory criminal ex-boyfriend, Ben, I'd swooped in. One call later, I'd recruited Tabitha to help me get close to Sin. Tabitha had convinced Sin of the value of getting an investor—specifically, me—to help her expand her business. In exchange, I'd agreed to take care of Tabitha's debt to Ben and send her on a very long vacation.

"But Tabitha didn't tell her everything." Zuri countered.

"And she wants money," I groused. It wasn't a question but a statement.

"Yes," Zuri replied. "Apparently, she's broke."

Tabitha could go fuck herself. Our business had been done the moment she took my money.

"She implied money was exchanged between you two," Zuri reported.

Fuck.

I hadn't twisted her arm into taking the money. And the recording of Tabitha and our business arrangement would surely enlighten Sin.

"Where are you?" I asked.

She rattled off an address.

"Max should be in the vicinity," I replied. "Hold tight. He'll be there to get Tabitha." I ended the call.

It was time to turn the screws on Tabitha and permanently shut her down. I had so much dirt on her shady dealings with

Vargos that by the time I was done snitching her out to the authorities, she'd end up in jail, designing uniforms for the entire prison.

"Max," I voice-dialed.

"Hey, bro," Max answered. "What's up?"

"We just got a text from Zuri. Tabitha has finally surfaced." I gave him the address. "I need you to get over there and shut her up. But don't kill her. I just want to make a statement that I can find her anytime, anyplace. Call me when it's done." I ended the call.

"I don't like this shit, Core. Too many fucking loose ends," Rocco grumbled.

I didn't need his ass telling me something I already knew.

Ram stared at me. "I guess the *talk* between you and Sin is going to happen sooner than you expected, huh?"

I ignored his gibe. "Let's get this Bigsby shit over with."

Ram nodded over to Rocco.

Rocco dumped the tub of water over Jeff's head.

Jeff's limbs jerked into action. His eyes snapped open. "What..." he garbled.

"Good. You're awake," I responded. "I wouldn't want you to miss this." I quickly swiped my finger over my cell, tapping the number and putting it on speaker. "Bigsby."

"McKay?" Bigsby answered. "What can I—"

"Bigs!" Jeff yelled, his voice so hoarse it sounded broken with panic ringing in it. "Help..."

"Jeff? What's going on?" Bigsby asked sharply.

I paced back and forth. "I have your ledger," I responded, "and a recording."

"What fucking recording?"

My nostrils flared. "Apparently, Jeff didn't trust your dumb ass and needed some insurance. Frankly, I don't blame him, given the fact that you've killed so many people—Greer, Ian, Stella, and her son." I wasn't going to reveal—yet—that I was Stella's son, the little boy he thought he'd killed so many years ago. No.

That little eye-opener would be unveiled right before I killed the fucker. "Poor Jeff was afraid he'd end up on your shit list, too. So he recorded you confessing to a lot of crimes."

"That dumb fucker!" Bigsby exclaimed. "I'll—"

Losing patience, I stopped him. "Let's cut to the chase, Bigsby. I can make this all go away for twenty million dollars and control of your empire. And, of course, I'll expect you to disappear." It was all a bluff. I wanted to know exactly what Bigsby would do now that his back was against the wall.

Bigsby sputtered before saying, "Fuck you, McKay. I've built this. I want the fucking recording and my ledger back."

"What about your boy Jeff? Don't you want him back, too?"

"I don't give a shit what you do with his ass. He wasn't worth shit to me anyway," Bigsby hissed.

Jeff started screaming because he knew he was going to die.

"I want my ledger and the recording. And if you don't give them to me, Sin's dead."

What the fuck?

I stopped midstride. The muscles in my shoulders bunched.

I didn't respond well to threats, especially against someone I cared about.

"What makes you think I give a shit if she dies?" I did... and I wanted to break every bone in Bigsby's body for threatening Sin's life.

Bigsby laughed. "I've been keeping tabs on you and Sin. And it seems like you've got something going on with Michaels. I can't really blame you. She's simply delectable."

He was trying to push my buttons, but this was not my first rodeo, dealing with assholes who thought they could best me. Every day, I ate motherfuckers like Bigsby for breakfast and enjoyed it.

I deliberately infused nonchalance into my tone. "Shit. I like a woman who gives good head. What man doesn't?" I laughed coldly. "But I ain't planning on marrying her."

Bigsby sneered. "There's no honor among thieves, McKay. So

let me make things very clear. I either get my fucking ledger back, along with any copies you've made of it and the recording, or your sweet little cunt, Sin Michaels, is dead." He rattled off an address. "I'll meet you there in seventy-two hours. Ticktock, McKay."

Our call ended.

"Fuck!" I banged my fist against the table.

Despite the fact that I'd just gotten what I wanted—a meeting with Bigsby—I didn't want to tell Sin the truth... today. Or that she already knew part of it—due to Tabitha's big mouth —and wasn't happy about it.

The only upside of this clusterfuck was that Bigsby's world was about to collapse. And that he was a desperate man on the verge of losing his power and wealth—equivalent to death for a social climber like Bigsby. I'd heard the desperation in his voice, and I knew he'd do anything to avoid losing it all, even if he had to lie, steal, cheat, and in this case, kill... both Sin and me.

Killing Sin or me? That shit is not happening. Not on my damn watch.

It was time to go to fucking work... meticulously planning Bigsby's death.

I looked over at Rocco. "Bury Jeff somewhere he won't be found, and then clean this place and get rid of all the evidence."

Rocco nodded.

"Please! Don't... I can help you." Jeff bucked against the rope binding him to the chair. "Give me a—"

"Time's up," Rocco revealed flatly.

Jeff struggled uselessly against the rope.

I looked over at Ram while grabbing my jacket. "Let's go. We've only got seventy-two hours to put things in motion." And for me to figure out how to finally tell Sin the truth and lay out the plan to protect her.

～

AS I WALKED OUT OF THE WAREHOUSE WITH RAM AT MY SIDE, my mind buzzed with all the things I needed to do to keep Sin safe from Bigsby. My team was already stretched thin. Rocco was getting rid of Jeff before cleaning up the warehouse. Max was hemming up Tabitha. Zuri was protecting Sin; it was a good thing Zuri was carrying a gun and knew how to use it. Kevin had intel work to get done. Ram and I had to start working on the logistics of my meeting with Bigsby.

And the clock was ticking.

Damn. Seventy-two hours. That's all we have to get our shit together.

My gut instinct urged me to go to Sin, but logic ruled. I had to work on a plan to take Bigsby down. There would only be one shot to get it right. Any mistakes would get us killed.

I ran my fingers across my hair. Logically, the smart thing would be to move Sin into my penthouse until this shit got resolved. But Sin agreeing to move in would be difficult... especially after I told her the truth tonight.

Ram loudly cleared his throat. "Bro, look... What I said about Sin earlier. Everything cool between us, right?"

"Yeah." I sighed heavily. "And you're right. This shit with Sin is a real fucked-up predicament. I had no business getting involved with her." I eyed him. "But I did, and there ain't no going back with her. Only forward. No matter the consequences, Sin's worth the fight to keep her by my side."

Truth be told, from the moment she'd allowed me into her body, I had known that our fates were sealed and she was mine to protect and care for.

Sin is my present and future... and I'll fight tooth and nail to keep her in my life.

"Shit," Ram said, "that's deep." He shook his head. "I guess I never thought any woman could replace Maya."

"Me either. Until Sin."

Maya had been my balance, my rock. But in one tragic

moment, she'd been taken away, leaving me emotionally void—until Sin had unwittingly turned my world around.

Now the thought of Sin walking away from me, from us, was totally unacceptable.

Despite losing every woman I'd ever loved—Maya and Mom —to death and the fact that I still felt haunted by their passing, Sin made me want to try again for another chance at a relationship, companionship, and hopefully... someday... even love. With her.

"Damn, I never thought I'd see the day Core McKay officially took his ass off the *Single and Available* list."

A smirk rolled across my face. "Life is full of compromises, and I'm more than willing to make them to be with Sin." There were so many sides to Sin—sexy, rebellious, sassy, smart, and vulnerable—and I wanted them all.

He clapped me on the back. "Okay. Well then, we'd better hurry up and sort this shit out with Bigsby because we're going to need to start working on *Operation Save Core's Ass*, pronto. How I see it, there's no doubt in my mind that when you tell her the truth... Sin's going to go Amazon warrior princess on your ass."

"Fuck, I'm screwed." I grunted.

"Yep. So gird your loins, motherfucker."

❧ 10 ❧

SINTHIA

PACING ACROSS CISCO'S LOUNGE, I dropped my bag before checking the fitting rooms, making sure each had the correct client gown.

"Still no call," I muttered after checking my cell clutched in my death grip.

Maybe he was busy.

Walking over to the soft, comfy gray couch and sitting down, I ignored the open complimentary champagne bottle and waiting glasses. No alcohol. I needed to keep a clear head.

I inhaled. Exhaled. Tried to chill the fuck out... then *bam*! My mind went right back to what-the-fuck mode.

What in the world is going on between Core and Tabitha?

It seemed like no one was who I'd thought they were. I recalled the conversation Tabitha and I had weeks ago when I asked her about my secret investor.

"WHY CAN'T I KNOW HIS DAMN NAME?" I DEMANDED.

Tabitha's eyes hardened. "Darling, the less you know, the better. Believe me. Sin, I swear to you he's legit. I wouldn't get you involved if he wasn't. You can't have it both ways. You asked me to find an investor, and I did. You've got the money. Isn't that all that matters now?"

Is it?

F RANKLY, I DIDN'T KNOW, BUT WHAT I DID KNOW WAS THAT I wouldn't have been able to complete my collection without Core's money.

But the nagging feeling that something was off wouldn't go away.

Why did Tabitha hook me up with Core? And what did she get out of the deal for doing it?

A second thought crept into my mind, and it was hard to dismiss. *What is Core really after? My business? Me? Or both? And why?*

Ariana finally breezed into the room, cell pressed against her ear, with her new bestie, Erika Watson, walking beside her. Both women—in their fifties, slim, and tall—wore their beauty and class well.

Ariana—the older, classically refined version of my bestie, Jade—had porcelain skin, a square face, blue eyes, an upturned nose, and wore her long black hair loose. She was stylish, and as usual, she was looking radiant, wearing a black mid-length sheath dress with peplum detailing around the waist. She'd paired the dress with a cozy gray cape, tan top-handled purse, and matching pointed-toe stilettos. A bold red lip and matching manicure completed her look.

Erika was stunning. The dark richness of her skin contrasted beautifully against her long, white belted coat, black Christian Louboutin pumps, and classic diamond jewelry. She'd styled the look with oversize shades and a slicked-back ponytail.

"Cate, enough!" Ariana screamed into the phone.

"Hello, Erika," I greeted.

Erika dramatically whipped off her shades and kissed me on the cheek before sitting down and saying, "The full moon must be coming tonight because everyone is losing their damn mind. Between Ariana and Cate going at it all day and you and that woman downstairs, everyone is either battle ready or battle weary. Which one are you?"

I replied, "Definitely battle ready." I poured her a glass of champagne.

Erika laughed. "A woman after my own heart. That must be why I like your ass so much." She winked at me. "Just let me know if you need backup, because I'm not afraid to kick off my red-bottoms and get to kicking ass."

I grinned at the television producer voted most likely to bitch-slap an actor. "And that's why you're my favorite client." I gave her a high-five.

I wasn't kidding. I adored Erika's vibe. She was remarkably laidback for a woman who'd achieved so much, so fast. She was an award-winning writer and producer who created hit TV shows. She was also the first black woman to create and executive produce a top ten network series—a series starring Jade, my best friend.

"Love the bracelet," Erika commented. "I meant to compliment you on your excellent taste in jewelry when you wore it to Bigsby's gala." She paused. "It's Victorian Scottish, right?"

"Yes. It's special... an heirloom that belonged to my Scottish great-grandmother. My dad gave it to me before he died." I swallowed hard over the emotions welling up inside me. "It's the only piece of my heritage and my family that I have left."

"Oh, sweetie." She comfortingly touched my shoulder. "I'm sorry for your loss."

"It's been years, but you know... the shit still hurts." It did, and the pain would never go away.

"I know. Losing people we love is never easy." Her eyes clouded over with emotion. "It leaves you hollow."

I nodded in agreement.

"Do you mind?" Her fingers hovered over my wrist with the bracelet clasped around it.

I shrugged. "Nope."

She examined the jewelry. "It suits you." Her lips curled up at the edges. "And I'm happy it finally found a home." Then she abruptly slapped my leg. "Enough of this sad stuff. *Viva la vida*."

We both held our glasses in the air before taking a sip.

"Wait... *viva la vida*... Isn't that a Coldplay song?" My lips curled up.

"Yep," Erika retorted. "It means *live life*. And you and I are going to rock the hell out of this life while we still have it." She winked. "So are you ready for me to get all sexy?"

"You're set up in the second room," I responded.

I completely forgot about the phone war Ariana was waging until she growled into her cell, "I'll be damned if I let you marry that sleazy bastard."

She didn't mention his name, but I knew exactly who the "sleazy bastard" was—Bigsby.

"Bigsby at it again?" I asked Erika.

"Of course." Erika rolled her eyes. "But what's new about that shit?" She pursed her full lips. "The man is an utter douche bag. After what Ariana just found out about him, at least I can finally convince my husband to drop his support of Bigsby for mayor of New York. Now my world is complete."

"I can't blame you." I shuddered. "Every time I'm around Bigsby, I want to douse my body with holy water to rid myself of his evil vibes."

"He creeps everyone out. It's his greasy used car salesman personality." She stuck her tongue out in disgust.

"Are we done?" Ariana yelled.

"And, as usual, Ariana and Cate are like two pit bulls in skirts." Erika grimaced, eyeing Ariana. "If I wanted to hear that shit, I could have stayed at work and listened to the overpaid divas bitch about who had more lines." Getting up, she swayed toward the fitting room, slamming the door behind her.

"Blah, blah, blah. I don't give a shit what he thinks. God, I hate that fucker Bigsby," Ariana hissed. "I made no damn secret about the fact that I'd hired Irvin to investigate his ass."

I recalled what Jade had told me—that Ariana, Cate, and Jade were the last members of the Bellisario dynasty and each worth millions. And if anyone wanted to date a Bellisario, they got investigated thoroughly. According to Jade, most guys just ungracefully bowed out because they couldn't deal with Irvin, the investigative proctologist.

"I'm done with this conversation, Cate. And no, I'm not going to tell Irvin to back off until you publicly call off your engagement. Good-bye. Yes, I'm hanging up, Cate," Ariana barked before tossing her cell into her handbag. "Family. Can't live with them. Can't fucking kill them."

She flopped down next to me and kissed my cheek. I loved Ariana because she was beautiful inside and out. When Dad had died and Grace had disowned me, Ariana had taken me into her family, treating me like I was her daughter.

"How are you, darling?"

"You saw that shit downstairs. I'm pissed, but I gather from your conversation, you're not too chipper yourself." I arched a brow. "So what's going on?"

Ariana Bellisario—a philanthropist, heiress, and successful businesswoman—was Jade's mother and also a member of the illustrious group of New York socialites. Her sister, Cate Bellisario, was older than Ariana by a couple years. To some, that made Cate the most powerful member of the Bellisario family. She was using that status among the New York elite to get her fiancé, Bigsby Calhoune, a wealthy shipping mogul, elected as New York City mayor.

"Irvin, my private investigator, finally found the skeletons in Bigsby's closet."

Erika peeked out of the dressing room, making eye contact with me in a *See, we were right about Bigsby* moment before disappearing back into the room.

My mouth fell open before closing with a snap. "What did

Irvin find out?" I had no qualms asking because Ariana and Jade were family. All three of us had been by each other's sides in the best and worst of times. And I would never reveal anything they'd told me because I loved and trusted them as much as they did me.

"The Feds are secretly investigating Bigsby over some shady business going on with Pomtonic International." Ariana scowled. "Irvin says his source told him it's a shell company that's cleaning sex traffickers' money."

I blinked in shock. "Sex traffickers?"

"Oh, it gets worse." Ariana took a huge swallow of champagne. "According to Irvin, those same traffickers are laundering money through UF-Star. That is why the Feds were digging into UF-Star in the first place."

My brows came together in a puzzled frown. "He's into sex trafficking and money laundering, and he has the Feds on his ass? That news bomb can't be good for Cate or the Bellisario name."

"Exactly. There's no fucking way we want our family name being linked to this shit. That's why I told Cate she has to break off her engagement to Bigsby and publicly denounce any association with him."

I replied, "Well, there goes his political ambitions and his bid for New York City mayor."

"Exactly. It's a wrap, and the only one who doesn't get it is Cate." She ran her fingers through her hair.

I pressed my lips together in a slight grimace. "Knowing Cate, her reaction must have been a hissy fit worthy of a reality show cast member."

Cate was a ruthless, conniving, manipulative woman who would think nothing about taking down the most powerful people in New York unless they played nice with her and kowtowed to her every whim.

"When I told her what I found out, it was a clusterfuck. Cate accused me of being jealous because she's finally found the love of her life and I'm still alone." Ariana's upper lip curled in disdain. "I'm not alone. I'm in a relationship with a lawyer Erika hooked me up with—not that I'd ever tell Cate that because she'd just use that shit against me and try to break us up because she can't stand to see me happy." She paused. "With Cate, it's always some damn competition that I've never been interested in participating in. She can't get past the fact that our parents always favored me when they were alive."

I snorted. "That woman only loves herself."

"Exactly. Anyhoo, things got ugly, and Cate left my house in a huff. She's been calling me all day, trying to get me to back off, but I won't. Push comes to shove, I'd even go as far as leaking the Bigsby information to the media."

"That's not a good idea, Ariana. The bad press might back-fire, hurting you and Jade in the end." I countered.

"Yes, but we're damned if we do and damned if we don't. I need to get ahead of the Manhattan gossip rags by putting my own spin on the information and releasing it first. But more importantly, despite the fact that Cate and I have never been on the best of terms, she's family, and blood is thicker than water."

I frowned. "Hopefully, Cate will dump him."

Ariana sighed heavily. "I know my sister. She's not going to turn her back on Bigsby. She's invested way too much of her time, money, and connections into molding him into her perfect Ken doll. No. She'll turn her back on our family first. In her eyes, I've just declared war against her and Bigsby."

"Does Jade know what's going on?" I asked.

"Yes. And she's angry with Cate, and she wants to come back to the US. You know, to have my back when shit gets ugly between Cate and me... and believe me; it will."

"You and Jade are not on your own. You both are my family." I grabbed her hand. "You're like my mother, and if I can help, I'll do it with no questions asked. Let me be there for you while Jade's away."

She squeezed my hand back. "Sin, you already have enough

going on in your life. Plus, I don't want you getting hit with shit when Cate starts slinging it. You know how cruel she can be."

"I'm not scared of her, Ariana. You and Jade are the only family I have, and I'll fight tooth and nail to protect you two."

She smiled at me. "What a damn tiger. I raised two beautiful women." She nudged me in the side. "So are you going to tell me what the hell happened downstairs between you and that woman?"

"That was Tabitha," I answered.

"Really?" Her eyes widened.

I nodded.

Ariana pursed her lips. "She looks different. Time out of the fashion spotlight has dimmed her remarkably."

"I know. She looked like a hot mess. Not that I feel bad about her predicament at all."

"Okay. Get me up to speed," Ariana said.

I leaned my head on her shoulder. "Where should I start?"

"From the top and leave nothing out."

She stroked my hair in her familiar, comforting way, and it didn't take long for the drama playing out with my townhouse break-in and the Tabitha reality show to come tumbling from my mouth.

SEVERAL HOURS LATER, ARIANA HAD ALREADY LEFT. AND ZURI had sent me a text saying she was in the vicinity, taking care of business and for me not to leave without her. And still... there was no return call from McKay.

Fucker!

We—Erika and I—stood before the floor-to-ceiling mirror while I made the final adjustments to her gown. I was proud of my creation; Erika was stunning in the gown that accented her perfect, tight, curvy body. The dark richness of her skin contrasted beautifully against the formfitting chartreuse drape-back dress. Next to Jade and Ariana, she was the best walking commercial for my clothing line.

"Damn!" Erika exclaimed. "My ass looks spectacular in this dress. It's like I've had a butt lift." She did a sexy butt shake.

I laughed. "Well, look at you. Twerk it."

"Age ain't nothing but a number." She shimmied. "I've still got it."

"Yeah, you do." I impishly tapped her ass. "But I'm gonna need you to stop watching Cardi B music videos." I smiled saucily before stepping back, examining her.

"Never!" Erika dissolved in laughter before walking over to her bag, reaching in, and pulling out a piece of paper. "This is for you," she explained, extending her hand.

Walking over, I took the check, blinking at the five-figure number written on it. "Erika, you're overpaying me again." I handed it back. "I can't take it."

"Nonsense." She waved away my objection. "Just the pleasure of my husband drooling over me in your design... that's worth the price of this gown and more, darling." She grinned at me. "When Mitch sees me in this, he won't be able to keep his hands off me. And let me tell you, the man's foreplay game is on point."

Ugh... no. Why do my clients insist on oversharing?

Her statement was the equivalent of realizing that your parents were still having sex. Hard pass on that kinky image.

"Well, if my designs get women laid, then my community service is done. You're welcome." I bowed playfully.

She cracked up before walking over to the mirror again. "What do you think? Up or down?" She gestured to her hair.

"Up." Coming up behind her, I twisted the hair hanging freely from her ponytail, wrapping it around into a tight, high knot. I stilled when I noticed the small infinity tattoo at the base of her neck. "Well, look at you. A tattoo?"

Erika didn't seem like an ink chick. I squinted at the letter G etched at one end of the infinity symbol and the letter A at the other.

She lifted her head, meeting my eyes in the mirror. "It's to remember someone I loved and lost years ago," she confessed, and her famous sassy smile was nowhere to be seen. There was an unmistakable sadness in her eyes.

I pressed one hand against her shoulder. "I'm sorry for your loss."

"Thank you," she whispered. My hand fell away when she turned around to face me. "He died too young, but when he was alive, he did give me the best gift a woman could hope for, his love." She cleared her throat. "Sin, I overheard your conversation with Ariana about your break-in and that horrid Tabitha woman." Her eyes locked with mine. "And I hope you don't get offended, but I'm worried about you. Is everything okay money-wise? I know how close you were to finishing your clothing line. I'd just hate for you to give up on your dreams because of every-thing that's happened."

My thoughts flashed to Core...

Would he do anything for me?

Or is he just running a game? Using me to get what he wants?

"I'm okay." I warmly smiled at her. "Believe me; I'm not remotely close to giving up designing for a job at a fast-food restaurant."

Erika drawled, "I know that." She reached out, grabbing my hand. "But if I can help in any way, I will. My show has millions of viewers, and I'd love to have your pieces on set. I want the world to know about your clothing."

Heat radiated through my chest at her generous offer. "I'll never say no to business or publicity. I'm game." Just the press coverage would be enough to keep the fashion hags talking for days.

"Good. I'll have my people contact you." Her hand tightened around mine before quickly pulling away as if she'd just realized she was still clutching mine. She smiled at me before walking away toward the dressing room, and then she stopped abruptly, turning around to stare at me.

"Sin, I—" She fidgeted and twisted her large, sparkling diamond engagement ring coupled with the diamond-encrusted wedding band. A look of uncertainty flickered in her eyes. "Uh… nothing."

Without another word, she dipped into the dressing room.

"Well… that was strange," I mumbled under my breath.

11

SINTHIA

AFTER LEAVING CISCO'S BOUTIQUE, I stood in Core's kitchen, fuming silently. "Fucker!" I mumbled under my breath while glancing down at my cell again. "Who does he think he is, not returning my call?" But I'd be damned if I blew up his cell. I refused to chase his ass for answers about Tabitha.

"Sin—" Zuri started.

"Nope." I cut her off. "No excuses."

And then there was another problem. The tenseness between Zuri and me that permeated the confines of the kitchen was uncomfortable.

There were so many unanswered questions.

What was going on between Tabitha and Core? Why had he sought me out through Tabitha? And why would a billionaire like him want to go into business with a fashion designer? And lastly, what does Zuri know about this debacle?

Even if she knew the answers to my questions, which she probably did, I suspected she wouldn't tell me. She was loyal to Core.

Besides, it would be unfair to interrogate her, given her close relationship with him.

My cell chirped. Glancing down, I saw it was a text from Core.

Dinner tonight. We need to talk. Max will pick you up at 8 p.m. sharp. C.M.

I promptly texted back. *Fuck off! S.M.*

"Take that, asshole," I muttered.

Zuri exhaled loudly. "That was Core, wasn't it?"

"Yes. Your lord and master has finally decided to acknowledge my existence, ordering me to be ready to go out to dinner with him tonight." I snorted. "That shit is not happening."

"Why not?"

"Because I don't jump to attention and salute when he snaps his fingers."

Zuri shook her head. "You two are the most stubborn, most bullheaded people I've ever met. All I know is that both of you need to talk this out, clear the air. Don't you think?"

"I called him hours ago... and nothing. Not an, *I'm busy right now, and we'll talk later.* Just crickets. This is not normal. He's not fucking normal." I huffed, plopping down onto the barstool nestled under the granite kitchen counter.

"I'm sorry... Were you under some perception that he was normal?" She arched a brow. "Because you and I know he's not. For that matter, you wouldn't want his ass if he were. Admit it."

I rolled my eyes. "Maybe not. But I do expect some level of communication."

Zuri sat down with a heavy sigh. "Then go out with him and let him communicate. Let him explain what the hell is going on. Don't you want to know?"

"Of course I want to know, Zuri. Hence my call to him hours ago." I eyed her. "Something is going on. I feel it in my bones, and my instinct is never fucking wrong. Never."

"Sin, I—"

I held up my hand. "Zuri, stop. I don't need you to explain anything. It's not your place to clean up his shit."

"Sin, you know me better by now. I'm not going to touch this whole Tabitha drama. That's between you and him." She leaned forward. "But I will say this—he's my family. I love him. I really do, but he's stubborn sometimes." Zuri sighed heavily. "When Core wants something, he goes after it with a single-minded, calculating focus, and he won't stop until he gets it. But he's a bull in a china shop. He doesn't give a crap about finesse. So all I'm saying is to be patient with his ass because he's going to make all sorts of mistakes when it comes to you. Just"—she cleared her throat—"try to forgive him when he does because he's really a good guy and worth it."

"Why are you telling me all this?"

"Because I want you to understand the man behind the mask. I want you to take the blinders off and really see him. And when the time comes when he pulls off the disguise he wears to protect himself emotionally, I want you to be open to forgive some of the things he does or says. Because sometimes Core forgets the human aspect of being human. You know what I mean?" She pursed her lips.

"No, I don't," I replied, feeling like she was passing on some secret message that I didn't quite have the code for.

"You will. Just give it time," Zuri finished, lightly touching my arm.

I could feel the beginning of a migraine when my cell rang. I smiled when I saw the name on the caller ID. "I've got to take this," I explained to Zuri.

"Sure. No issues," Zuri replied, getting up. "I'll be in Core's office," she finished, striding out of the kitchen, giving me privacy.

"Hey, Jade!" I answered.

Jade was scheduled to be away on her shoot for months, and even though she hadn't been gone long, I already missed her something fierce. We'd been friends since high school. We pushed each other further. Our friendship had tightened over the years, creating a perfect synergy unmatched by any other relationship to date. We were an unstoppable team who stuck by each other, no matter how rough the circumstances.

"Don't *hey* me." Jade countered. "My mom just told me about what happened at your place. Are you okay?"

"Yes."

"Thank God." I could hear the relief in her voice. "Shit. Where were you when it happened?"

"With Core." I leaned forward, putting my elbows on the counter.

"Wait! What?" There was a beat of silence. "Core? As in Core McKay?"

"Who else?" I answered, nibbling on my bottom lip.

"Oh, please tell me you fucked my favorite bad boy."

"Sure did… several times."

Jade squealed. "About time!" She followed that with a rambunctious rendition of the "Bad Boys" song, and then she abruptly asked, "Wait. You did come, right?"

I burst out laughing. "Yes… and it was magical."

"Ah, shit… I knew he had potential. Damn. My favorite alphalicious billionaire rained pixie and fairy dust on your vajay-jay. Leg on his shoulder. Boom! Fairy dust. Doggy style. Bam! Fairy dust."

"Jade." I interrupted. "You want to hear my story or not?"

"Hell yeah! And since it's been such a pathetically long time since I've had sex, I'm going to need details. Lots of sweaty, hot, and hopefully very filthy details." She paused. "Hold on a second. Let me take a sip of coffee and get all comfy." I heard shuffling sounds, and then Jade shouted, "And… go!"

Putting my phone on speaker, I gossiped. "So Friday, he invited me to his McKay Club's private playground—Noire." Thirsty, I went over to the refrigerator.

"I've heard about that place. The gossip hags say Noire is the anything-goes section."

"More like anything your kinky little heart desires," I replied, grabbing a bottle of Pellegrino, cracking it open, and taking a long sip. "Believe me; the gossip is nowhere near the reality of Noire. It's total sexual energy and chaos."

I opened the cabinet, looking for a snack. "Oh, jackpot! Macarons." Pulling out the box, I ripped into the package, biting into the cookie's crisp outer shell that gave way to a soft, chewy center with an intense burst of flavor. "Lordy... it's yummy."

"Wait. His cock was yummy?" Jade asked.

"I was talking about my macaron. But his cock was quite tasty, too," I sassed cheekily.

"Sin!" Jade screeched in an impatient tone. "Focus. Details."

I chewed. "Put it this way." I swallowed. "If I threw his cock up in the air, it would rain sunshine. That's how good he is."

"Oh, I want one of those." Jade gasped comically.

"You know... he does have a friend named Ram."

"Ram?" she sputtered. "What kind of name is that?" She paused. "Never mind. I don't even want to get into that topic."

I laughed. "Yes. Let's not go there."

"Anyhoo," she replied, "I'll hard pass on the *Ram*."

I nearly choked on my mouthful of cookie at her dramatic emphasis on the word *Ram*. "Girl, you're a hot mess."

"I'm just saying..."

"Anyway," I quipped, "after the club, when he dropped me home, my front door was wide open. And when I walked in, my place was destroyed." I swallowed hard. "Everything, including my collection."

"Jesus," Jade hissed. "This story just turned left." She paused. "Not that I don't care about your work, but I'm happy you weren't home when they broke into your place. You can re-create your collection. Your life and safety are more important," she remarked. "Was anything stolen?"

"Nothing I could pinpoint but that ledger of my dad's."

Jade had been with me when I was looking in Dad's ratty trunk and found the well-worn leather ledger that had been deliberately concealed in the false bottom.

"You sure you didn't just misplace it?" Jade asked.

"I'm sure. I put it right back where I'd found it. I had every intention of looking through it again when I had time, but I never did."

I also remembered that while the police were at my house after the break-in, I'd found the large chunk of old, splintered wood that had once covered the false bottom of Dad's old trunk on the floor, and the trunk had been lying on its side with all the contents spilled out. When I'd righted it and scanned inside, I could see the false bottom was missing and so was the red leather ledger that had been hidden in the secret compartment.

"That's odd," Jade uttered. "Why would someone want to steal that?"

I shrugged. "How would I know? There was nothing in the ledger that made any sense to me." I guzzled my water.

I recollected lifting the cover and flicking through the thin paper. The first several pages were a collection of names, which were not in my father's handwriting. Then there were the initials G.L.C. scrawled in red ink at the bottom of every page, along with random numbers and phone numbers. All the pages had codes running along the margins.

"Anyway..." I carried on. "It's gone, but all my jewelry and other expensive stuff remained untouched. Not that I give a shit. Material possessions can be replaced, but my collection can't."

"Sin, it's going to take hard work, but you can reboot your collection," Jade responded. "I'm just relieved that my bestie didn't get hurt."

I heaved a sigh, twirling the bottle between my fingers. "You're right, but what's messing with my head is that the intruder just destroyed everything, down to the smallest details. It was spiteful, as if they were trying to break me emotionally."

"You see, that... I just don't get," Jade said. "Unlike me, you don't have any enemies or rivals. It's just fucking freaky that someone would do that shit to you. Sin, I don't feel comfortable with you staying alone at your townhouse. Why don't you stay at my place while I'm away?" She urged. "I have twenty-four-seven security. You'll be safe there."

I seriously contemplated her offer. Staying at Jade's place seemed like the smart thing to do. I had no guarantees that the intruder wouldn't come back, but next time, I could be home. Staying by myself wasn't ideal, particularly since the intruder was still out there, but what were my alternatives? Definitely not camping out at Core's place... especially not after he'd ignored my phone call. But the townhouse was my home, and no one was going to chase me away from it.

"I can protect myself, Jade. Shit, I've been doing a damn good job for twenty-six years."

"Don't get all huffy with me, Sin Michaels. I'm worried about you; that's all."

I sighed heavily because I was being irrationally bratty. "I know. I'll be okay. I promise."

Jade confided. "I don't feel right about being so far away from Mom and you right now. That's it. I'm coming back home. Fuck shooting this movie. You two are my family. We have to stick together."

I banged my fist against the counter. "Don't you dare, Jade." This was exactly what I didn't want to happen. Her dropping everything just to come back to New York. "You worked too damn hard to make your project a reality. I'm going to be fine. I swear."

"Dammit," she swore. "I hate being so far away. Especially when everyone I love is going through some major, real-life crisis shit. My mom is feuding with Cate over that fucker Bigsby. And now you and your break-in. I can't just sit here with my thumb up my ass. I feel useless."

I hated hearing the despair in her voice.

"Jade, we'll both be okay. Stay where you are. Your movie is important to you... to all of us."

"Not as important as you two." Jade countered.

My jaw hardened. There was no way I could live with myself

if she gave up her dream just to come back here and babysit me. That was exactly why I hadn't called her when everything in my life went to shit… starting with the break-in. I didn't want her to worry, and I damn sure didn't want her to give up her dream because of me.

"You are not coming back to New York until you finish what you started. At least one of us has to have their dreams come true. This movie is yours."

"But—"

"Enough, Jade. If shit gets unmanageable, I'll call you. And only then will you hop on a plane and come home. Okay?" I insisted.

"Okay." She confirmed in a tired voice. "Well then, tell me something… anything to distract me from the clusterfuck of my life."

"Well…" I bit into another macaron, chewing thoughtfully. "I can officially cross *have an all-night sexathon* off my to-do list."

"All night?" Jade interrupted.

"And morning," I shot back.

"Holy shit! You stayed until morning?"

"Yes." My lips pressed together in a slight grimace.

"Interesting…" Jade murmured.

I furrowed my brows. "What do you mean by that?"

"Oh, nothing. So you know the drill. What's his performance score?"

"Eleven." I grinned. "No, scratch that. He's a twelve. I forgot to add points for this genius and wildly creative thing that he does with his tongue that makes me so delirious every time he does it. Like this morning when he was mid-swirl, I swore I saw a unicorn frolicking through a meadow."

Jade screamed, "Oh. My. God. You've never rated a lover a twelve."

I shrugged. "Because he's that good."

"Okay, bonus round. What's his conversation score?"

I thought about all the conversations Core and I had. But

there was one moment last night that stuck out—when I'd decided to lay my feelings out like a rug before Core...

"You don't know how much this means to me—you being here for me," I whispered to him.

His eyes were passionate, and his words were fierce in response. "I always protect what I care for."

My heart had jerked at the truth laid out in his words. They confirmed what I'd secretly suspected—that Core would destroy anyone and everyone who dared try to harm me.

Frankly, I liked that kind of devotion because it was something most men didn't have anymore.

"Same score," I answered. "Twelve. He's intelligent, funny, and very intense, but he keeps me interested."

I bit my lip, contemplating the enigma that was Core. He was the complete opposite of everything that I'd thought he was, and little by little, Core McKay was unveiling who the man truly was.

A man who cared about me.

A man with a damn heart.

"But he's complicated," I started, "and dangerous with a whole lot of crazy mixed in." I stared into space. "Plus, Tabitha's back."

Jade scoffed. "Back from where? The asylum?"

"She sure as hell looked like it... but it was more than that. It's the unnerving shit she mentioned today."

"Like what?"

"That Core had sought me out. He came to her to broker an introduction to me—like he used Tabitha just to get to me. Worse, they're not even friends. What do you make of that?"

Jade snapped, "Anything that comes out of Tabitha's mouth is utter bullshit. I warned you about her years ago. I never liked or trusted her. She's a pretentious bitch who's fixated on outshining you—her protégé."

"And you were right."

Jade and Tabitha never got along. Jade hated Tabitha's biting, acidic personality, and Tabitha resented Jade's privileged lifestyle.

"But today, what Tabitha disclosed about Core rang true. Though, for the life of me, I can't figure out why he wanted to meet me."

"Did you ask him?"

"I called him and left a message for him to call me back."

"Nope," Jade simply stated.

"Nope what?" I asked.

"Not the way to go about this shit. In person. Have the discussion with him face to face. You'll be able to tell whether he's lying then."

I sighed heavily. "You might have a point."

"I always do," she quipped and then yawned. "I'm exhausted already. I haven't been sleeping well lately."

"Try that sleep app with white noise that I nagged you to buy before you left." I urged. "You should be asleep in no time."

"Okay, but call me... no matter what time, and tell me how it goes with him."

"I will."

Jade sighed. "And, Sin... please be careful, all right?"

"I will. Love you, girlie."

"Love you more, Sin."

12

SINTHIA

STRIDING out of Core's building, I felt sexy but warrior-tough in my little black dress, paired with thigh-high boots and a leather jacket. Now I was ready to do battle against Core at dinner tonight.

Zuri was talking to a sandy-haired man who was leaning against a sleek black SUV.

The man pushed away from the vehicle, tilting his head toward me. "Well, hello, sweet cheeks. Remember me?" He grinned.

I eyed the man who was built like a tank. "How could I forget? You and your sidekick—"

"My brother, Rocco." He interrupted. "I'm Max."

I arched a brow. "Well, Max"—I widened my stance—"you and Rocco refusing to let me onto the rooftop was a prick move."

"Oh, come on, sweet cheeks. Don't hold that against us," he replied. "At the time, the roof was reserved for Core. But I do recall we did let you onto it to spend some private time with Core." He suggestively waggled his eyebrows at me.

Zuri rolled her eyes before jabbing him in the side. "Don't be crude, Max."

"Ouch!" he grumbled. "Woman, don't poke me with that bony elbow of yours." He glared at Zuri. "I was just pointing out a fact."

She eyed me. "He's like a little boy sometimes. You'll get used to him... eventually." She pursed her lips. "I'm going home. Max will be driving you over to the restaurant to meet Core." She touched my elbow. "Sin, you have my number. Call me if you need to talk, okay?"

I smiled at her. She looked exhausted.

"Yes. We'll chat." I hugged her before stepping back.

She winked at me. "Have a good time tonight." She got into her vehicle and drove away.

Max opened the back door to his SUV.

"Thank you," I replied, maneuvering inside.

Shutting the door, he strode around to the driver's side before sliding in and driving off into the Manhattan traffic.

After a few minutes of zipping in and out of the snarl of taxi-cabs and buses, it didn't take long for Max to pull up in front of a restaurant that I recognized from a foodie magazine —Redemption.

Anxiously, I smoothed out the nonexistent wrinkles in my dress, waiting for Max to open my door.

"Have a good time," Max remarked as I stepped out.

"Thank you," I replied before striding toward the inconspic-uous doorman, who opened the door, allowing me to step into the dim, upscale restaurant. I was trying to hide my excitement and morbid curiosity. This was my first time at the well-known private restaurant owned by a former model named Vivica.

I observed the celebs inconspicuously sauntering around before a willowy redhead with ample cleavage on display approached me with a huge smile, which I returned, immedi-ately recognizing that she was wearing one of my designs.

"Love the dress," I complimented, trying not to act like a total fangirl. But inside I was jumping up and down. One of the most recognized and famous models in the world—Vivica—was wearing something I'd created.

"Well, I love your designs, Sinthia Michaels," she answered.

I was flattered that she'd recognized me. "Thank you. Believe me; it looks fab on you."

"Thank you, darling." She winked. "And welcome to my sinful establishment"—she gestured dramatically—"Redemption."

"I'm meeting Core McKay," I replied.

"I know. He's waiting for you," she replied. "Right this way."

We sliced through the space, and I admired the exquisitely designed restaurant draped with rich fabric across the ceiling. The Moroccan flair made the space feel both exotic and elegant. Bypassing the seated patrons, we eventually arrived at a long hallway that led to a flight of stairs. At the top of the staircase, she pushed open the door.

"And here we are," Vivica announced. "Have fun, darling," she drawled before sauntering away.

My gaze swept across the lit rooftop with its medieval architecture and vines hugging the bricks. Candles were strategically placed, giving the space a sultry, romantic vibe. A table nestled in the center of the rooftop was set with candles and an elaborate table setting.

Core stepped out of the shadows, studying me with no smile. In fact, his eyes were the most serious I'd ever seen.

I tilted my head, and my eyes traveled up his tall, well-built body. Muscles bunched beneath his crisp, tailored white shirt, and his rolled-up sleeves displayed the tattoos on his forearms. His collar was unbuttoned, and all I could focus on was the all-seeing eye tattoo on his neck. He looked delicious and dangerous.

My stomach popped and gurgled like a freshly opened bottle of Pellegrino.

Damn. This doesn't bode well for me.

I felt my hands grow moist.

His searing steel-gray eyes made me visualize seriously wicked, naughty things.

Shit. Shit. Shit. Sin, focus.

Keep your eyes on the prize. He has some damn explaining to do about his relationship with Tabitha.

He regarded me for a long time before smoothing a hand across his blunt-cut midnight-black hair.

"You look absolutely beautiful," he drawled in that ridiculously gruff tone.

My cunt clenched like it recognized its master's voice. As the cool air whirled around us, I sashayed toward him. Stopping before him, I tilted my head, and my eyes traveled up his body. Core under the bright moonlight was like a work of art.

"And you're late," he informed me with a velvet voice.

I considered him from head to toe and looked back again to his hard lips. "Well, hello to you, too," I replied before leveling him with an irritated stare.

He arched a brow.

I coolly glared at him before gliding around him to take in the beautiful views of downtown and uptown Manhattan, as well as the Hudson River.

There was a loud clearing of a throat from the entrance to the rooftop. Laden with dishes, the waiter and another server stood looking at us as if asking for permission to enter.

"Sin, let's have a seat." Core urged.

I nodded, allowing him to escort me to the table where he pulled out my chair, and I sat down while watching him take the opposite seat.

Both waiter and server approached the table.

"Bone marrow with veal cheek marmalade, foie gras fried rice with shredded duck and coriander, crispy duck wings with yuzu kosho, grilled clams flecked with Calabrian chilies, pasta spiked with pink peppercorns, and squash-stuffed ravioli with hazelnuts," the waiter announced as the server grandly set the small sharing plates down in the center of the table, carefully avoiding a stack of papers held down by a glass. "Enjoy," he finished with a bow of his head.

"Are you feeding an army?"

Core smiled, a slow lifting of perfect lips to reveal straight white teeth. "I didn't know what you'd like, so I took the liberty of ordering some of their popular dishes for you to try."

"I see," I croaked before clearing my throat. I kind of liked that he had taken the initiative to make sure I was properly fed with a well-selected sampling of a foodie's wet dream.

The server poured water into our glasses while the waiter beamed at me. "What would you like to drink?"

"I'll have a Moscow mule," I answered.

"And I'll have a Jack on the rocks," Core replied.

The waiter and server roamed away.

We eyed each other for a full minute before I couldn't stand the silence anymore. "Busy day?" I asked.

"It was very... enlightening." He narrowed his eyes as he continued to assess me with a combination of curiosity and intense interest.

"For me, too." I knew he was toying with me, but I was in no mood for games.

Core put a small plate in front of me, scooping a teeny portion of foie gras fried rice and putting several crispy duck wings with yuzu kosho onto it.

With butterflies fluttering in my stomach, I was not in the mood to eat right now, despite the delicious offering. "So are we going to talk about Tabitha or not?" I brought the glass of water to my lips, sipping slowly.

"We'll talk about Tabitha, but first, I need to get this out of the way. There's something on the table for you." He gestured to the stack of papers under the glass before filling his plate with food.

What is Core up to now?

I picked up the papers. "What's this?" I asked.

"A contract giving you back full control of your company." Core leveled his gaze on me.

My breath hitched. "Why?" A flush of adrenaline tingled through my body.

He ate a forkful of rice while staring at me. He swallowed before asking, "Isn't that what you wanted?"

"No!" I snapped my mouth shut, gathering my thoughts. "I mean, yes. It's just... sudden. Only weeks ago, you seemed pretty adamant that our business relationship was going to remain intact, and now... this?"

Yes. I am happy but also perplexed.

"Sin, sign it."

I scanned all the papers, and the contract was exactly what he'd explained. He was giving me back full control of my company. Happiness zinged through me, and then I froze.

But what does this really mean?

Is Core withdrawing all financial support for my business?

And if he did, I would be screwed. The only reason I wanted a financial investor from the get-go was because I needed money, lots of it. And now that my collection was ruined and I was starting from scratch, I needed Core—I mean, his money... more than ever.

My heart raced when another horrible thought filled my head.

Is he breaking up with me?

I wasn't egotistical, but a woman had to have her pride. It was all good when I was considering walking away from him, but for Core to beat me to the punch? That shit was frankly ego-bruising.

Heat flushed through my body. My emotions went from calm to rage in seconds.

Oh, hell no! Who the fuck does he think he is?

Then the numbness set in, and my emotional walls went up.

Fuck him. I'll survive.

I zeroed in on where it was flagged for me to sign. My fingers shook a little before I steadied myself.

He quickly signed, too. "It's done." He confirmed, pushing the documents back under the glass.

The server arrived with our drinks on a silver tray. Swiftly, he placed them in front of us before scurrying away.

My throat was parched for liquid courage. Picking up my Moscow mule, which was in a cool copper mug, I drank thirstily, feeling the smooth burn of alcohol before placing the cup down. "All right, Core. Now tell me what the hell is going on." I looked in his direction, my eyes suspicious.

He studied me for a moment, long and hard. Then he frowned, deep creases forming around his brow and lips. He rubbed his fingers over his lips, and more time passed before he spoke. "What if you had to tell a person the most important thing that they needed to know, and you knew they wouldn't believe you?"

Uh-oh... this is bad.

I'd never seen Core this somber.

"I'd tell them," I whispered.

"Bigsby is the man who killed my mother."

I blinked and then blinked again.

Wait. What?

"Bigsby Calhoune?" My question came out with a tinge of hysteria because right now, I felt like I was losing my fucking mind. "How did you come to that conclusion?"

"The man who placed the gun to my mother's head still wears the custom-made gold ruby-and-diamond-encrusted horseshoe ring on his middle finger."

A ring?

I let the words roll around in my head before I sputtered, "You're basing such a serious accusation on a damn ring?" I frowned. "Do you know how many men could have that same piece of jewelry?"

"One," Core answered, holding up a finger. "Bigsby told me he's had his ring for over forty years and that it's custom-made."

Okay... none of this shit makes any sense.

"Cut to the fucking chase, Core. What the hell does this shit have to do with me?" My heart was racing like a rabbit because I suspected I wouldn't like his answer.

"The man who shot me and my mother wore a gold ruby-and-diamond-encrusted horseshoe ring. I've been looking for years for that man. When I finally found the owner of the ring—Bigsby—I had Kevin dig up everything he could on him."

My eyes narrowed. "And?"

"Kevin found out that Bigsby was looking into your business. And I knew if he was interested in your business, there had to be a pretty damn good reason."

That was the truth bomb I'd been waiting for.

My mind screeched to a stop, and slowly, I began to reverse-engineer all the information I knew. And the pieces to the puzzle that had been plaguing me for hours all started to fit together.

Why Core had sought me out through Tabitha—because she was my friend and his only way to get close to me. That was the answer to the riddle about why a billionaire like Core had wanted to go into business with me, a fashion designer.

Core couldn't give a rat's ass about me. He'd needed my business as the bait to lure Bigsby in. That simple truth cut my heart like a dagger.

I was nothing to him.

Nothing but a pawn he'd used to get him closer to his end game... Bigsby.

My blood started to boil. Rage slithered through my veins like poison.

Breathe, Sin. Breathe.

Picking up my glass of water, I drank quickly. There would be no more alcohol for a bit; I needed to keep my mind focused for this conversation.

I was mad as hell right now, but I needed to think logically, not emotionally. And when I did exactly that, more pieces clicked into place. "You purchased my company so he had to deal directly with you." It was a statement, not a question.

"Yes," Core replied. "Kevin did a thorough investigation, but he couldn't find anything linking Bigsby to you. But I was sure if Bigsby was interested in you, there had to be a sinister motive, which was why I had to acquire your business fast. I had Kevin search through your background again, looking for anything that could be used as leverage."

My heart clenched and then dropped to the pit of my stomach. His words confirmed what I'd suspected—that all I was to him was a resource to be used to suit his needs.

"Leverage?" I asked in a low voice and through clenched teeth.

He furrowed his brows as he continued to stare at me. He slightly tilted his head, and then his frown deepened.

I inhaled a deep breath and held it for a beat before speaking. "You dirty fucker."

He spoke in a low, soothing tone. "Sin..." He leaned forward to touch my hand.

I snatched it out of reach. "Don't. Touch. Me. McKay," I gritted out.

His angular, rough-hewn face clenched.

"Continue..." I ordered before I steepled my fingers, cool eyes on him. "I want to hear exactly how I've been used for leverage."

Core inhaled a long, ragged breath before dragging his hands over his face. His cool, controlled demeanor dropped for just a moment before it reasserted itself. "I found out that you needed money, and I had lots of it." He sat back and cocked his head. "But I couldn't find a way to get into your small inner circle without raising suspicion or scaring you off. That was when Kevin found out you were friends with Tabitha."

The more Core had unveiled, the more pissed I got at myself for trusting Tabitha Thorp.

So this was all part of his big game plan... to maneuver me like a chess piece.

Everything that had occurred right before and during our relationship sank in. It was no happenstance when Tabitha had called me out of the blue, all excited about one of her business connections willing to provide financing in exchange for a small percentage of my future profits.

Core had put her up to making the business arrangement and the call. And that truth stung like a motherfucker.

My brain started working overtime. *What else don't I know about Core and Tabitha's relationship?* I knew for sure that they weren't friends; Tabitha had told me that much. *So if they weren't friends and didn't run in the same social or business circles... then how did they know each other?*

Then a horrible thought occurred to me. In the past, Tabitha had recounted her many excursions to the McKay Club to hook up with prime hotties—her words, not mine. Tabitha unapologetically slept around.

Is Core one of her many lovers?

"Did you fuck her?" My lips mashed together.

"I did." Core confirmed grimly.

I sucked in a sharp breath as the anger sparked inside me. "You had sex with Tabitha?" I jumped to my feet, toppling the chair behind me. "I knew it! Something about you two just didn't feel right." I clenched and unclenched my fists.

He stood, towering over me. "Sin!" he barked. "I slept with her years ago. Back when Tabitha and I were young. Way before I met you, we hung out in the same criminal circles. The only difference was, back then, the now-famous Tabitha worked as a mule for her seedy drug kingpin boyfriend, Ben Vargos."

Keep it together, Sin. There's more. I can feel it.

I held a breath before releasing it. "I'm listening," I replied in a sharp tone.

His jaw clenched so tight; if it were glass, it would have shattered. It seemed like he had to unhinge it just to speak. "When I found out she had a shitload of debt, I recruited her to help me convince you of the value of getting an investor—specifically, me—to help you expand your business. In exchange, I agreed to pay off Tabitha's debt to Ben and send her on a very long vacation."

"That's why she cleaned out her house and abruptly pulled up roots as if she never existed. You made her leave."

"Yes." He intensely watched me for a few moments. "It was part of our deal."

"Deal? That's all I am to you, isn't it?" A bitter tang coated my mouth. "An object. An acquisition to add to your collection." My hands were shaking with anger. Deep down, I knew that was all I meant to him, but it still hurt like hell to hear him say it.

I briefly closed my eyes, still processing what he was telling me... the truth. Despite my best efforts to calm the hell down, the warmth from my rising anger became an inferno.

I launched at him. "You lying, manipulative fucker!" I punched my fists against his chest. All of the anger and pain from being lied to and manipulated like a pawn on a chessboard erupted inside me like a volcano.

I can't believe I actually thought Core could be the one...

This man had inspired me to do and want things sexually that no other lover could.

This man who I'd thought did sweet, genuine things for me without me even asking...

This man I had been falling for...

Was this all part of his grand plan?

To trick me into trusting him? Falling for him? Wanting him? Maybe even... loving him?

My stomach twisted with pain because he was just like every man I'd encountered over the years, selfish... a liar... a manipulator.

A man who would use people—me—for whatever he needed without giving a shit.

Who the hell is the real Core McKay? Because everything I thought I knew about him—and liked about him—was all an illusion. Smoke and mirrors.

My voice was harsh when I whispered, "I let you into my body... my life... and you used me like a whore." I wanted to wrap my hands around his thick neck and squeeze the living shit out of him. I pummeled his body with all my might.

"Sin!" He easily grabbed my hands. "Stop!" he pleaded in a gentle but warning voice that didn't have the desired effect. Instead of calming me down, it just added fuel to my fire.

"Let. Me. Go. Now!" I yelled.

"I will if you just calm the fuck down." His voice was softer, calmer, and in direct contrast to mine.

I took some deep, cleansing breaths. "Let go," I ordered.

He released me, slightly stepping back. The uncomfortable tension between us didn't vanish.

I moved back to maintain the distance between us. All the trust that I'd had in him was gone... and there was no coming back from this shit. I knew that, and from the look of remorse in his eyes, he did, too.

"Core, you used me as fucking bait, like my life and business meant nothing." I cocked an eyebrow, putting a hand on my hip. "Really?"

"Sin, I needed closure." His voice was hard and decisive.

I threw my hands in the air. "Oh, to hell with you and your fucking closure." I stormed away from him, nearer to the railing. Being close him was making me claustrophobic. "You fucked me... literally and figuratively."

"I am who I am, Sin." His usually vibrant gray eyes seemed dulled by regret and intense thought. "I can't change that." He sighed. "Could I have done things differently?" he asked in a coarse voice, and deep brackets formed around his mouth as he frowned. "Fuck yes, but I did what I did because Bigsby needed to be destroyed."

"At my expense," I whispered.

I shook my head. For the first time, I really saw the man behind the veil. He was a broken man who'd waited his whole life to get revenge on his mother's killer. Core didn't give a shit who he had to use to get it.

Then another horrible thought occurred to me. "You were the one who caused all of my retailers to pull out of their deals."

He studied me for a long moment, and when he spoke, his tone was quieter, apologetic. "Yes."

I flinched as if he'd physically slapped me.

No. No. No. This shit can't be happening. I'm such a damn idiot. I allowed myself to do what I'd promised myself I'd never do again... trust a man.

"And was Lily Sanchez a part of your plan, too?" I inquired, looking for more traitors in his web of deceit.

Lily Sanchez was a buyer who'd pushed her bosses to carry my Sin Michaels collection in their Fifth Avenue luxury goods department stores. But when the stores had mysteriously backed away from my deal, Lily had seemed just as puzzled as I was.

"No," he replied sharply. "Lily was insignificant in the food chain of New York City power. I went above her head and called in some favors. She didn't know why her bosses had decided to pull out of your deal because I'd ensured that everyone involved in killing your deal kept their mouths shut... or else..."

All the information was painful to hear, but I had to know.

"Or else?" I asked.

He didn't blink. "I'd destroy them."

I studied Core, a scowl etched over his features, his nostrils flaring.

He is a monster.

And if by chance I'd forgotten Core was a powerful predator, it was abundantly clear at that exact moment.

Clearly, Core was a ruthless man of action.

What would he have done to me if I'd refused his proposal as my business investor?

Would he have destroyed my reputation? My business? My life? All three?

Now knowing everything about him... the answer was a resounding, *All of the above.*

After moments of uncomfortable silence, I asked, "And how exactly did you kill my deals?"

"Sin, that's not important. I just did." His voice turned commanding.

Wrong answer.

I didn't give a shit if he was the baddest motherfucker in New York. Because in this moment, I felt like the baddest bitch around, and I wasn't backing down from him. Not one damn inch.

"You don't get to decide anymore what's important for me to know. I do, McKay." I moved closer to him. "Now how did you destroy my retail deals?"

His face tightened. "I called all my connections at the retailers and had them end the agreements."

Exactly how powerful is Core that he could so easily destroy deals I'd worked months to get?

I straightened my spine and glared at him. "I want to know, Core. I want to know all the dirty details. What types of connections would do such a despicable thing?"

"Let's not play games, Sin. You know I'm not some fucking Boy Scout." He walked over to me, tracing a finger across my cheek.

His touch incensed me. I stepped back.

His hand fell away.

Irritation glinted in his eyes as he continued in a low voice. "My connections are shadowy, wealthy, deadly, and ruthless. I've built alliances while doing things like blackmail, coercion, and extortion, and that made me one of the wealthiest and most feared men in New York City."

After a long moment, I said, "So in essence, you're their

puppet master, pulling the strings and making everyone, including me, dance for your sheer amusement."

His face hardened.

Oh... did I hit a nerve, McKay? Good.

I wanted him to fucking hurt just as much as—no, more than —I was hurting right now.

I'm a vengeful bitch.

"Sin—"

I cut him off. "Did Bigsby tell you why he wanted my business so badly?" My lips flattened.

"Yes," he snapped. "When he found out I was a stakeholder in Sin Michaels Corporation, he requested a meeting with me. During which he told me he knew you were set to manufacture in Thailand, and your first run to the United States would be in weeks."

"And?" I inclined my head for him to continue.

Core cleared his throat. "He wanted a small area within your cargo shipment to put his merchandise—women. If I agreed, he'd ensure there were no issues at Port Authority when your shipment arrived in New York."

My heart clenched before speeding up.

What. The. Fuck?

My business and sex trafficking?

"And let me get this straight," I croaked. "You agreed to get my company entangled in sex trafficking?" The thought of it made me angry all over again.

He studied me in silence. His nostrils flared. "Yes, and—"

"You fucker!" I screamed before swallowing several times and then sucking in a slow breath that didn't help. I began to pace, aware that he was watching me.

Now Bigsby's interest in my business made more sense. No one would ever suspect a naive designer was part of a sex trafficking ring. Frankly, Bigsby's plan was brilliant.

My heart started to pound in my chest at the thought of

women, men, and children being robbed of both their lives and freedom by sexually depraved predators.

It's disgusting.

I glared at Core, and I didn't like the man I saw.

Who is this man? And why the fuck did I let him into my life?

Did he ever care about me?

Or was it acting?

Dammit! How did I let this shit between Core and me even happen?

"Let me finish," he requested in a rigid voice. "I had no intention of trafficking women. That's not my shit. You should know that. You know me."

I shook my head. "No, I don't... but please, continue."

"Sin, I just wanted to know exactly what he had planned for your business."

I shouted back, "Oh, go fuck yourself, Core!"

I started to storm away, and he grabbed me from behind, pressing me against his body. I stiffened and then tried to pull myself away, but the heavily muscled arms that encircled me refused to budge.

"Let me go."

"Only if you calm down," he said, his mouth brushing against my ear.

My skin prickled. I struggled hard to get free.

His arms tightened. "Sin, just let me finish what I have to say to you." His voice was soft, lighter than I would have expected from him, but firm.

"Okay. Whatever... just get off me," I croaked.

His touch repulsed me. I had given him everything, and he still made a mess of things.

His hold loosened.

I scrambled away from him before swinging around to face him. "I hate that you did this to me." I pointed at him. "You used me like I meant nothing."

My face felt like it was on fire.

Core was a horrible mistake.

And I had done everything with him that I'd sworn I would never do with another man. I had opened up and shared a piece of me, all because he'd weakened my defenses, made me believe that he cared about me and that I could trust and be trusted.

All of it was a damn lie.

"Sin, what was I supposed to do when I found out Bigsby had killed my mother? Let him walk away?" he replied in a cool, level voice. I could tell he was trying to get a handle on his anger.

"I never said that," I protested.

There was no doubt in my mind that Bigsby deserved to pay for his crime. But using me to do it? That shit was inexcusable.

"Good," he barked. "Because that wasn't fucking happening. My mother deserved better than to remain some unsolved crime sent away to the cold case unit that the police officers didn't give a shit about anymore."

I saw the raw pain and fury in his eyes and understood the emotions. It was what I'd felt when Dad died. I blamed the police for not searching day and night for the person who had run him off the road, killing him. I remembered calling the cops for months, pleading with them not to close his case and for them to keep looking for his killer. But they didn't.

"And what do I deserve, Core?" I pointed at him. "To be treated like some stepping-stone? An expendable object to be used just to get what you want... justice?"

I recognized this topic was a slippery slope for both of us. He'd lost a mother, and I'd lost a father. Each death and loss had torn us apart.

But how many lives had to be destroyed in the process of him getting his mother's killer? My life? Core's life? Just how far was he willing to go? From everything he'd done... very far.

The moments of silence drifted to minutes, and his eyes narrowed. "There are always sacrifices in war." His voice dropped to a growl.

His words were like a dagger to my heart.

"So I'm the damn sacrificial lamb?" My words were clipped.

The silence stretched.

I waited for something...

Anything...

That could erase this vile *I want to firebomb his damn car and then go to his penthouse and destroy all his shit* feeling that took up residence in my soul. I despised that he was the cause of these foreign, dark, heavy, sordid emotions.

This isn't me. I never look for drama, but dammit, why does drama always come looking for me?

"Sin." He blew out a hard breath before sliding his hands over his face. "You and I shouldn't have gone this far. I didn't want this." He chewed on his lip for a moment in consideration and seemed to be carefully choosing his words. "But I've come to understand there's a big difference between what I want and what I need."

I ignored everything he'd just disclosed, except for one word. *This?*

Irritation colored my words. "What part of this"—I gestured between us—"didn't the great Core McKay want?" I jammed my hands on my hips. "Because it seems to me like you've gotten everything you wanted. Your mother's killer. My business. To fuck me... literally."

What an arrogant asshole!

Every time he opened his mouth, I had to resist the urge to shank him... repeatedly.

"Sin, I won't say that I'm sorry. I do what I have to do. That fucker took my damn mother away from me. Do you understand me?" he asked in a coarse voice. "Bigsby shot me and my mother..." His eyes looked haunted while his fists clenched and unclenched. "And he walked away like we didn't mean a goddamn thing. What would you have done if he did that shit to you and to someone you loved? Walk away? Or make him answer for his crime?"

I swallowed hard. He had me there. Memories marred my mind. Dad's senseless death had destroyed me emotionally and burned me to the core. It'd changed me in ways I didn't even really understand until recently. Even years later, with his murder unsolved, it burned me that someone had gotten away with murder.

I turned my back on Core when I felt a tear—from anger—roll down my cheek.

Looking out on the cityscape, I rubbed my damp cheek on my shoulder. "You think I don't want retribution for my dad's death? But at what cost?" I shook my head. "Using you to get what I want? Manipulating you? Fucking you? I'm not that type of woman. I've never done shit in my life that made me question my morals—whether you believe it or not." My lower lip trembled. "I have a code of honor, and I tell the straight-up truth. I'm simple. Transparent. Real."

"And where the fuck has that gotten you?" he lectured in a low, even voice.

I shot a glare at him over my shoulder. There was a quick flicker of emotions—anger, then regret, to confusion, and then back to neutrality—in his eyes.

Is Core so blinded by his need for revenge that he didn't give a shit about anything or anyone? Including me?

Jerking my eyes away, I stared at the bustling city below. With a voice deliberately devoid of any emotions, just matter-of-fact, I replied, "At least I can look at myself in the damn mirror and know that I haven't backstabbed my way to the top. And if that shit makes me naive in your eyes, well, fuck you and the horse you rode in on."

"Well, in my world, it doesn't work that way," he retorted, his voice cold, hard. "Watching my mother getting killed changed me."

I felt rather than heard him come up behind me. A tsunami of energy swirled along my hypersensitive nerves.

Core pressed his body to my back.

"Core. Don't." I stiffened, clutching the railing for dear life, trying hard to ignore how comforting the heat emanating from his body felt pressed against mine.

Damn. Damn. Damn.

I swallowed hard.

Focus on the matter at hand. I scolded myself, but I had a hard time redirecting. I was so pissed off with myself that he still affected me this way. *Don't fold, Sin.*

"Sin." He pressed his hands over mine. They were so much bigger and darker than my slender, feminine ones that trembled underneath. "I will not apologize for what I am."

"I never asked you to," I mumbled.

"No. What you're doing is even worse. You're condemning me for being broken and, yes, fucked up in the head," he replied hoarsely. "But I am the product of my environment. Seeing what I saw and living through what I lived through... those things aren't easily forgotten." He paused. "Waking up in the middle of the night to sounds of people being gunned down. Coming home from school and witnessing single mothers giving blow jobs in alleyways so they could pay rent and put food on the table..."

I calmed a bit as I listened to him. The horrible sense of rage faded slightly.

"Sin, the things I've seen either break you or make you. I chose the latter."

"Core, you don't understand."

"Please... make me understand then." He lowered his head on top of mine.

After a few moments of uncomfortable silence that were riddled with distrust and tension, I asked, "How can I trust you anymore?"

"Sin, you never did." His breath puffed the delicate hairs at my temple.

I pulled one hand out from under his.

I bit my bottom lip and remained silent. He was right. I never did trust him—and with good reason. He had done everything that I'd feared a man would do if I ever lowered my defenses and let him in—hurt and betray me.

"What? Did you think that I didn't know? That I couldn't feel you were ready to bolt from us, from me, like some nervous rabbit? You had one damn foot in and one foot out of my bed."

I frowned. "I'm not good at trusting men. And everything you've done just proves why I never let my guard down. You manipulated me to get what you wanted, with no damn consideration for my feelings or how it would affect me."

"We both didn't trust each other," Core answered in a deep, velvety voice. "And without trust, there's only fear." He turned me around to face him.

I studied him as he studied me.

He carried on. "I trust you now, Sin. Despite the things I've done, given time, don't you think you can come to trust me?"

I rolled my eyes skyward. "Are you kidding me right now? Of course I can't trust your ass! Not after all the lies you told me."

"Not once did I lie to you."

I arched a brow. "Oh, really? Then what would you call it?"

"I omitted information, but I didn't lie."

I sputtered, "Don't play word games with me, Core. The way you manipulated me—your lies of omission—was infinitely worse. I can't forgive you for that shit."

Core angled his head and watched me. "Putting all my cards on the table, it did start out as me using you and your company to get to Bigsby. But it all changed when I got to know the real woman that you are. You became more than business; you became someone I needed in my life. And you can call bullshit on this if you want, but in my world, the less you know, the safer you are."

I stiffened. "Safe from what?"

He intensely watched me for a few moments. "You're going to need to sit down for this, Sin."

"No. I'm good. Just tell me," I declared with quiet resolve.

He furrowed his brows as he continued to stare at me. He

slightly tilted his head, and then his frown deepened. "Kevin's investigation into your family background unearthed that you have two birth certificates, each one showing a different set of parents."

I sucked in a sharp breath and held it for a moment before releasing it. "What are you talking about?" I croaked.

"The first birth certificate had your father listed as Ian Michaels and mother as Grace Michaels. The second certificate had your father listed as Greer Lorne Cruickshank and mother as Aubrey Cruickshank."

"What?" My knees buckled.

Core caught me and escorted me back to the chair. I plopped down, feeling light-headed.

"I don't understand. Ian Michaels is my dad."

"Sin, no... he's not."

With those four words, my world shattered, along with everything I'd ever thought I knew.

13

SINTHIA

MY APPETITE HAD VANISHED after hearing Core's earth-shattering revelation, so the waiter and server cleared the table of food and plates. Core had also instructed them that we no longer needed their services for the rest of the night.

I sat stiffly in the chair on the rooftop as the Manhattan air chilled me, staring at Core in disbelief. "Let me get this straight. My supposed parents, Greer and Aubrey, started having an affair behind Bigsby's back and then cut business ties with Bigsby?"

"Yes," Core replied.

"And Bigsby got so pissed," I started after moments of uncomfortable silence, "that he killed Greer in an apartment fire. But Greer gave his brother, Ian, the ledger just in case something went wrong?"

"Exactly."

Tilting my head in quiet consideration, I studied him. "And Jemma, whom you suspect is my real mother, disappeared while on bail after Bigsby snitched her out to the Feds?"

"I know this shit sounds crazy, but it's true." He spoke in a soothing tone.

I bit my bottom lip, examining him for a beat. "And during

all this drama, Bigsby had no clue that Jemma was pregnant with me—until now?"

"Also true," Core answered.

I eyed him like he'd lost his fucking mind. "So Ian is not my father. He's my uncle and Greer's brother?"

Core nodded.

"Oh God," I whispered. I felt like I was about to hurl. My emotions were churning from anger to confusion to dread and back to anger. "My whole life is one big lie."

Dad is not my biological father?

He's really my uncle who loved and raised me as his own?

Part of me wanted to reject everything Core had just told me, and the other part... wholeheartedly believed him because this was the answer to the question I'd been asking myself for years.

Why didn't I look anything like Dad or Grace?

Because I was not their biological child.

I stared into space while images of my dad flashed through my mind. He had been the doting dad who took me to zoos, aquariums, and planetariums, and I always marveled at how fortunate I was to have a parent who loved me unconditionally.

But now those memories were complicated by this extraordinary drama that was unfolding.

Once again, Core spoke in a simple, even tone. "Sin, I have information to verify everything I just told you."

Jerking my eyes away, I stood and began to pace the terrace, aware he was watching me.

I stopped and stared at him. "But if Bigsby killed all of them—Greer, your mother, and Ian—isn't it plausible that he killed Jemma, too?"

He pushed up to his feet, striding over, and stood just inches from me. "Bigsby is a psycho, so if he killed her, I'm sure he would have bragged about that, too, on Jeff's recording. But as far as I know, he's still looking for her."

Sex trafficking.

A Manhattan madam who is also my mother.

Greer is my real father.

What. The. Fuck?

But the crazy thing was Core's story did make part of my life make a hell of a lot more sense—like how much Grace disliked me, especially after Dad's death. Grace was probably pissed that she was stuck with me... still having to pretend to be my mother. Given how self-centered and selfish she was, having me around as a constant reminder that I wasn't her biological child probably sucked big time—especially in light of the fact that she didn't have a damn maternal bone in her body.

I stiffened when I recalled an argument between Dad and Grace years ago that I'd buried. It was one of their vicious spats that took place on Thanksgiving. My mind traced back to the memories of that fateful day.

GRACE WAS IN THE MIDST OF ONE OF HER INFAMOUS TIRADES, AND Dad hissed, "Shut up, Grace. She can hear you."

And Grace shouted back, "I don't care because I've never wanted her. She's not mine."

YES, HER WORDS HAD CUT LIKE A KNIFE, AND I HAD CRIED hysterically because of them, but I'd thought Grace had said them to hurt me and Dad—not because what she'd stated was actually the truth. Now I knew that all of her actions and barbed words were because she resented the fuck out of me since I wasn't her child.

"Bullshit! This doesn't make any sense. There's no way someone with Bigsby's past can run for mayor of New York, much less attract a socialite like Cate."

He studied me for a few minutes. "What past?" he requested in a low, rigid voice. "Do you know how hard it was for me just to get this much information on him?"

Three deaths—possibly four, including Jemma. All orchestrated by one man—Bigsby. I wasn't sure which feeling was more overwhelming—anger, frustration, or rage.

I paced back and forth, still trying to make sense of it all. "I believe everything you revealed about Bigsby being involved in an escort service. Ariana—Cate's sister—hired a private detective, who dug up information about some trafficking ring Bigsby's involved in. According to Ariana, the Feds are close to nabbing him for money laundering." I skidded to a stop, glaring at Core. "But what I don't understand is why Bigsby would pay someone to kill my dad."

"Which one?"

The headache from stress had been just a minor ache earlier; now it was raging. "Ian. Despite what you've told me, I'll always consider him to be my dad."

Maybe he wasn't my biological father, but he'd raised and loved me. That shit counted for something... my loyalty and devotion to his memory and all that he had given me unconditionally.

Core replied, "Ian had incriminating evidence about Bigsby's sordid past. A ledger—essentially the escort service's little black book."

"That's why Dad hid it in the trunk." I swallowed several times and then sucked in a slow breath that didn't help.

"How did you even find it?" he asked.

"The night of Bigsby's fundraising gala, I was looking for an heirloom piece of jewelry that I'd stowed inside my dad's old trunk. When I was digging inside, I saw red leather peeking out of the broken bottom, so I tried to yank it out. But when I hit the bottom, a secret compartment shifted, completely revealing the leather ledger."

"Didn't you think it was strange that Ian had put it there?" Core's lips pulled into a straight line.

After a long moment of consideration, I confided, "Yes. But when I looked through the ledger, nothing in it made any sense to me. There were several pages of names, and I knew it wasn't my dad's handwriting. And there were the initials G.L.C. scrawled in red ink at the bottom of every page."

Core interjected, "G.L.C. Greer Lorne Cruickshank. Your biological father."

"I knew there had to be a good reason my dad had hidden it because he was the most transparent person I knew." I paused. "But it's obvious now that he had a whole lot of damn secrets." And the unveiling had turned my reality upside down, forcing me to question every core thing I'd ever believed to be true. Now I was struggling to come to terms with all these shades of gray. I needed to make sense of them and hopefully achieve some sort of peace with them.

"So what did you do after you found the ledger?" Core asked.

I shrugged. "I pushed the journal back into the false bottom, banged the base back into place, and then dumped everything I'd pulled out back on top of it, promising myself to further investigate the ledger over the weekend. I just never had a chance to—"

"Sin, that ledger documented all of the clients who frequented your parents' and Bigsby's escort service. Those clients are rich, powerful people whose lives would be destroyed if that information got out. It's leverage Bigsby can use to blackmail people to do anything he wants. Greer knew that, and it's probably why he gave it to Ian for safekeeping. The ironic part about all of this is that Bigsby thought the ledger had burned along with Greer. Ian probably knew if Bigsby found out that he had the ledger, Bigsby would kill him to get it back."

"That's why my dad kept us moving from state to state like we did." I gasped. "We never settled anywhere for too long until... right before his death. I remember being so happy that we were staying in New York permanently, and then out of the blue, my dad decided he wanted to move again." I bit my bottom lip. "Core, shit, that ledger was stolen during the break-in." I froze with my eyes wide. "Wait. Did that fucker Bigsby steal it?"

My body shook with rage at the violation of my space... and my home and, worse, at the destruction of my clothing line that I'd spent months creating—all because of a ledger. And if Bigsby had wrecked my house just to get his hands on it, was my life now in danger since I'd had the ledger?

Fear weighed heavy on me as I considered the possibility of Bigsby coming back to my townhouse when I was home alone to tie up loose ends—me. Adrenaline and fear didn't mix well, and the combination was coursing through me, making me anxious and jumpy.

"Core"—the tension and fear were there, tightly bound around me like a cocoon—"did Bigsby break into my house just to steal the ledger?" I worked hard to control my breathing, steady my heart rate, and temper my fear.

He scowled, and his voice dropped to a rumble. "He ordered Jeff, his little minion, to break in and steal the ledger."

Fury chased the fear away. "But why did Jeff have to destroy my clothing line?" I asked through clenched teeth. "Was he trying to send me, or maybe you, a message?" Bitterness burned in my belly. It all felt like a blanket that wrapped around me too tightly.

"Sin, I don't know who destroyed your house. But what I'm sure of is Jeff didn't do that damage. He told me that he stole the ledger, but he didn't do all that shit to your house."

"And you actually believe a word that fucker said?" I arched a brow.

I was still trying to make sense of it all when a horrible thought raced through my head. *If Jeff didn't destroy my house, who did?*

"Yes, I do," he growled. "Believe me. With the shit we put him through last night and today, it wasn't in his best interest to lie to us. Trust me. No one can withstand—" Core stopped, jaw clenched, and shook his head as if clearing away whatever he'd been about to say.

"Torture?" I squeaked.

My thoughts flashed back to Core's telephone conversation yesterday morning and his statements about "ice for hours" and "softening him up."

"Exactly what type of criminal shit are you into, Core?"

When he finally spoke, he carefully chose his words. "Not something you need to know about. We got the answers we needed about Bigsby via the recording that Jeff had secretly made."

"What happened to suddenly put Da—Ian on Bigsby's radar?"

"Ian's greedy-ass wife."

"Grace?" I asked.

He nodded. "Ian told Grace about the ledger, and apparently, she figured out the value of the book. She snuck behind his back and went to Bigsby, asking him for money in exchange for giving him back the ledger."

"That bitch!" I hissed.

"Well, she was the one who put a bull's-eye on Ian's back," Core replied. "Bigsby thought the ledger had burned up in the fire, along with Greer. And when Ian found out what Grace had done, he met with Bigsby and threatened to expose him with the evidence contained in the ledger if he didn't leave him and his family alone. And you know how well Bigsby took that threat. He decided to put a hit on Ian."

"But why did Bigsby wait so long after that to come after the ledger?" I asked.

"My best guess is he figured that once he acquired your company and got you wrapped up in his illegal business, you would just turn it over with no questions asked."

"Oh God." My tears welled up, more so out of anger than anything else. "For years, I blamed myself for my dad's death"—tears rolled down my cheeks before I dashed them away—"because the morning of his death, I argued with him and then deliberately disobeyed him by not coming home straight after school. He died because he was out looking for me when that driver slammed into him. But now... Bigsby hired someone to kill him?" I stared at Core, blinking back the tears. "His death wasn't because of me."

The memory of that morning and the shouting match I'd had with Dad still made my heart heavy with emotion. Now I couldn't hold back the tears that fell. I was still racked with so much guilt and self-loathing about that day. Instead of telling him, "I hate you," I wished all I had said was, "I love you, Dad."

"Sin? Sin, come on. Please don't cry."

He wrapped an arm around me. I struggled, but he pulled me into his broad chest anyway. I nestled there, enjoying his warmth.

"When I arrived home," I mumbled, "a cop car was pulling away. I raced up the front stairs and slammed into the house to find Grace sitting on the stairs with a drink in her hand, reeking of alcohol." My mouth felt like sawdust had made a home inside. "She told me that Dad was... dead. That he'd gone out searching for me and a car crashed into his, sending him off the bridge."

"It wasn't your fault, Sin. It was Grace who had gotten him killed."

"I know that now! But why did she let me believe all these years that it was my fault that Dad—Ian—had died?"

It was still so hard for me to believe that he wasn't my real father. But despite the fact that he wasn't my biological father, I loved him as such. He had been my lifeline, the man who'd wiped my tears and loved me so much.

"She doesn't hate you, Sin. She hates herself."

"No. I'm pretty sure Grace hates me. I'm not her child. I'm just some other woman's baby that she has been forced to parent. It is a recipe for disaster because Grace doesn't have a nurturing bone in her body. She is a selfish, hateful bitch who has never loved me, but how could she betray her own husband?" That I couldn't understand.

I'd always suspected by her actions and words toward Dad that she didn't love him, but if she'd resented him so much, why hadn't she divorced him? I shook my head. There was no way to figure out why people did the crazy things they did, but as far as Grace was concerned, her ass could rot in hell.

"And all those lives destroyed because of one man... Bigsby."

I hated Bigsby for taking so much away from me. Maybe if my real parents were alive, I wouldn't have had such a fucked-up life, being at the mercy of Grace's emotional abuse. Dad had done his best to shield me from her, but frankly, he hadn't done enough.

"Your mother," I started, "my dad, my biological parents are all gone because that fucker Bigsby thinks people are disposable, like razors." I pushed away from Core, staring at him with narrowed eyes. "Their lives were nothing but damn footnotes. He has to pay the price for taking away their lives."

I was teeming with a level of rage that was new for me, and I didn't know how to subdue it. Vengeance rode me hard.

"I agree. He has to be stopped before he tries to hurt you." His tone was hard and sharp. His lips twisted into a snarl.

"Hurt? What the hell are you talking about now?"

"Bigsby gave me an ultimatum. If I don't give him back the ledger and any copies I've made, plus the recording that Jeff made, within seventy-two hours, he's threatened to kill you."

"Great!" I threw my hands up in the air. "This shit just keeps getting better and better. He's going to kill me." Bile crept up, and I pushed it down.

With a dismissive wave of his hand, he intoned, "That shit will never happen. I'm going to end him before he can even try to kill you or me."

I sighed heavily. "And the ledger and recordings are the only leverage you have to bring him down?"

"No." He scowled. "There's a gun stowed away in Bigsby's safe. Kevin's working on finding out how we can get that, too."

"What's with the gun?" I asked.

"It's the gun he used to kill my mother," he stated in a low, ominous voice.

I narrowed my eyes. "He kept it?"

Core just nodded.

"Damn. Bigsby is a real piece of shit."

There was a special place in hell for a man like Bigsby, who had taken at least three lives without any remorse and then kept a trophy from his kill. Anger rolled over my skin, raising the hair on my arms.

"We can't let him go unchecked," I breathed out. "You've got more than enough evidence to bring him down, Core. So what's the fucking problem?"

Silence stretched for long moments. Core's eyes shone with a clear understanding. Behind them, I saw the same ire and exasperation I had felt.

"Bigsby disappeared," he snapped. "But my intel says he hasn't left New York City... yet."

More silence. The muscles in Core's forearms bulged from clenching his hands into fists.

"Oh shit! Bigsby went underground? That's not good."

Now Bigsby was lurking in the shadows, just waiting to kill me if he didn't get the ledger.

"No. The situation is not good."

I sucked in a sharp breath as the fury sparked inside me. I was not going to let Bigsby get away with taking and destroying so many lives. My dad's life had stood for something. Core's mother's life wasn't just some afterthought, never to be revisited. And rage burned deep inside me that Bigsby had taken away the life I could have had with my biological parents. I'd be damned if I was going to cower in some corner, waiting for Bigsby to come after me, too. I would fight for my life tooth and nail. And if I lost the battle against Bigsby—which I damn well hoped I didn't —I was going to make sure he paid the price for his misdeeds one way or another.

"Well, you're not giving him that fucking ledger or recording back," I snapped. "I don't give a shit what happens to me. Bigsby took my family away from me. He has to pay. How do we make that happen?"

"We're meeting him in seventy-two hours. That's Thursday. He's expecting me to hand over the ledger and recording then. We'll use that meeting to kill him."

Bigsby has to be dealt with strategically and with brute force. And if that means his death... so be it. No one will mourn a world with one less psychopath in it.

"So we just sit around waiting for seventy-two hours?" I ranted. "Are you out of your mind?" I shouted. "He could be plotting anything by now."

Fear and apprehension coursed through my veins. Fear was something I hated to experience because it made me impulsive, which was the worst way to handle things and people like Bigsby.

"We're trying to track his money because he's going to need cash to leave the country. The minute we have some good intel, we'll try to take him down before the meeting. But you won't be safe, Sin, until we get him."

Core is right. I'm not safe. Shit. This situation has turned into the clusterfuck of all damn clusterfucks.

Bigsby was a psychopath, willing and capable of taking a life —mine. Fear shook me to the bone. But when the image of my dad's face flashed through my head, resolve steeled my nerves. There were only two ways to handle Bigsby—flight or fight. I decided to take the latter route. I couldn't control Bigsby's actions, but I could control how I felt about them, and I wasn't going to go down without a fight.

"Safe? Honestly, Core, I don't give a damn."

But that was the furthest thing from the truth. I gave a lot of damns. Because at the end of the day, there could only be two outcomes from our battle against Bigsby—me ending up dead or remaining alive—and I had too much shit to live for, so I chose to duke this shit out gladiator-style until the bitter end.

Core grabbed my face between his hands. "I care for you,

Sin... and you're mine," he proclaimed while one hand slid down. His thumb stroked my lips.

I barely held back the urge to run my tongue over the callused pad of his finger. "I'm not your property, McKay."

"You can deny it." He traced along my cheek, down my jaw, across the curve of my neck, and over my collarbone. Gentle, languid movements. "Argue about it. Try to run away from it. But you're still mine. I will not hurt you, and I will always protect you. And when you realize that you and I are forever... you'll begin to trust me." He paused. "I'm a patient man, Sin."

My heart thundered. I liked that he wanted to fight for me... for us.

Is it too late to salvage our relationship?

"You're insane, McKay. You manipulated me for your own ends. I can't trust you anymore."

And while knowing I had to trust Core in order to survive a Bigsby attack, actually doing it was a completely different thing.

"Sin"—his voice was still low, a sultry, deep rumble—"in the beginning, it was business, but that changed for me a long time ago. You mean so much more to me now. Just give me time to prove it to you."

"Crazy—that's what you are," I whispered.

"That makes two of us." He curled his mouth into a smile. He slowly lowered his head, watching me. When I tensed, he whispered, "I haven't tasted you in hours. One kiss, and then you can go back to being mad at me." His hands pressed into my lower back as he pulled me closer.

He waited inches above my lips for consent.

Shit. This is wrong on so many levels.

He'd manipulated me into his business spiderweb, claiming ninety-seven percent of my business, all while using me as a pawn to get revenge on the most repulsive man I knew—Bigsby.

Frankly, everything Core had done earned him a top spot on my shit list because he could have come clean with me a lot sooner.

I sighed heavily, pushing aside the dark, ugly thoughts, and considered the positive things that came out of having a mutual enemy—Bigsby. Everything Core had done was in my best interest, too, since we were tied together because of Bigsby's nasty deeds.

If Core hadn't come into my life right when he did, my life would have turned out a lot differently. If Bigsby had gotten what he wanted from me—to become a major stakeholder in my business—I would have been unwittingly shoved knee deep into his sex trafficking business. And given how devious Bigsby was, he would have figured out how to easily get the ledger from me. And when Bigsby was done getting everything he wanted from me—business and ledger—he probably would have killed me because I knew too much.

I took a deep breath. For better or for worse, Core's and my destiny, future, and very life were tied together. For how long... I didn't know. But there was no doubt in my mind that Core and I would be stronger working together than apart.

I glanced from Core's smoldering eyes to his ridiculously sexy mouth. The tension melted from my traitorous body.

He felt my resistance disappear. His mouth covered mine.

My eyes fluttered closed. His lips, warm and firm, moved with a featherlight touch against mine, as if he were discovering their shape and texture all over again.

His kiss was slow, confident, unhurried, and sensuous. I tried to hold on to the anger, distrust, and hurt from everything he'd done to me when pleasure zinged through my body and grew liquid. Lost in the sensation, I touched his jaw. He licked and nibbled at my lips, his breathing deepening.

My fingers traveled up from his jaw and threaded through his hair. He opened his mouth and drove into me with his tongue. The pleasure spiked higher, sharper. He growled deep in his throat before reaching down to hike up my dress and pick me up. My legs wrapped around his waist as he carried me over to the corner of the rooftop where there was a long bar, and he plopped me on top.

He angled my head, so he had better access and could plunge deeper into my mouth, his body hardening. He drove his thigh between my legs, pushing up against the area that had grown wet in response to him.

I made another muffled noise as I kissed him back with escalating excitement. He growled and pushed harder with his thigh, deeper with his tongue. He hit just the right spot.

I gasped and arched my pelvis. Both of my arms were now wrapped around his neck. He cupped my ass and pulled me up more tightly against him. He wound his other arm behind my neck, holding me pressed along the length of his body.

He found a wicked rhythm with mouth and thigh that stole all thoughts from me until I was so torched that I was wantonly eating at him.

He devoured me with starved greed. My hands ran over his muscular shoulders while his thick, hard erection pressed against me.

If we were undressed, Core would have slid inside me.

The feel of his cock burning against me made me wiggle closer, trying to settle my throbbing heat against him to get that fraction of an inch closer. I felt his breathing slow.

I want his clothes off.

I want him inside me... holding me down as he pounds into me hard and fast, making me temporarily forget the ugliness of the Bigsby mess and Core's violation of my trust.

But there was still so much residual stuff between us due to all the manipulative crap he'd done.

There was a part of me that was furious with Core. I wanted to shout at him, tell him how much he'd hurt me by not telling me the truth about Bigsby sooner, that I didn't know if I could ever trust him again, that he was the first man in a while I'd let get so close to me emotionally, but that he'd gone and fucked up everything.

And without trust, aren't we building a relationship on a foundation of sand?

The fact that he hadn't been forthcoming with the truth about Bigsby from the get-go contaminated every area of our relationship.

How can I believe anything he says anymore without the urge for me to play detective to confirm it's true?

Trust was a pretty big fucking deal in any relationship, and I wasn't sure if I could wholeheartedly trust him again.

I had to pull way the hell back now.

I yanked my mouth away. "Stop," I pleaded. "It's too much."

He reared back his head and hissed. He crushed me to him and didn't move, his body strung tight.

I turned and buried my face against his hard, bunched biceps. I whispered, "I'm going home. I need some space to think... alone." I looked up at him, determined to make it clear that he wasn't forgiven for his transgressions.

And even though I was terrified of the possibility of Bigsby attacking me, I needed breathing room from Core. As soon as I got inside my home, I planned on having my cell in hand at all times with 9-1-1 on speed dial and ready to call at the slightest sound of trouble.

He was looking down at me, the planes and angles of his dark face cut sharp. "It's dangerous with Bigsby underground and plotting against you and me. It's better if you stay with me until we catch him."

"What didn't you understand? I can't be around you right now." I became decidedly defiant, a scowl pulling my face tight.

With a piercing gaze, he studied me for a long time. "You'll stay at my penthouse, and that shit is not negotiable." He snarled.

I glared at him even though, internally, I conceded to the fact that I was acting on emotions and he was the voice of reason. I knew Bigsby wanted to kill me. I wasn't an idiot, and I damn sure didn't have a death wish. "Separate rooms."

"If that's what you want." The tension in his body eased.

"Yes, that's what I fucking want," I replied. "But I need to go to my place to pick up some essentials for a longer stay at your house."

He lifted me off the bar, giving me a long, lingering once-over, his eyes roving over me inch by inch as I fixed my dress, smoothing it into place.

His eyes blazed with raw sensuality as they raked over me. "Let's go. I'll drive you home." He placed a hand on the small of my back, escorting me off the rooftop.

The deeper I went into Core's world, the more I understood him.

Core was dangerous, deadly, and focused—all traits that, instead of repelling me from him, drew me closer like a magnet.

❧ 14 ❧

SINTHIA

ONCE WE WERE in the car after leaving Redemption, we had a brief conversation about Jaxon, and then time ticked by as we drove in silence. The hush made the rest of the drive to my townhouse seem longer. Much longer.

Moments stretched, and Core spent more time glancing at me than looking at the road.

I felt as though I'd been through a tornado. Resting my head against the soft leather headrest with my eyes closed, now that my brain had started working again, I grappled with the fact that my entire view of the world had been proven false.

Ian is not my dad. He's my uncle.

Grace is not my mother... which, frankly, is a blessing in damn disguise.

Greer and Aubrey—Jemma—are my real parents but are both dead.

I frowned. Scratch that. Greer was conclusively dead, but Jemma... that was still an open question. But she had to be dead. *If she were alive, wouldn't she have contacted me?* My stomach hardened. Not if I was some sort of pregnancy mistake and she didn't want anything to do with me. Given my lifelong experience with a non-maternal woman—Grace—that was likely the situation.

Then there was Bigsby, who was planning to kill me unless he got the ledger back—his little black book.

Fuck. My. Life.

I felt like someone had hit me in the head with an ax. Really. All I wanted to do was lie down. Everything I'd believed to be true was now called into question.

Since Dad—Ian—had died, I'd never had so much go wrong with my life in such a short span of time. And all of my bad luck, misadventures, and misfortunes centered around one man... Bigsby.

I peeked at Core. The muscles of his neck bulged as he clenched his jaw. I wasn't sure if he was silent out of respect, giving me time to gather my thoughts about everything he'd just told me, or because he was plotting how many different ways he'd torture and kill Bigsby once he found him.

Turning my head, I stared out the window at the passing Manhattan landscape. I wasn't quite sure what I wanted to do about Core or his deception.

On the one hand, I really did understand his burning desire to find his mother's killer—Bigsby—and seek retribution for her death. On the other hand, he'd mercilessly used me as a pawn to get what he wanted—revenge.

Then there were the other things I now knew about Core. He was a very dangerous man who'd outright told me that he'd torture, kill, bribe, and manipulate to get what he wanted.

Can I really open up my heart to a man like him? Not to mention trust him again?

Is he even the one I can open my heart up to?

Shit. Is it even worth my while to spend more time with him to see where our relationship can go?

Damn. There were so many questions that I didn't have the answers to right now. Not with my mind churning with all of the information about my biological parents and Bigsby's ultimatum fogging my brain. But what I did know was if I did decide to go down the relationship rabbit hole with Core, there would be no going back. Any life with Core would be all-consuming and utterly dangerous.

I slid my eyelids closed to soothe the headache now emerging.

The sound of Core's phone ringing echoed throughout his vehicle.

"What's up, Max?" Core answered. "I'm with Sin and on my way to her place. She needs to pick up some stuff before we head over to the penthouse."

My eyes snapped open. I studied him in silence.

"Got it. But..." Max started.

"Go ahead, Max. Sin and I talked, and she knows everything." He glanced over at me. "So speak freely."

Core pressed a hand to my thigh and squeezed. I pushed his hand off. His face tightened.

"We can't find Jaxon," Max's voice boomed out. "We had a solid lead from his credit card purchases. There was a pattern of Uber rides to the same location in the span of a month."

"And?" Core requested in a tense voice.

"I broke into the apartment he was renting, but it's empty now. I suspect he was doing a stakeout in the joint; essentially, it was stalker central. And here's the kicker... It's only a few blocks away from Sin's townhouse."

"Oh God," I mumbled. "This is bad." My heart clenched and dropped into the pit of my stomach.

Core's hands tightened around his steering wheel. His nostrils flared. "Did you try his parents' house? Their law firm?" He frowned, his anger showing as he accelerated, passing the cars that had the audacity to go the speed limit.

My head got a little lighter from holding my breath. I kept thinking about what Max had reported.

"We can't find Jaxon."

Damn. Damn. Damn. I swallowed hard.

"Come on, bro," Max replied. "Of course I did. I staked out both locations—their office and home. At the latter, there was no sign of activity. So I talked to the security guards and administrative assistants at their law firm. His parents aren't even in town. They're in Europe on vacation." He paused. "But everyone I talked to said they hadn't seen Jaxon. They said he was still in Europe."

Core pressed his lips into a thin line. Several moments passed before he spoke again. "How do you know they didn't lie to—"

"Core." Max cut him off. "None of the people I interviewed today lied to me. For fuck's sake, I'm a former Green Beret who's faced all kinds of liars. Nothing slips by me... ever. You know that shit."

"I want that stalker caught so I can show him exactly what I do to anyone who fucks with mine." His hands clenched the wheel.

"Come on, man. Relax," Max urged. "I know how bad you want to get Jaxon. We all do."

"Tell Kevin to stay on the trail. I don't care how much money it costs for more intel. And I need you to meet me outside Sin's townhouse. I'll be there in a few." He pressed a button on his steering wheel and ended the call. "You okay?" he asked, glancing over at me.

My lungs relaxed into an exhale. *This is what breathing feels like.*

The restricted feeling had gone away.

"With Jaxon loose? Hell no," I sputtered, glaring at him.

He scowled, and his voice dropped to a rumble. "Sin, you're safe."

"I'll never be safe," I pointed out. "Not with Jaxon stalking me."

"We'll catch him and then get rid of him—permanently." His voice was matter-of-fact.

"You're going to kill him?" I finally replied after moments of uncomfortable silence.

His features clenched as he drove down the street. "After everything I've told you about him, do you really care if he lives or dies?" He was silent for a while, allowing me to contemplate and consider his words.

It didn't take a genius to figure out that Jaxon was a big problem for me.

"No, I don't."

Not after everything Jaxon had done to me and now that he was back to stalking me. He had to be stopped—by any means possible.

I stared out at the passing city scene of looming glass towers, along with spectacular architectural sights like Grand Central Terminal, the Chrysler Building, and the Seagram Building.

Before long, we pulled up in front of my house with Core parking behind the SUV Max was leaning against. He stood up, striding over to us, and waited for us to get out.

Turning off his car, Core unbuckled his seat belt and then reached over to the glove compartment, unlocking it. My eyes widened when he pulled out a gun.

"Are you expecting trouble?" I asked.

"I'm always expecting trouble, darling." He threw open his door, hopping out while simultaneously holstering the gun, hiding it underneath his jacket. It didn't take long before he was at the passenger door, opening it for me.

Max grinned at me. "Hey, sweet cheeks!"

"Hi, Max," I replied, taking off my seat belt. I stepped out, ignoring the hand Core held out for me to grab.

"Eventually, you'll forgive me, Sin," he answered in a deep, velvety voice.

"Overly confident, aren't you?" I replied as he pressed his palm to my lower back, ushering me up the stairs with Max pulling up the rear.

I became hypersensitive to the way Core's firm hand pressed into my back. His thumb lightly stroked me, and I liked it—too much.

"No, just realistic." When he spoke, his warm breath brushed lightly against my ear.

For a brief moment, I thought about all of the wicked, sensual things his talented lips and tongue had done to my cunt just yesterday morning.

Sin, focus.

Ruthlessly, I pushed all the sinful thoughts out of my mind.

Turning around, I poked him hard in the chest. "Well, I think you're aiming too high, McKay. I'm not so forgiving. In fact, I'm a card-carrying vengeful woman, and you are now on my *To Be Shanked* list. So if I were you, I'd sleep with one eye open," I stated coolly before whirling around to resume my climb toward my front door.

"Damn," Max grumbled. "I like her." He laughed huskily.

"What's not to like?" Core countered. "She's a pit bull in a skirt with an amazing ass."

"Keep your eyes off my ass, McKay." Pulling my key out of my mini clutch, I pushed the key into the lock and then opened the door. I felt both Max and Core present behind me. "Okay, I've got it from here." I turned around to eye them. "You two wait outside. I don't need your help."

I felt secure that if Jaxon were to do a stalker drive-by, he wouldn't even think about stopping after the mere sight of a muscular, scowling Core and hulking Max standing outside my door like warrior sentinels.

Core frowned. "That shit is not happening." He gently tugged me back, pushing his bulky body in front of mine. "Sin, let me go inside first."

He nudged the door, and both he and Max stepped over the threshold.

With them both tall and built like a wall of muscles, I barely squeezed around them to turn on my lights.

With eagle eyes, they scanned the area.

I remembered the last time Core had been at my place—when we found out the break-in had occurred—and the door had been open when we arrived. So I felt pretty sure everything would be fine while I gathered my things.

"Will you both leave? You're hovering, and I need some space." I eyed Core. "Especially from you."

Max replied, "Damn. Zuri was right. She's the perfect match for you, Core. I'm loving her take-no-shit attitude." He clapped him on the back. "It's going to be interesting seeing her keep you in check." He stared at me. "Core's one lucky man. Do they make more like you?"

"You wouldn't be able to handle another of me. But my bestie, Jade, is a ballbuster like me and will give you a run for your money."

"Many have tried," Max revealed, "but I've yet to meet a woman who can handle a man like me." With a gleam in his eyes, he added, "But I'm willing to give Jade a shot."

I scrutinized his tough military demeanor.

Shit. He looks like he could bench-press a car—easily.

I was intrigued about a possible hook-up between Jade and Max.

Would it be fireworks? Or oil and water?

Knowing Jade, probably the latter. She liked her men pliable and ready to succumb to her every whim and demand in and out of the bedroom. But something told me that shit would never work with Max.

Max's cell rang. He scanned the caller ID and relayed, "It's Kevin." He turned to Core. "I'm out. Core, I'll meet you outside." Then he left.

Core strode over to me. He wasn't smiling, but he didn't look angry, more contemplative than anything. "Now back to us."

I rolled my eyes. "I'm sorry if you haven't gotten the memo." I gestured between us. "But the whole *us* situation has been put on hard pause... by me." Jamming my hands on my hips and looking him up and down, I continued. "Like I said, I need my space. So I'm going to need you to exit left." I wasn't budging on my position. I needed alone time to decompress before I was shuttled over to his place for God knows how long.

He lowered his head to mine, eyes open, almost daring me to

look away from him. It was predatory, determined... and primal. He was letting me know that he was top dog and what he said goes.

In the bedroom, I'd allow him to dominate me.

But outside? Hell no.

And it would be my pleasure to set his ass straight.

"Does your mean-mug expression actually work on other people?" I asked. "Because all it's doing is annoying the hell out of me," I sassed.

"You can have your space while I wait right here," he explained. "And pack enough clothes for a couple of weeks. It might be a while until we wrap up this Bigsby and Jaxon situation."

I scoffed. "Weeks?"

"I'm hoping sooner," he replied grimly. "Do you need help with moving your packing along?"

Okay, that's it. His "Me, Tarzan; you, Jane" *attitude is pissing me off.*

"Out, McKay." Marching over to the door, I yanked it open. "I don't need your ass micromanaging me while I pack up my shit." I desperately needed the time alone to come to grips with my feelings.

His eyebrows lifted in amusement, and then he shook his head. "Damn, your dirty mouth is making me so hard right now."

He's not making adulting easy at all.

I pointed at him. "Is that your attempt at sweet nothings?"

Core tilted his head as he considered me. "Yes. Is it working?" He gave me an honest-to-goodness, panty-melting bad-boy grin.

I sighed, running a hand through my hair. "No, it's not. And as far as you and I are concerned... you're on a pussy diet." I pointed to the door again.

He stared at me with his mouth open.

Look at that. I got him quiet.

He swallowed the distance between us, and when he spoke,

his warm breath brushed against my lips. "No pussy for me. And no cock for you." His voice was low and sensuous. "It's going to be a rough couple of days for both of us, huh?" He leaned in and kissed me. He didn't move when he finished. He kept his lips gently pressed against mine.

A few moments passed before he kissed me again, more commanding, hungry, urging a response that I freely gave before my brain caught up with what my body craved. Quickly, I put a hard stop to Core's seductive play by breaking our kiss.

"Don't worry about me, McKay." I softened my voice to saccharine sweet. "My vibrator, Beast, and I will be A-okay."

He licked his lips, as if still savoring my taste. "Normally, I don't share when it comes to you, but I can definitely get with a threesome—you, me, and Beast. Can't wait for our date. Say... in three days? In my bed, when you're not so pissed off at me?" He winked at me.

"Don't hold your breath, McKay." I countered, even while my cunt tingled and my nipples puckered as I envisioned a gloriously naked Core lying between my legs, pressing Beast against my slit while he finger-fucked me.

Oh, sweet Jesus... I've found the trifecta—a man with a big cock and a wicked tongue and who loves playing with sex toys. Damn. Damn. Damn. It's like Christmas and my birthday wrapped into one. Surprise!

As if he could read my sexy, dirty thoughts, he grinned. "I'll be right outside, waiting." He leaned into me, his voice dropping to a low purr. "And don't forget to pack your toy, darling."

Dammit. Focus. Eyes on the prize. Give him hell for betraying my trust. He's an asshole—a sexy one, but an asswipe nonetheless.

My racing thoughts revved up my anger all over again.

He strode out the door before I could launch my final shot.

"Whatever," I clipped out before closing the door but leaving it unlocked. I knew no one had a chance in hell of getting past him and Max—two mixed-martial-arts-looking fuckers.

I padded over to the kitchen and grabbed a bottle of sparkling water from the refrigerator. The cleaning company did an excellent job. I leaned a hip against the kitchen counter and stared at the rows of empty racks that were in part of my townhouse. Racks that had once held around twenty outfits, ranging from shredded organza dresses with flowers at the hem, cobweb gowns that fluttered from neck to floor, crystal tank tops over short sequined skirts, to peacock-print silk dresses tumbling off one shoulder.

I'd have to make the outfits again. Trying to calm the anxious ball of energy bouncing around in my stomach, I took a deep, cleansing breath. It didn't help.

I wasn't a quitter, and despite the daunting task of starting over, I'd do it because being a fashion designer was my life and getting my designs into major retailers was a dream I'd never let go of.

"Okay, Sin," I muttered, "no wallowing in sadness. Get your shit together." Pushing away from the counter, I made my way upstairs, mentally cataloging what I needed to pack for my stay over at Core's place.

Finally in my bedroom, I kicked off my stilettos before walking over to my dresser. I started pulling out my neatly folded lingerie when I heard something drop in the hallway right outside my bedroom door.

I rolled my eyes. "McKay," I yelled over my shoulder, not bothering to stop what I was doing, "what part of 'I need my space' didn't you understand?"

There was no response. I sighed heavily. My back was facing the door, but knowing Core, he was probably standing there with his usual *I'm the king of the world* glare.

I huffed. "I'm not going to move any faster with you cracking the whip. So go on. Get." Gathering my stacked pile of bras and panties with one hand, clutching it against my chest, I swiveled around to face him, my resting bitch face firmly in place.

I screamed. The muscles in my arms went slack, everything in my hand dropping to the floor, as I watched with disbelief and then horror as Jaxon, dressed in all black, strode toward me with a knife held in one hand.

Panic quickly took over the darkest parts of my mind, and the fear blossomed into terror. I had to escape.

He was blocking the path to the door—the only exit. I spun on my heels, running to the left, where my bathroom was located. If I could just make it inside, lock the door... I'd be safe.

He grabbed me. There was a sharp yank on my hair and then the burn of strands being ripped out of my head as he jerked me backward.

Damn. He caught me.

I still fought the backward momentum by pressing forward, ignoring the sting of my hair being pulled out at the roots, courtesy of his brutal tug. My head throbbed, but I didn't give a shit about the pain because I knew Jaxon had much worse planned for me.

Slamming me against his hard body, he pinned my back against his chest with one muscled arm. My fight response amped up, and I was immersed in survival mode.

"Let me go." I snarled, wildly swinging my arms, scratching and punching and kicking. I felt like a rabid animal foaming at the mouth until I felt the cold, sharp prick of his knife against my throat.

"Cut it out, or I'll fucking slice that pretty little neck of yours." His words came out in a growl, his anger was blistering, and the muscles of his arms were taut.

I froze. *Oh my God, he's going to kill me.*

How the hell am I going to get out of this mess?

And where's Core?

The headache from stress was raging.

Why the hell did he have to listen to me when I told him to get out?

Fuck. Fuck. Fuck.

This is it. This is how I'm going to die.

Panic threatened to consume me, but I fought for mental

control. I took a calming breath as my brain raced with multiple scenarios of how this night would end. None of them were good.

Sin, it's time to reason with the psycho.

"Jaxon, what is it that you want?" I worked hard to control my breathing, steady my heart rate, and temper my fear.

When Jaxon spoke, I felt like he was taunting me. *Asshole.* "You. I've always wanted only you." His sour breath made me gag, but when he pressed the knife harder against my skin, my body tightened. "We belong together. Do you see?"

"Jaxon, there is no *us*," my voice shrilled.

"I've been waiting for you," he muttered. "I wanted to talk. I wanted to apologize for destroying your clothes and your house."

Everything in my mind froze. "That was you? You were the one who destroyed my collection?"

"Yes. When I saw you all dressed up and then getting into that car, I knew you were going on a date with lover boy. You're cheating on me." His hand trembled. He was becoming more enraged. I felt the knife piercing my skin as a little bit of blood trickled down my neck. "How could you do that? To me? To us? I needed to teach you a lesson."

He's a damn lunatic.

This fucker had broken into my house, destroyed my shit, and now he was violating me because he had some delusional notion that I was his girlfriend because I'd fucked him years ago?

But I knew his crazy went deeper. He was pissed and obsessed with me because I'd said hard pass to anything more than a one-night stand.

Rage coursed through my veins.

I wanted to claw his eyes out. Kill him. Bathe in his blood. That was what I had been reduced to. Primal urges—attack, maim, kill, using whatever was available to succeed, including kicking Jaxon in the groin, which became a priority.

I remained silent, emotionless, knowing that would bother him more than me talking. He wanted my attention, my adoration, my begging. Well, that shit was not happening.

He leaned in, and his tone dropped to a low growl as he spoke. "And now you show up again with lover boy? Are you fucking him, Sin?"

I kept a sharp eye on the entrance to my bedroom. *Come on, Core. Get a clue.*

It had been ages since I kicked him out.

"I'm talking to you, bitch!" Jaxon shouted.

I'd seriously had enough of his shit. "Bitch? Is that the best you could come up with? I've been called worse by a better class of people than your ass," I pointed out.

Core's voice bellowed from downstairs. "Sin? What's taking you so long?"

"Good. Your boyfriend's here," Jaxon whispered.

I croaked, "Core—" But I was quickly silenced by a sharp dig of Jaxon's blade. At first, it felt like someone was pinching my skin with a metal claw—like a nipping feeling but a lot worse—and then I got pins and needles before it went numb.

"Time for some fun," Jaxon jabbered before dragging me over to my open closet with the blade firmly pressed against my throat. Then he flung me inside.

His gaze rested on me, and then his eyes traveled along my face, down the curve of my neck, and to my breasts. Then they lifted lazily to my mouth again. "It's been so long," he chattered. "I can't wait to kiss you."

"I'd like that, too," I replied in a saccharine tone, "so you'll be close enough for me to rip your cock off."

He grinned. "I find our banter amusing."

I frowned. "Banter?" I spit. "That's a fucking threat."

"Sin?" Core's voice called out again, and this time, he seemed closer.

"Co—" I shouted.

"Shut it," Jaxon warned while simultaneously lunging at me with his knife.

Dodging his blade swipe, I clumsily fell back onto my ass—

hard. "Goddammit." That was going to leave a mark. "Asshole," I groused, scrambling onto all fours and scooting farther away.

Jaxon narrowed his gaze on me. "Keep your damn mouth shut," he warned, "or you'll both die." He slammed the closet door shut.

My heart raced with fear as I stumbled to my feet in the dark space.

My mind raced with all of the horrible possibilities and scenarios psycho Jaxon had planned and would inflict on Core and me, given the opportunity.

The only bright spot to this clusterfuck was that Core was one tough motherfucker and could handle Jaxon. And so could I.

My counterattack strategy quickly came together. As soon as the closet door opened, I would be ready to brawl. Scrambling over to my shoe shelf, I snatched one of my highest stilettos and tightly gripped it with the thin, long heel pointing outward like a deadly weapon.

"I'm no one's bitch," I mumbled while making practice swipes with the shoe, slicing it through the air.

I never realized how deadly my stilettos were. One stab with full force would easily cause serious injury, and with laser focus on a soft part of the body—like the throat or eye—it could give me enough time to escape from Jaxon... or piss him off. Either way, it was him or me, and I chose me.

I blew out a breath. "Okay, Sin," I mumbled, "no fear."

Bouncing on my bare feet, I readied myself to go full-on survival-of-the-fittest beast mode. If Jaxon somehow made it past Core—highly unlikely—then it would be a shoe to Jaxon's face.

"It's go time, motherfucker. Stiletto fucking city."

There was an audible bang that pierced the air. I knew it was gunfire.

I heard Max's voice bark, "Clear."

The closet door was thrown open with Core standing at the

threshold. Dropping the shoe, I rushed into his arms, relieved as hell that he was alive and so was I.

"Thank God," I whispered, clutching him for dear life. I wanted to cry, laugh, and yell—all at the same time.

"I've got you, Sin," he declared huskily before kissing me.

Warm, soft lips covered mine. The kiss became more fervent, and when it ended, I leaned into him, lingering in his arms that protectively engulfed me as if he never wanted to let me go.

He released me, clutching my face in his palms with eyes sweeping me for injuries. "Are you okay?"

"Some cuts to my throat, but I'll be fine," I answered. "How did you know he was here?"

"Because Max smelled cologne when we were downstairs. He didn't think anything of it, but when you were taking so long, he put two and two together, and we knew something was wrong."

Glancing over, I saw Max standing there with a gun in his hand and a fierce look on his face. "Core, go. I'll take care of it. I already sent a text to both the cleaner and Rocco. They're all on the way. We'll make sure to clean up the body."

I blinked and then blinked again.

Cleaner?

Clean up the body?

Both Core's and Max's expressions were *There's nothing to see here, folks... just a dead man lying on the bedroom floor* neutral. It was as if we were standing in a grocery store, waiting for a cleanup on aisle ten.

What type of world does Core live in that makes this situation remotely normal?

And is this a world I can learn to get used to?

My heart started to pound in my chest at the thought of it.

My gaze landed on Jaxon, who was lying faceup.

"Sin, don't look." Core's voice became low and commanding.

But I couldn't help myself. My eyes zoomed in on Jaxon's body crumpled on the floor with blood running out of his head, eyes wide with shock, and lips parted slightly in death's awe.

I felt nothing about his death. Jaxon was going to kill me. So it was either him or me. Yet there was a part of me that was a little concerned that my conscience was silent, on a hiatus, unmoved at the loss of life. But I also knew that the body on the floor could very well have been me, and just the thought of that near-miss tragedy settled my lack of emotions toward his demise.

I croaked, "Who's the cleaner?" I split my attention between Max and Core.

Max's lips flattened into a straight line.

Core narrowed his eyes. When he finally spoke, his tone was slow and restrained as he carefully chose his words. "It's our connection that takes care of messy situations like this for us."

My eyes widened.

What the fuck?

Exactly how many situations like this has he been involved in?

My lips parted to ask more questions.

"Sin, the less you know, the better." He grazed his finger along my cheek. "You got me?" Fastened on me were determined and unwavering eyes.

I nodded because, strangely, I did.

They'd killed Jaxon with a weapon they probably shouldn't have. Plus, I'd watched enough police procedural shows to know that calling the police would only land the three of us in jail while the cops sorted out the who, what, why, and how of this major clusterfuck.

And I damn sure didn't relish the probability of spending time behind bars, fending off sexual passes from Big Bertha, who was eager to make me her new prison yard bitch.

"Good. Let's go," he demanded, grabbing my hand. Escorting me toward the door, he led me out of the bedroom. "Don't bother with your stuff. I'll buy you whatever you need. Right now, we have to clear out of here. I'm not sure if your neighbors heard the commotion that took place just now."

Still in shock from everything that had gone down, I didn't look back. I didn't need to.

Jaxon was gone, and I had one less person out to hurt and kill me. Then my new reality sank in. I'd never be able to be in my bedroom... in my home... without the memory of what Jaxon had done and his eventual death tarnishing the peace and sanctuary that I'd built.

My home was where I'd felt the freest of worries. Where I'd felt comfortable and safe. Now not only Jaxon, but also Core and even Bigsby had broken that barrier in my home as well as in my life.

I felt vulnerable and scared.

I didn't know how to process the fact that my world had shattered around me.

What do I do now?

And how do I move on from this?

And will it be with or without Core?

$\maltese$ *15* $\maltese$

SINTHIA

UNABLE TO SLEEP, I sat in the serene environment of Core's private terrace overlooking Manhattan. It was late, a little after midnight, and the sky was dark. The crisp fall air whipped around me as I tucked my legs under me.

"Now this is living," I murmured under my breath, enjoying the panoramic view of the Manhattan skyline, East River, and Central Park.

Cradling a cup of coffee in one hand, I sighed heavily. It was Thursday, only four days after my world had imploded due to Core's truth bomb about my real parents and Jaxon getting killed at my house. The situation had gotten worse when Grace was found dead inside her business. The police had speculated that it was a robbery, but we—me, Core, and his team—all suspected it was Bigsby's doing. He was systematically going down the list, killing everyone who knew about his connection to the ledger. It didn't take a genius to figure out I was next, so Core and his team went on high alert, putting me on lockdown at Core's penthouse until his meeting with Bigsby today.

Adding to the tension permeating the house, I'd moved myself into Core's guest bedroom, deciding I needed time to get my shit together emotionally. I'd asked for space, and he was giving it to me.

"Be careful what you wish for..." I muttered.

I hated to admit it, but I missed him.

Compounding my feeling of isolation, I hadn't spoken to Jade since Sunday, even when there were so many times I had wanted desperately to call her. Jade had her own little family drama brewing after the press had gotten wind of the authorities linking Bigsby to a sex trafficking ring. The media circus had kicked into high gear when Bigsby went into hiding. The tabloids had become dogged in their twenty-four-seven news coverage of the Bellisario family—following them around and camping outside of both Cate's and Ariana's homes. I was relieved as hell that Jade was still in New Zealand, avoiding the public drama this Bigsby fiasco had become.

Taking a sip from my cup, I voice-dialed the only person I wanted to talk to right now.

"Jade?"

"Sin? Why aren't you sleeping? It's past midnight in New York. Is everything all right?"

I grumbled, "Nothing a couple of shots of Patrón can't resolve."

"What's going on? Issues with Core?"

I sucked in a ragged breath and held it for a long time before exhaling. "Yes," I replied.

"And?"

The silence stretched.

"And my life is so fucked up right now." Dammit, I needed to keep it together. I pressed my fingers along my temple, trying to ease the pressure from the stress. It didn't work.

"What does that mean?" Jade countered.

"My life is a reality show, and the results are in. Ian is not my father, and Grace is not my mother," I responded flatly, curling up into the plush cushions. "My real parents are essentially a pimp and a madam."

Jade was silent.

"Did you hear me?" I asked in a strained voice.

"I did, but what's the damn punch line?"

I swallowed hard before launching into the full details.

Moments later, Jade cleared her throat. "Oh my God! This explains a lot," she hissed.

I frowned. "Like what?" I finished my drink and carefully set the mug down on the table.

"Why you look nothing like Ian or Grace."

I sighed. She was right about that fact. I had olive-toned skin and dark, exotic features. Grace had ethereal, porcelain features, and Ian had been just as fair.

I inhaled a ragged breath. "Is that all you got out of the fucked-up lowdown I just went into?" I nibbled on my bottom lip.

"Sin," Jade replied in an even voice, "what you told me about Bigsby frankly isn't surprising. My mom and I have never liked or trusted him. So Core taking that fucker down is just community service in my eyes."

I jumped up, wincing when I hit my toe on the coffee table. "And the fact that Bigsby is planning on killing me?" My heart started to pound in my chest at the thought of it.

I started slowly pacing the terrace and twirling my tresses around my finger, holding my cell in one hand.

Once again, she spoke in a simple, even tone. "Core sounds like a badass, so that shit is not going to happen." She paused. "I mean, come on. He took care of stalker boy. You can give him my thanks for that shit."

In Jade's typical MO, she was trying to calm me the hell down, but it wasn't working. I was too wired... too frustrated... too conflicted... too damn everything.

"Great!" I threw a hand up in the air. "So now you're a member of the Core McKay fan club?"

"Hell yeah! I don't have to worry about your ass while I'm away. He has your back."

"He manipulated me, Jade!" I snapped.

"And did you slap his ass for being a naughty boy, telling him not to do that shit again?"

I couldn't help the laugh that slipped out. Only Jade could lighten my dark mood.

"Jade, come on. This is serious. He manipulated me to get what he wanted."

"I got that, and knowing you, you laid into his ass about it."

"Yes. I told him if he lies to me again, then that's his ass."

"So what's the problem?"

"I can't trust him," I replied.

She exhaled an exasperated breath. "You mean that you won't."

"Can't. Won't. It's the same thing."

Jade snorted. "Come on, Sin. You and I know what this is really about. You're terrified of being hurt by a man again. Look, I get that what he did was fucked up, but the why is valid. Bigsby had killed Core's mother and left him for dead. That shit would stick in anyone's teeth like corn. Life is too short to stand on the sidelines because you're scared to trust and love. Zone in on the bad boy and make him yours."

"It's not going to work. I can't trust any man to do the right thing." I sighed. I hated feeling this way, but a whole lot of shitty life lessons had taught me nothing good came out of trusting men.

"Bullshit. You're just scared. Just let the past go, Sin. Scars remind us where we've been, not where we're going."

My heart raced. Trying to hide from the truth wouldn't alter the reality of this clusterfuck. "He scares the shit out of me. He's the one man who changes everything I thought I knew about myself." He was the one man who had stripped away my mask and laid me out, bare and vulnerable. "I've spent my whole life building a fortress and defending myself from being hurt again."

"Listen to me, Sin," Jade whispered. "Every relationship is

different, and you can't carry your past issues into the future. Keep the ex baggage where it's meant to be—in the damn past."

I remained silent.

"If you don't open yourself up and trust him, your relationship will go nowhere. And without trust, you're putting a dead end on a future partnership. Now pull on your big-girl panties and be brave and open. Let him in."

I dashed away the tears rolling down my cheeks. That was exactly what I was afraid of doing. "I hate that I'm so fucked up in the head."

"You're not fucked up. We're both emotionally challenged, but I think it's time for a change."

"Jade, I've only known one good man in my entire life, and that was my dad. He was way more man than Grace deserved."

My upper lip curled in disdain. Even though Grace was now dead, she'd caused a hell of a lot of emotional damage while she was alive. I hoped her soul could find the peace she needed.

I walked over to the railing, staring down at the bustling city below. "I don't think I'm built for the level of commitment that a relationship takes."

Jade sighed. "I think that's what we've been telling ourselves for so long that we actually believe it. This much I know. Someday, I want kids and stability. Don't you?"

My mouth went dry. For the first time in my life, I was thinking about a future with children... with Core. "Maybe. I'm just so afraid that I'll be a cruel monster like Grace. I would never want to do that to a child. So I decided a long time ago that I didn't want children."

My life growing up had been an emotional roller coaster, all due to Grace. Dad had done the best he could to shield me from her verbal and emotional abuse, but still, it just hadn't been enough.

"Grace was a bitch. You're nothing like her."

"I hope not." My pulse sped up. "She never loved me or my dad, and it changed us for the worse. We both morphed into people who lived just to please her—hoping if we changed, if we could be everything she wanted, she would love us. It took me years to learn that loving myself was good enough."

"Loving yourself is important, but having the right man to love you for who you are is important, too. And a partnership of equals? That's icing on the fucking cake." Jade paused. "Just think about it, okay?"

"I will." I bit my lower lip, changing subjects. "I spoke to your mom today. She's holding up well. But how about you?"

"Stressed about being here while she's being chased by the media every day. But she's right; staying in New Zealand is best until all this shit dies down. That said, it helps that Cate is getting the brunt of the bad press and not Mom. Did you watch that freak show she orchestrated on Monday?"

Cate had called a press conference, tearfully announcing she'd called off her engagement to Bigsby because, according to her, "Like the good citizens of New York, I, too, was duped by the former mayoral candidate."

I snickered. "Hell yes, I watched it. In typical Cate, over-the-top, diva fashion, she gave a television performance worthy of an Emmy."

Jade laughed. "I guess I'm not the only actress in the family. Well, enough of my family drama. It's late... and you need to wrangle yourself a bad boy."

"Damn right I do. I'll call you later."

"Hopefully with good news that you and Core fucked it out, and there's a happily ever after," Jade replied. "Call me and let me know either way."

I ended the call, letting out a sigh of despair.

Jade was right. I wanted—no, I *needed* more with Core than sex. Deep down, I was a woman who wanted to be cherished and cared for. And given a chance, Core wanted to do both. Even though I knew he wanted more from me, from us, together we were facing a whole new set of challenges.

Can I trust him after he's manipulated me? The answer was

unclear, and the only way I could find out if he was a man of his word was to break down the walls I'd built around my heart, allowing him to get close.

But I was afraid of letting Core into my life.

I was afraid of letting him see me weak and vulnerable.

I was afraid of getting attached and then losing him.

I was just so afraid of getting hurt. I knew it was going to happen—with Core or with someone else—but I was still terrified.

He'd wanted a chance to redeem himself in my eyes—a do-over.

Would it be so bad if I just gave it to him? Especially when he had the courage to ask for forgiveness?

I was far from perfect, and I damn sure couldn't promise him that I wouldn't make mistakes. All I knew was that any man I let into my life would have to have the strength to forgive me when I said I was sorry.

Not only that, but he would also have to have the ability to move forward without holding a grudge, leaving the past in the past.

In the same vein, the man I was with would have to be coura-geous enough to ask for forgiveness. Given that I knew how hard that shit was to do, I would respect him even more when he was able to admit his blunders—like Core had.

My pulse raced at the thought of belonging to him, and deep down, I wanted him. I walked into the penthouse.

Shit. Am I really doing this?

What would my reaction be if he changed his mind and he wasn't interested in a relationship with me anymore? Relief? Hurt? Anger? All three? The fucked-up part is I have no damn clue which of the three I'd feel.

I'd either have the pain of opening up and maybe getting hurt or have the pain of shutting down and being alone. There was no pain-free choice.

No one was in the living room, so I walked farther into the

apartment, moving toward two male voices. One was distinctly Core's, and the other sounded like Ram. I hesitated outside Core's office, shamelessly eavesdropping on their conversation inside.

"Ram, the clock is ticking," Core stated. "And we have to get our shit together for our meeting with Bigsby today. Did you scan the perimeter of our meeting location with the drone?"

Ram shot back, "Of course we did, Core. This is not my first mission. I know what the hell I'm doing."

"I just want to be sure we're ready for anything during our meeting. I don't want any surprises," Core grumbled.

A shiver ran down my spine. *What if things go wrong at their meeting with Bigsby?*

"We'll be ready. Our game plan is airtight. Once you hand over the ledger and recording to Bigsby, our sniper will pick him off, and then our cleaning crew will take care of the body. Kevin will be handling the surveillance remotely. Rocco and Max will be sniper A and B. And I'll have your back on the ground during the exchange." Ram paused. "That means we won't have anyone to guard Sin during our meeting. What are you going to do about her security?"

I frowned at the mention of my name.

"This penthouse is an impenetrable fortress, but I've asked Zuri to stay with Sin just in case shit goes south at the exchange."

"Bro? You actually think Sin will just sit here twiddling her thumbs and wait for you to get back?" Ram argued.

I snickered under my breath. Ram was damn right. There was no way I was sitting out this faceoff.

"If I have to handcuff her ass to the bed, then that's exactly what she'll do. I can't risk putting her in even more danger." Core's voice got louder.

"Core, calm the fuck down."

"Ram, I can't risk losing her. My mother and Maya are gone

because I couldn't protect them. I'll be damned if I lose another woman I care about."

Butterflies fluttered in my stomach. Core really cared about me. Then it dawned on me just how much I cared about him... so much that I'd risk my heart just to have him in my world.

"Core, bro, you're not going to lose her. Besides, from what Max told me about how she handled herself with Jaxon, she's one tough chick."

I smiled at Ram's words. He was right; I was tough, but I knew I wasn't invincible. Jaxon had taught me that shit... more than once.

"She got lucky. That fucker could have hurt her."

"No. Not lucky. She's brave, Core. And now she knows enough about you and our world to understand exactly what she's getting involved with."

Between how efficiently he'd handled the cleanup of the Jaxon incident and what I suspected he'd done to Bigsby's lackey, I knew exactly the type of man Core was. He took care of his own, no matter what it required. And that was the kind of loyalty and protectiveness I knew firsthand, given my feelings toward everyone in my inner circle. My friends had my back, and I had theirs, no matter what.

"Yeah. But what's fucking with my head is that she didn't know the truth when she got involved with me," Core snapped. "Maybe if she did, she would have walked away from me." He paused. "Shit. All I can think about right now is that maybe she should have hightailed her ass away from me a long time ago. If she had, then her life wouldn't be in fucking jeopardy right now."

My heart thudded with joy. Core was truly bothered by the fact that he hadn't been upfront with me from the beginning. The man had a conscience when it came to me and the damage he'd done.

But Core was right. Maybe if I had common sense, I would have walked away from him, but I wouldn't because I was just as fucked up in the head as he was. I wanted Core, and I wasn't walking away from him, not anymore. I'd made up my mind to see this thing with him through before I walked toward his office. But now, after I'd overheard his conversation with Ram, I was here to stay by his side for as long as our relationship lasted.

I stormed into Core's office. Ram stared at me while Core's eyes narrowed at my presence.

"Core..." I started and then stopped when something on the television flashed, catching my eye. "Do you see that?" I pointed to the television. "The news ticker on the TV says there's breaking news on Bigsby Calhoune. Can you turn up the sound on the television?"

The three of us stood before the flat-screen with our eyes fixed on the news anchor.

"We have breaking news," the anchor said. "New York mayoral candidate Bigsby Calhoune has been charged in one of the nation's largest sex trafficking rings." The hypnotic, repetitious evenness of her voice continued. "Federal authorities just announced charges against Calhoune and forty-three others in a conspiracy that allegedly trafficked hundreds of women throughout the United States. Now let's go to Anne, who's on location outside of Calhoune's campaign office. Anne, any sign of Mr. Calhoune?"

Anne smiled with excited eyes. "No. But we've just gotten word that Bigsby Calhoune is a fugitive and on the run. The former mayoral candidate is now on the Most Wanted list. Back to you, Jessica."

Core turned off the television and stared at Ram. "Well, we already knew the Feds were going to make this announcement, but now we have the news sniffing around for a scoop on Bigsby. So this is bound to turn into a media free-for-all. We know that Bigsby is dead set on getting back the ledger and recordings, so he'll show up for our meeting today. We just have to be ready to take him down. No errors."

Ram nodded. "Got it. I need to catch a couple hours of sleep.

I'm going to bed. I'll see you both in a few hours." He strode out of the room.

Core eyed me. "What are you doing up?" He leaned against his desk, crossing his beefy arms.

I locked eyes with him. "I couldn't sleep. But that doesn't matter now. I heard your conversation with Ram about Bigsby."

"Eavesdropping, huh?" Amusement danced in his eyes.

I threw my arms up in the air. "Of course. I'm not going to lie about it. There's no shame in my game. I'm nosy." I invaded his space, giving him a peevish look. "So what?"

"So now that you know what's going on"—he gently grabbed my face—"take your sexy ass to bed and let me handle this shit," he stated flatly before his hands fell away.

I cupped his cheek. "Baby, I don't take orders. You should know this by now." I tapped his face hard before letting my hand drop. "But since I like you so much, I'm going to be clear so we don't have these communication issues again. I don't like *you woman, me man* caveman shit. Now I'm not asking you to get all poetic while communicating with me, but I—"

Core's eyebrows drew together. "Good, because that shit isn't happening."

I blew out a breath. *Patience, Sin.*

My gorgeous lover was going to take more work than I'd envisioned, but I was up to the job.

"Like I was saying before I was rudely interrupted..." I pursed my lips. "I don't expect you to be poetic. Shit, you're incapable of not grunting every other word."

He grunted.

I shook my head in dismay. "But I do expect you not to bark orders at me. I'm your equal, and I expect to be treated as such. Now, I'm capable of being reasonable, contrary to your belief."

He snorted.

I scowled. "So if you think I'm in fucking danger, communicate with me in a way that won't make me want to smother you in your sleep."

The vein along his jaw pulsed. "Do you even get that I'm worried about Bigsby trying to hurt you? Sin, you mean the world to me." He fiercely looked at me, his words barely above a whisper. "I wouldn't survive losing you." His own admission appeared to surprise him.

The tender affection in his words and in his eyes washed over me, making me feel cherished and desired. I hadn't realized until now that I'd needed to hear him say how much he wanted me.

He glanced at me with pained eyes. "So if you're expecting me to apologize for wanting to protect you, that's not going to happen."

I sighed, grabbing his hand, kissing his fingers one by one. "I get it, but you don't have to be so fucking abrasive about it. That's all I'm saying, Core."

"I'll work on my delivery," he answered. "But you're not going to the meeting."

"I'm going, Core. We're partners, remember? In business and…" I paused. There was a flutter in my belly. I was nervous about uttering my next words, but I had to push myself not to play it safe… to believe that everything would be all right… that he wouldn't make me regret giving him all of me—heart and soul. "Now in life. Fifty-fifty. And I'm not going anywhere, McKay." I stared at him. "I'm yours, mind, body, and soul."

He fisted his hand into my hair at the nape of my neck—a sign of his possession. "Sin, you don't know what you're saying."

"The hell I don't." My heart raced, bracing for the impact of telling him the truth. I bit my bottom lip. "I'm a hard woman, Core. What man will take the risk of loving me?"

"Me. I know who you are, Sin. You hide yourself with men who have no chance in hell of getting your heart or loving you. Give us a chance. Let me in."

I licked my dry lips. "I've spent my life hiding from relationships so I could feel safe. But I don't want to feel safe anymore. I want more with you. But I'll walk the fuck away from you, from us, if you ever lie to me again."

He released my hair. "I never lied to you, Sin—"

I held up a hand. "If you ever lie to me or are deceptive in any way, I'm gone. The only way this can work is if you go all in with me, because I fucking love myself too much to accept anything else. And even though you're a pain in the ass and way too cocky, I think every bit of the work our relationship is going to take is worthwhile."

"I belong to you, mind, body, and soul. And now that you're mine, I'm never letting go." He kissed my jaw, down the column of my throat, and to my collarbone. There was more tenderness, passion, and meaning in those precious, gentle kisses, and they claimed me like no words ever could.

"Good, because I've decided to keep your crazy ass." I kissed him hard.

"Really? Decided? You had no choice, woman. Now let's get the formalities out of the way. You belong to me and no other... and I belong to you."

I frowned. "You'd better. I'm selfish, and I don't share."

"There's no other woman for me. I'm a mean SOB some-times, but you'll deal like I can deal with your crazier-than-hell attitude."

I grinned. "Oh, fuck off, McKay. I don't have an attitude. I'm Brooklyn sassy."

He arched a brow.

"Well, I am." I ran my tongue over his firm lips.

I had let go of the terror. He was the man for me, the man who destroyed the fear.

"And for the record, I accept everything you're offering, McKay." I flattened my hand on his stomach. "There's no other man like you. I know this. And I'm crazy turned on right now." I ran my palm along his muscular thigh.

He regarded me with half-open eyes. "Like how turned on?" he demanded with a rasping voice.

I desperately wanted him. I stared at him, wondering how the hell this shit happened.

"Like on-my-knees hot," I blurted out without blinking. There was no shame in my game. I asked for what I wanted always. And I wanted him... now. I ran a hand over his crotch and winked. "Let the fucking commence. And I plan on keeping you busy until it's time to meet Bigsby."

He took my mouth with a kiss that sent me barreling into another world. His kiss left me with no doubt of his dominance as he explored my mouth with a thoroughness that rendered me breathless. His tongue tangled with mine, leading me in an erotic, sexy dance that made my senses reel.

I followed where he led with every stroke of his tongue on mine. I felt the power of his possessive seduction in every cell of my body.

Core broke off our kiss before standing, and in one sinuous motion, he lifted me and placed me on the edge of his desk.

I licked my bottom lip with anticipation as he shoved up the hem of my dress, grabbed my thighs, and pushed them wide open. I shivered deliciously as cold air brushed against my womanhood before he slid a hand between my legs, pinching my clit.

My lips parted. "Yes. Harder," I whispered.

He squeezed my thigh hard and then soothingly rubbed it.

"Ready to fuck, McKay?" I licked his lips and unzipped his pants, grabbing his cock. "Impressive." I bit his lower lip. "I want you—now."

The sultriness of the air skimmed across my skin. All the fun and games were over. This was the truth. There was no compromising.

"I'm never letting you go," he growled.

I reached up, digging my fingers into his hair, scratching my nails across his scalp.

He carried on. "This will never work until you trust me, giving me your submission, surrendering your heart, body, and soul, as I am willing to do for you. Trust is the only thing that can keep us together. Trust that you accept the man I am. And trust my acceptance of the woman you keep hidden."

I calmed my breathing. He'd stripped away my mask, leaving me bare, vulnerable, and raw. For the first time in my life, I would have a protective, caring man who would cherish me for as long as I allowed it. And I was pretty sure I wanted forever.

"And what if the woman you think I am isn't there?" I paused. "I'm more than what you see."

"That's what I'm counting on. Nothing is perfect. I'm far from it, but I'm half the man without you." He grabbed my face between his callused hands. "On your knees, darling. Now." He tilted his head. "Submit to me." His voice was hard and unyielding.

"Submission," I whispered as if rolling the word over my tongue like a fine wine. "And do you think you've earned my submission?"

"Make no mistake about it." He narrowed his eyes. "I'm wild and ruthless, and I don't give a shit about anything but what belongs to me. You."

After spending a lifetime of overthinking everything in my life, it was freeing to put my trust in his hands.

He gripped my hair, tilting my head back. I knew what he wanted now. It wasn't about sex... not anymore. It was about sharing a piece of me I had long hidden away, a part of me that needed nurturing, love, and acceptance. I knew he wouldn't push or force. He would wait for me to submit—not because it was what he wanted, but because it was what I wanted to give. That piece of me reserved and owned only by him.

I angled my head in submission. His body tensed. I wrapped my hands around his penis and squeezed hard.

He slightly stepped back, intently watching me. There was no need for words. He knew I was meeting him halfway. I slid off the desk and then started to get on my knees before him. He stopped me by grabbing the back of my neck, pulling hard on my hair, ushering me to stand.

"I want you." I trailed my fingers over his chest.

With our eyes locked, he asked gruffly, "Are you mine to enjoy... to taste... to explore?"

I couldn't look away from the stark need in his eyes. "Yes. Always."

Core's smile stole my breath.

"Good." Effortlessly, he nudged my back down onto the desk, pushing my knee-length slip dress up around my waist.

"Well... I thought we'd finish this in the bedroom. But I'm down for—" I swallowed the rest of my words.

Quickly, he removed my panties, tossing them aside.

He lightly ran a finger down my body, making every place he touched quiver.

"I want your sweet pussy," he demanded.

I watched, transfixed, as Core settled himself between my thighs. The first swipe of his tongue on my slit had me panting, my hips arching, before he held me down with one hand on my stomach. He dipped his tongue into my pussy, lapping at me, his slow, torturous caresses driving me insane.

"Please, Core. Faster." I needed more.

He knew just where and how to touch me.

He took his time and thoroughly explored my slit, his tongue caressing my folds before slipping into me again. He circled my clit with an unhurried precision that made me scream from frustration. Using my arms, I tried to rock, but Core slid his arms under my thighs, one hand pressing down on my abdomen, keeping me from moving, while his other hand cupped a breast, teasing my nipple.

With my thighs over his shoulders and his face buried between them, I couldn't move while he showed me no damn mercy as his tongue flicked my swollen nub until I screamed, "Oh my fucking God."

His warm breath blew over the throbbing bundle of nerves and set off another wave of sizzling heat. His long strokes had me writhing, my fingers clawing the desk. He thrust two fingers into my trembling channel, pumping me, drawing out my climax. My eyes rolled to the back of my head, and I swore I saw dancing spots. I panted, drawing ragged breaths—the experience more intense because I'd given myself to him fully. Mercifully, he relented, pulling away, his eyes blazing with wildness.

I was greedy for more. *Holy hell, I can't even form a coherent thought.*

"Fuck me," I demanded.

He growled, his expression savage. "I'll give you five minutes to get into my bedroom." He ran a callused thumb over my bottom lip. "And then you'll show me all the things your sexy mouth and sinful body promise."

He lifted me off the desk, securely holding me as my legs wobbled, my body a shuddering mass of jelly.

He softly kissed me on the lips. "You okay, darling? You look a little... dazed."

"Not dazed. Fucking amazed. Believe me; that's not easy to do." I smirked while cupping his hard cock. "McKay, we are going to do great things together." I wanted him right now.

He slapped my ass. "Off you go, vixen."

"Whatever you want, McKay." I squeezed his girth, smiling with satisfaction when he hissed. "I'll be waiting, McKay," I taunted before turning on my heel and walking away. I basked in the heat of his gaze as he stared at me all the way out of the office.

I padded through the penthouse and then up the stairs that led to his bedroom. Once inside, my heart thumped as I perched on the edge of his king-size bed.

Core stormed into the room. "Strip," he ordered as he walked over to the chair positioned next to the bed. He sat on that chair, facing me. He looked hard, sexy, and in control.

I flipped my hair. "Why, Core, you've read my mind. I'd love to strip." *Hell, I am adventurous.* It didn't hurt that I'd taken a few pole dancing classes with Jade for fun.

I swayed over to him.

"Strip. I want to see you take off your dress while I watch, thinking about all the dirty things I'm going to do to that sexy body of yours."

The thought of stripping before him ramped up my adrenaline, making me giddy with lust. I circled his chair, giving him my best smoldering gaze while trailing my fingers along his neck.

As I passed behind him, I leaned over, brushing my breasts against his back, whispering, "When I first met you, I wanted you to fuck me. Now I'm greedy. I want more. Now I want you to love me." I ran my tongue along his ear, trailing it across his neck.

He reached up, grabbing the back of my hair, and said in the sexiest voice I'd ever heard, "Loving a woman like you, who's so beautiful inside and out, won't be difficult."

I blinked back the tears of joy. "Damn. You're a romantic. Who would have thought?"

He shrugged. "Not romantic. Realistic. If I wanted sex, I could get it anywhere, and that gets real empty. But finding that... connection we have, well, that's priceless."

I twirled around him, stopping in front of him and bending over so he could peek down my dress. I spun around, placing one foot on the bed, bending over from the waist, practically putting my ass in his face. "Do you want to touch it, baby?" My breath hitched as I felt his fingers run along my ass seam.

"You have the sexiest ass I've ever seen. I can't wait to take you from behind."

I tauntingly wiggled my ass. "You sure you know what to do with all this ass?"

"Tease."

He slapped my ass cheek so hard that I knew I would have a handprint. I moaned when the delicious zing went straight to my cunt. He rubbed his hand over the cheek, soothing the pain of the sting.

I spun around, walking over to him. "Did I displease you, McKay?" I asked with a flirtatious smile.

"There's nothing your sexy body could do to displease me... besides disobey." He sternly looked at me. "Continue to strip."

"What if I don't? Will you punish me?"

Please say yes! Punish me, McKay.

"Take the dress off," Core demanded in a hard voice.

I inched the straps off. There was something so intimate and hot as I stared into his eyes while removing my dress, letting it drop at my feet. "Like this?"

He grinned, his teeth flashing white. "Just like that, darling."

Tweaking my nipples to make them erect, I asked him, "Do you like it when my nipples are hard?" I walked toward him, swinging my foot up onto his shoulder, stroking my womanhood.

"Shit," he groaned. "I didn't realize you were that limber."

I leaned in, licking the shell of his ear. "If only you knew how limber," I whispered.

"If you kiss my neck, it's done. We're fucking," he hissed.

Pushing back, I straddled one of his legs, lowering myself onto it, and then briefly rubbed my crotch against his thigh, making sure to press on his hard cock, giving him a lap dance. "If you like, you can touch it, baby."

"To hell with taking it slow. I need my cock lodged so deep into your pussy you can taste it in the back of your throat," he barked in a voice that was deep and smooth as he sprang up from the chair.

"Do your worst, baby." Instinctively, I wrapped my legs around his lean waist, digging my heels into his ass as he effort-lessly carried me over to the bed and lowered me onto it.

His firm lips curved a little into a smile. He stroked my hair. "Ready to be tied, darling?"

"Yes," I whispered.

His eyes never left mine as he picked up my hands and lifted them toward the head of the bed, wrapping a soft strap around them.

Excitement bubbled up as he moved to lie beside me. He

cupped my face in one huge hand, forcing me to meet his sensual gaze. "Do you trust me to take care of you?"

I nodded. "Yes. Always."

He brushed a tender kiss across my lips and nuzzled my temple.

I lay there, hands tied over my head, staring up at him. I remained as still as possible as the sexual tension heightened to a level that made it nearly impossible to breathe.

He stripped naked. His skin was a golden tan, tight over the bulging muscles beneath. He was without a doubt the sexiest man I'd ever seen... and damn, he was all mine.

I dropped my eyes lower. His huge erection was thick, hard, and jutting toward me. He joined me on the bed. He caressed my cheek before his tongue took full possession, darting in and out of my mouth.

"So beautiful," he murmured with approval.

I could hear his heart beating in a steady rhythm as he slid down. His fingers traced over my tattoo—*Love all. Trust few. Do wrong to none*—written horizontally from my abdomen to my back. He pressed his mouth against my stomach, nibbling and kissing until all I wanted to do was burst into flames.

He knelt between my legs, hungrily looking at me. He pushed my leg out a little. He cupped my pussy. "You know how I want you. Now assume the position, Sinful."

I brought my knees up to my stomach.

"Spread your legs, darling."

I did it without hesitation, eagerly following him into the world of decadent pleasure he'd created for me.

He gazed straight into my eyes while sliding his fingers between the wet folds of my heat. "Do you know what it does to me to see you this way?" Cupping a breast, he stroked the underside before tapping my nipple.

I wanted him more than I'd ever wanted anything, wanted his cock deep inside me.

I wanted his eyes on mine as he took me.

I arched up, wiggling closer as he slipped his fingers inside. His thumb circled and played with my clit.

"This pussy is all mine."

I was dying for more even though I was on the edge of my first orgasm. As I stared at him, my mind went numb. I needed more, but I was helpless.

He stroked my heat. I shivered, on the verge of exploding. I knew he had no intention of pushing me over the edge until I said what he needed to hear.

"Please," I whispered. "I just... Please... lick me."

"Was that so hard, darling?"

His huge hands curled around my thighs, spreading me wider, and his tongue thrust into my heat. That one lick sent me spiraling over the edge, and I screamed his name like a prayer.

He pulled his head back and watched me as his fingers continued to stretch me. "Scream louder, darling."

I was writhing and panting as his fingers thrust harder. I moaned louder when his finger found my clit again and mercilessly played with it.

I screamed and came again, feeling light-headed from the passion.

I am his.

I belong to him... and him to me.

"Core." I breathed his name and whimpered, all the fight going out of me.

As if it were the sign he'd been waiting for, he lifted his head, his smile gentle. "Nothing is sweeter than my strong woman's surrender."

I caught my breath. Core was right above me, his weight on his knees between my thighs. He directed his condom-sheathed cock into position, smoothly slipping in, looking at me with burning possession all over his face.

"So tight," he whispered.

I struggled to breathe as his cock stretched me.

He gave me a slow smile. "I've never wanted anyone more

than I want you right now," he grunted, fully seated with his balls bumping against my ass.

The tender affection in his words and in his eyes washed over me, making me feel cherished and desired.

He kissed my lips, my jaw, and my eyes. I basked in his tenderness and love. He pulled out and sank back in, hitting my G-spot with precision.

My legs wrapped around his waist as he continued to stroke me just right, making my legs quiver. My pussy sucked him in farther as he pumped deeper. I tilted my hips forward, and he adjusted his movements so with each stroke, he brushed deliciously against my clit.

The deeper he pumped, the more I wanted him.

My head snapped back as he slid in and out. I writhed beneath him, meeting him thrust for thrust. I was trembling, moaning low and deep. He stilled my hips so I felt every inch of his pulsing cock.

He swooped down, taking a nipple into his mouth. He lifted his head, his eyes boring into mine. "Take me, Sin. All of me."

Instinctively, I knew that he meant more than just taking his cock, that he was asking me to take him the way he was—flawed and dominant.

Tears pricked my eyelids, and I wished my hands weren't tied so I could caress him.

I sucked in a breath as he withdrew and plunged deep again.

"I accept everything that you are," I declared.

"From you... I'll accept nothing less." Core's dark eyes raked over me. "It's going to last all morning, darling. No rushing," he growled in my ear as he released my arms from the bonds.

Dropping my head on his shoulder, I felt so connected to him.

Wrapping my arms around his wide shoulders, nails digging into him like a wild woman, I buried my face in his neck and breathed deeply, the scent of him somehow reassuring me. He continued pumping, hard and controlled. I was going insane from the heat building.

My breathing was fast and shallow with periods of whimpers intermixed. "Please... harder." I grabbed his head, pulling him closer, biting his lower lip. "Please?"

He let himself go, moving faster, pushing me into another orgasm. Arching, I screamed as my pussy clenched around him, my body collapsing right after, worn out and sweaty.

His face was harsh and controlled as he pulled himself from my pussy, flipping me over onto my belly. He pulled me up onto my knees. I moaned when he kissed my neck and shoulders and then rained kisses along my spine.

Nudging me forward onto my hands, he gripped my waist with his strong hands as his cock smoothly thrust into me. I cried out with pleasure when his one hand gripped my hair and the other wrapped around my waist.

His body rocked into me. The slickness of our bodies was in perfect synchrony. I gripped the sheets as he reared back and pushed forward with every inch of him sheathed inside me.

My body shook and my legs quivered as my core pulsed, racing toward blissful release as he thrust faster.

"Sin, you're mine to cherish, love, and protect." His thrusts grew stronger as his body slapped against mine.

I clenched the sheets as I rocked back into his body. My body burned for sweet release. A strangled shout escaped his lips before I came so hard that I screamed his name at the top of my lungs. My inner muscles contracted, milking him. He roared as both of us crested.

He kissed me on my shoulder before pulling me up farther onto the bed. Clutching me against his body, he kissed me, and with eyes closed, I kissed him back.

I couldn't stop trembling. I wanted to laugh. I wanted to cry. I wanted to be held in his arms this way forever.

There is no going back... not that I want to.

I knew with every fiber in my body that this man would love me hard and cherish me until his last breath.

I sighed, content, as we held on to each other, lips melding over and over as the tremors passed.

"So I guess you're stuck with me, McKay," I sassed, letting out a little laugh.

He nuzzled my neck. "I wouldn't have it any other way," he quipped, nibbling on my ear.

16

CORE

I STEPPED off the elevator with Sin by my side, and we stormed down the hallway leading to my war room.

I'd tried everything in my power to make Sin change her mind about going to my meeting with Bigsby, but she was determined to come with me tonight.

I flattened my lips. Heat flushed through my body.

Why the hell does she have to be so fucking stubborn?

When it came to Sin, my protective instincts were on high alert, and all I wanted to do was lock her ass up in my penthouse, keeping her safe until I could take care of Bigsby.

And even when I'd pointed out to her—several times—that Grace's recent death was a perfect example that Bigsby had no qualms about killing anyone he deemed disposable, she'd calmly rebutted, "Core, I have a stake in this shit. Bigsby ruined my damn life. Just like you. I need closure. I'm coming with you. End of story."

She was right about needing closure, but I would get it for both of us. She didn't need to be there to get it. But when I had seen the damn determination in her eyes, I had known she wouldn't just sit around at my place, waiting for the end of the Bigsby saga. Like me, she needed to witness the job being done.

And if I'd left her behind, denying her that right, she'd only resent me for it... and a pissed-off Sin was not what I wanted to deal with when I got home tonight. So my reluctant concession was agreeing to her request. I wanted no doubt in her mind that she was my partner in every way.

But what if Sin gets hurt... or killed, despite my best efforts to protect her?

I could lose her just like I lost Mom, Maya, and my child. Shit. If anything happened to Sin, it would literally break me.

I couldn't remember the last time I'd wanted someone—not even Maya—with the intensity I felt for Sin. Now the thought of living a life without her, in solitude, filled me with dread.

I would kill for her, live for her, do anything I needed to protect her.

I clenched and unclenched my hands by my sides as I took a deep breath. Somehow, I'd have to control my primal instinct to wrap her ass up in bubble wrap, protecting her from the hard-core shit that was about to go down in a couple of hours. And knowing Bigsby's sordid history of violence, there was no doubt in my mind that I was walking into a trap, which we'd planned for with our own counterattack strategy. But all of the damn planning in the world couldn't account for every possible scenario, which also meant there was a real possibility of Sin getting hurt. Again, I'd explained that to her several times but to no avail. She still wanted in.

Fuck my life.

I sighed heavily.

She grabbed my hand. "Core, stop worrying. It will be all right." She finished with a squeeze of my fingers before releasing them.

I growled menacingly, incensed that she was putting herself in unnecessary danger. "This is utter bullshit!" The words were out of my mouth before I could stop myself. "I can't focus on this mission and you at the same time." I was mad as hell, and it was making me act out emotionally instead of logically.

She stopped in her tracks, turning to stand in front of me. "Then don't." She countered. "I can take care of myself. Focus on taking down Bigsby."

"That shit is easier said than done."

"Core"—she reached up, touching a hand to my chest —"we're going to be all right. Everything I need is standing in front of me. Through the ups and downs, baby, I'm going to stick around." Leaning up, she pressed her lips against mine.

Damn, I never want to let this woman go.

I leaned into her body, sucking her tongue into my mouth. The nagging fear of losing her like Maya threatened to drown me. Her tongue slid around the tip of mine and then rubbed under it. I gave her one last swipe of my tongue before I retreated, bit her lower lip, and then pulled my mouth away from her, keeping my hands on her face. I inhaled deeply, smelling her sweet scent lingering all over me.

"I promise we will be all right," she insisted. "Now let's go."

I released her, reluctantly stepping back.

She grabbed my hand, and we continued toward my war room.

I shook my head to clear my mind. I needed to focus. The sooner we could launch our attack on Bigsby, the sooner I could get Sin back to my penthouse, safe and sound.

We stepped into the war room, and I glanced around, taking stock of my team. Ram, Max, Rocco, and Kevin were gathered around a mini mockup of the warehouse and the surrounding area. Zuri was walking around the room with her cell pressed against her ear.

Sin assessed the team. "Wow. You guys are not fucking around. Y'all are ready for war."

And we were, including Zuri. They were geared up for battle in our standard uniform—black tactical clothing with a sidearm attached to their legs and black combat boots.

The guys' bodies tensed with their eyes locked on Sin.

And here we go...

I ran a hand through my hair, hoping I didn't look as stressed out as I was feeling.

Before I'd left the penthouse, I'd told my team that Sin was coming with us. They weren't happy about the idea—just like me—but we'd quickly adjusted our strategy to factor in her presence, protecting her at all costs.

Zuri ended her call, striding over to Sin and pulling her aside. Their conversation was animated but in low tones.

Shifting my attention, I stared at the myriad of monitors that hummed with energy. Pacing back and forth, I narrowed my eyes on the streaming aerial images of the warehouse area where we were scheduled to meet Bigsby tonight.

In my peripheral vision, I saw Sin sway to the center of the room with Zuri trailing behind her.

"Let's clear the air, shall we?" Sin started.

Everyone around her—except Zuri and me—stiffened, and an uncomfortable hush fell over the room.

"From the look on everyone's faces"—she glared pointedly at Kevin, Ram, Rocco, and Max—"I can tell no one is happy I'm going with you tonight."

"I am." Zuri raised her hand like she was in school.

Sin smirked. "Besides you, Zuri."

Zuri air-high-fived her. "I've got your back, girl."

"Now," Sin replied.

"What?" Zuri pouted. "But you just said that you and I were cool... and we're starting with a clean slate as of tonight."

Sin pursed her lips. "We are, but I want everyone in this damn room to be absolutely clear that there will be no more lies or omitting info, and there will be no putting Baby"—she pointed to herself—"in the damn corner. I'm all in with Core and everything that shit entails."

She didn't even flinch under their scrutiny; she boldly met their hard stares. And it occurred to me that it was very possible I'd found someone who could outstare all of us. Sin was a force to be reckoned with, and she was obviously not going to take any shit from my team.

"Preach, sista," Zuri chirped, throwing her hands up like she was in church.

Kevin, Ram, Rocco, and Max frowned at Zuri.

Ram snorted, crossing his arms over his chest. "Just what we need... another member of the I Heart Sin Club."

Zuri rolled her eyes at him before retorting, "Whatever."

Sin turned to Zuri. "I'm loving your support, but you're stealing the thunder from my epic vagina monologue. So hit the mute button." She ended with a smile, eyes glimmering.

Zuri gave her a wide grin with a thumbs-up.

Sin eyed my men. "Anyway, like I was just saying... You might not be thrilled that I'm coming along." She jammed a hand on her curvy hip. "But I am, so just suck it up."

I smiled, feeling some of the tension leave me. *Damn, I loved her feistiness.*

Max finally did something other than scowl; a faint smile brushed his lips. "Well, look at that... Sweet cheeks ain't afraid of the big, bad alphas."

Ram quipped, "She has balls of steel for sure." He waggled his eyebrows. "I like that."

Kevin tilted his head as he considered her. His expression clearly relayed his conclusion about Sin. She was a science experiment gone wrong.

A muscle twitched beneath Rocco's left eye. He was annoyed, but he remained silent.

Sin continued. "Look, I'm not planning on getting in the way or doing something stupid like pretend I'm Lara Croft or some shit." She glanced around. "But I have a right to be at that meeting, given what Bigsby has done to my family and me. I have to be there to see him get his due justice. So just tell me what you need me to do, and I'll do it, no questions asked. But I'm going with my man." She nodded at me.

The corners of my lips lifted into a smile.

Damn, how fucking lucky am I to have Sin, who is everything I need and a force to be reckoned with?

Now all I could think about was fucking her so hard she would taste my cock in the back of her throat.

I was proud of her for not cowering in a room full of alpha personalities. I loved it. She was the special woman in my life and here to stay, so it was important for her to assert her place, by my side as alpha female, among the team. Especially since she'd be seeing them a lot because, despite the fact that each team member had their own luxury apartment, it never failed that command central was always at my penthouse. I didn't know how, but over the years, our living quarters had turned into a quasi fraternity house with the one elevator giving us unlimited access to each other's space. Our living situation worked because none of us had a significant other in our lives—until me.

Kevin replied, "We've already got your security covered, Sin. You'll be with Zuri and me in the surveillance van." His lips kinked into a smile.

"Got it," Sin replied. "And nice to finally put a face to the voice, Kevin." Her lips twisted into a smirk.

Kevin and Sin had interacted in the past when he contacted her—at my request—about taking care of all her business financial matters, including providing the money to continue her line.

"So I've met the rest of you." Sin confirmed. She turned to stare at Ram. "And we've met twice. The first time at Core's office. The second when you were Core's sidekick at the gala."

Ram retorted, "You forgot to add *sexy* before sidekick." He gave her a salacious smile.

"Cocky much?" Sin countered with an arched brow.

"Just saying... the ladies love me," Ram answered. A smile spread over his face, brightening his eyes and his voice.

Zuri rolled her eyes heavenward. "So says the king of dirty hook-ups." She pointed at Ram. "He's our resident man-whore."

"I'm just spreading love." Ram countered with a suggestive pelvic thrust.

Kevin mumbled, "I hope that's all you're spreading."

Ram punched him in the shoulder. "Shut the fuck up."

Sin snorted. "Anyhoo, moving on... So Max and Rocco." Tilting her head in quiet consideration, she studied them. "We first met at Bigsby's fundraiser gala."

Max answered, "Where you threatened to kick our ass... which was the single most thrilling moment of that whole damn boring night."

"What can I say? I'm a very bad girl." Sin batted her eyelashes, almost comically. "But that will teach you not to fuck with a woman not afraid to street fight in a couture dress and stilettos." Sin countered, ending with a grin at Rocco.

Rocco scowled before his muscular forearms crossed in front of him while he stared pointedly at Sin.

Sin quirked a brow in his direction. "Well... ain't you the chatty one?"

Rocco grunted before running a hand over his blond five-o'clock shadow.

"Lovely... another one who loves to grunt like a caveman." She shot me a look.

I felt my mouth twitch into a smile. "Yep. And for fun, my team and I like to knock stones together to make fire."

Sighing in exasperation, Sin perked her lips into a half smile. "Smartass."

"I don't have time for this shit," Rocco muttered before making his way over to the monitors.

Zuri jabbed a finger at Rocco. "See? He talks."

"Uh-huh," Sin replied with an eye roll. "Anyway, now that we're all cool with shit, I'll let you all do your mission prep thingy." She took a seat next to Kevin, who seemed to consider-ably warm up to her when she pointed at his screen, saying, "Wow! Cool graphics."

With eyes spanning the team, I asked, "What's been done so far?"

Ram responded first. "I've done the radio communications in

and around the warehouse perimeter, and snipers, Max and Rocco, will be positioned in the vulnerable areas."

"We're ready," Rocco and Max replied in unison before opening their arsenal supply, a weapons closet. High-tech weapons were anchored to the walls, and shelves were full of stacked cash.

Rocco smiled like a kid in a candy shop as he pulled out the weapons and quickly checked them before handing one to Zuri.

Sin stared, slack-jawed, as Zuri proficiently checked the gun.

Zuri was a gun expert even though you'd never know it by looking at her. She was graceful, beautiful, and feminine. People outside our circle thought she was just my pretty eye candy personal assistant, but she was way more. Zuri was an integral part of my team. She was tough as nails and could hang with the boys with ease. Once she'd joined the team, knowing how to handle a weapon was mandatory—as it would be for Sin after I warmed her up to the idea—because of the enemies we'd made over the years. So being ready to protect ourselves was top priority.

Kevin glanced up from his laptop. "I checked the perimeter with the drone," he disclosed. "We're good to go."

"I want this mission tight and everyone on their game," I added gruffly. "When Ram and I step into the warehouse to meet Bigsby, I'm expecting an ambush, but we'll be ready to handle it. But just in case something goes wrong, our body cameras will record everything."

This wasn't our first mission; my team was professional and specialists, and we all knew the drill. We might not make it out alive. But I'd never had something so precious at stake... Sin.

"Knowing Bigsby, there'll be plenty of firepower on both sides. Does anyone have any questions before we head out?"

Everyone responded in unison, "No."

Max and Rocco barked, "Hooah!"

I saw Sin's flushed expression. She was worried. I could see right through her anxieties.

We all marched out of the war room, silently getting into the elevator. Quiet prevailed on the ride down as we mentally prepared for our dangerous battle. Without pause, we quickly slid out of the elevator—private garage level—moving toward the waiting military-style vehicles.

I pulled Sin aside, brushing a few stray strands of hair off her forehead. "Don't leave Kevin's and Zuri's side, no matter what you see or hear on the live video feed to the surveillance van. Okay?" My chest constricted at the thought of ever losing her.

She nodded. "Got it. And you be safe, McKay. I need you back alive."

Lifting up on her toes, she kissed me hard on the lips. My fingers pushed through her hair as I devoured her mouth with sweeping strokes of my tongue, slow and deep, needing the comfort of her taste and touch. I kissed her neck, her chin, and her cheek as the recollections of Mom's and Maya's deaths echoed through my mind. Memories of fire engulfing my SUV, taking Maya with it... the moments frozen in time of the gun being pressed against Mom's head. Tragic events that had shattered my world into a million pieces, leaving me emotionally vacant until Sin came into my life, making me want to move on from the past and build a future with her.

My family—Max, Ram, Rocco, Zuri, and Kevin—and business gave me direction. But Sin... she gave me purpose. And I would fight tooth and nail to protect her and our future together.

I stepped back and then escorted her over to the van where Kevin and Zuri were waiting. Once she was safely inside, I slipped into killer mode. Ram, Rocco, Max, and I loaded the vehicles with black crates filled with weapons. When we were done, I pulled on my body armor, black baseball cap, and mirrored sunglasses.

I nodded as we all piled into the vehicles with grim faces.

"Let's roll," I snapped.

17

CORE

I POWERED the military-style vehicle around the corner, gathering speed toward the warehouse. Rocco and Max had already driven off to secure their sniper positions. Kevin, Zuri, and Sin were parked on the perimeter of the warehouse but out of sight.

I dropped a gear and floored it right inside the large warehouse filled with forklifts, cranes, and various forms of heavy machinery.

After sharply hitting the brakes and throwing the truck into park, I grabbed the ledger and the thumb drive with the recording of Bigsby's confession and jumped out of the vehicle. With Ram following, I stalked toward the black SUV parked in the middle of the warehouse. We stopped midway, assessing as much as we could of the vehicle with tinted windows. We then panned the area with our eyes for any of Bigsby's people hiding in the wings.

"You seeing this, Kevin?" I asked, just checking that Ram's and my body cameras were sending the video and audio feed as they should.

"Yes." Kevin's answer echoed in the hidden earpiece receiver I was wearing. "Scanning for body heat signatures in the warehouse. I only see two at this time, and they're in that black vehicle in front of you."

I replied, "I need you to keep it tight and stay alert. This could be an ambush."

"I'll be scanning for any other radio transmissions or heat signatures," Kevin announced.

"You're on it," I answered. "Out."

The driver's door to the parked vehicle opened, and Bigsby hopped out, followed by what looked like his bodyguard.

"McKay," Bigsby greeted.

I deliberately said nothing, letting the cooling sound of silence speak volumes.

The chunky gold ring on Bigsby's middle finger glinted as he nervously adjusted his cuff. The ring was the stark reminder that this man standing before me was a cold-blooded killer... the man who had murdered my mother. I shoved down the rage that threatened to surge through my body. I needed to stay calm... collected... keep my emotions from spurring me to make fucked-up decisions that could jeopardize this mission and my team's lives.

"You're late," Bigsby snapped.

"I'm here." I countered, walking toward him and his body-guard with Ram at my side. "So let's make this quick. I've got things to do." My lips flattened when we stopped mere inches from him.

Ram crossed his arms, widening his stance, as both he and the bodyguard silently sized each other up. Ram could easily take him—with or without having to use his weapon.

I studied Bigsby for a few minutes.

Bigsby shifted uneasily. "Before you pulled up, my men informed me that a van just parked on the edge of this property." He tilted his head. "More backup?" His eyes flicked to Ram.

I kept my face neutral, but I knew from his statement that he had eyes outside, watching our moves. Hopefully, the guys had picked up that detail on the audio.

"Are we going to do this exchange or what, Bigsby?" I replied in a sharp tone.

"You're one impatient fucker." Bigsby's jaw tightened.

"I'm just cutting to the chase." I countered tonelessly.

The vein along Bigsby's jaw pulsed rapidly. "Fine. Let's get this business done. Once I have what I came for, my dealings with you and Sin are finished."

I handed him the ledger and thumb drive. Bigsby accepted the items and then turned to walk away.

He skidded to a stop, turning to glare at me. "Did you make any copies of these items, McKay?"

"I won't need it," I replied. "Because our business is not finished." I pulled out the trophy gun I'd retrieved from Bigsby's safe after ransacking his home, looking for anything and everything to bring him down.

Bigsby's mouth flopped open and then closed. "What the hell are you doing with my gun?"

The bodyguard reached behind him, pulling out a 9mm handgun from his waistband, but Ram drew his weapon first, aiming at the man.

"Drop the gun or make my day," Ram hissed.

The bodyguard threw the gun to the ground.

"Kick it away," Ram ordered.

The bodyguard anxiously kicked the gun across the ground.

With eyes locked on Bigsby, I aimed the gun at his head. "Isn't it ironic?" I hissed. "You'll die by the same gun you used to murder my mother."

"That," Bigsby croaked, "was you? You little bastard!"

"Yes." My lips thinned. "That was me. Now I'm all grown up. And I bet you're wondering how I knew it was you," I spit.

Bigsby nodded, swallowing hard.

"You fucking idiot. You still have that same fucking ring. The same piece of jewelry you wore the night you killed my mother." I widened my stance. "Now I'm here to finish what you started... and I won't miss."

Bigsby laughed. "Do you actually think it's going to be so damn easy? That van that I mentioned to you?" He grinned. "I wonder if your sweet-ass bitch Sin is inside it."

"It's not going to make any difference to you," I finished and then pulled the trigger.

The bullet pierced Bigsby's head. He slumped to the floor—dead.

The bodyguard scrambled to the ground to retrieve his weapon, but before he could touch his gun, Ram pulled his trigger. The man was dead.

I seized the ledger and thumb drive from Bigsby.

Kevin shouted in my earpiece, "Here they come."

Outside the warehouse, gunfire erupted.

"Ram, let's get the hell out of here," I bellowed. I knew Kevin and Zuri could take care of themselves if attacked, but Sin, she had no weapon experience. "And make sure Sin's safe."

We jumped in our vehicle. Tires squealed upon our exit out of the warehouse.

"Core," Kevin called in my earpiece, "incoming. Several hostiles coming at you."

Bigsby's men shot at our SUV.

Ram launched a grenade out the window.

Boom!

Some of Bigsby's men fell to the ground. Ram raised his gun, shooting and taking the rest out. But more men streamed out from the buildings that encircled the warehouse.

"Fuck this." Ram grabbed a walkie-talkie, yelling into it, "Sniper A and B, take the bastards out."

I drove down the street, gathering speed. I saw bodies slumping to the ground from sniper gunshots. I dropped a gear and floored it away from the warehouse perimeter.

Looking into the rearview mirror, I could see Max slipping off the overlook of the warehouse like a ninja.

I grabbed the two-way radio receiver from Ram. "Kevin. Status?"

There was no response.

My heart raced.

Is Sin okay?

"Zuri?"

Nothing.

Shit! Are Kevin, Zuri, and Sin injured? Oh God... don't let them be shot or... dead.

18

SINTHIA

KEVIN, Zuri, and I watched and listened to Core's verbal exchange with Bigsby while sitting inside the back of the completely furbished van with plush seats and a bank of monitors tracking the activities going down inside and outside of the warehouse.

My fists unfurled and the tension disappeared when I heard the gunshot. Then I saw Bigsby fall to the ground. Core had finally gotten his revenge for his mother, for my dad, and for Greer.

It was finally over. Bigsby was no more.

It was as if the dark cloud that shrouded my past and threatened to consume my future had disappeared, and my future looked—

I blinked in confusion when I saw several dark-clad men creeping toward the adjacent building I'd seen Core and Ram drive into earlier for their meeting.

Jabbing a finger at the monitor, I asked, "Kevin? Do you see that?"

He gave me the side-eye. "Of course, Sin," he muttered with exasperation in his tone. "Sniper A," he barked into the intercom. "Sniper B. Hostiles approaching Alpha and Beta."

"Sniper B. Got it," Rocco replied.

"Sniper A. Engaged," Max relayed. "Shit!" he snapped when we saw on the monitors that more men were streaming from the buildings. "Too many hostiles. I'm going in closer. Sniper B, cover me."

We saw someone dressed in all black slip behind some packing crates.

"Who's that?" I asked.

"Max," Zuri answered before Max swung into action, squeezing off a series of shots, taking out a swarm of men.

More men converged to Max's left, turning in unison and firing their guns. Max dived for cover.

"Sniper B. Shoot!" Kevin ordered.

One body collapsed to the ground, then two more, and then the last two. Max looked up from behind cover. All five were dead.

My heart was in my throat. I'd only seen moves like those in action movies. "Who the hell are you people?" I muttered in amazement.

"Max and Rocco are former military," Zuri answered. "The elite of the elite—Special Forces."

"Well," I muttered, "I'm glad they're on our side." And I made a mental note to thank them for their service.

Max started to retreat when a hostile came out of nowhere. My stomach plummeted with fear. Max lunged, wrestling the man's rifle away and knocking it down. The man drew a knife and slashed at him, but Max grabbed his knife arm, twisting it at an awkward angle that caused the knife to drop, and then he seized the man in a two-handed neck-breaker.

"Jesus. He broke the man's fucking neck," I whispered, both terrified and awed by his badass but brutal display, "with his bare hands."

"That's what he gets paid for," Zuri stated, nonplussed.

Boom!

The sound echoed outside our van.

Startled, I swung my head to the side, wildly glancing around.

I gasped in a strained whisper when our vehicle tilted slightly to one side, followed by the sound of lots of pings against the metal shell of the van. All of the monitors flickered and then went black.

Silence pushed from seconds to minutes.

"Kevin?" Zuri hissed. "What the hell was that?"

"Bigsby's men," he replied. "Grenade." His fingers flew over the keyboard and then the console, pressing several buttons, as if trying to get the monitors online. "Then bullets." He sat back, frowning. All systems were down. "Fuck!" he hissed, standing up.

I backed up a bit, giving him space. He was a massive man who had to be at least six-seven and looked like he could bench-press a car despite his Clark Kent nerdy appearance.

Staring directly at us, Kevin simply explained, "Now it's our time."

"Dammit!" Zuri's lips drew into a straight line. "This is the last thing we need."

Without another word, Zuri and Kevin pulled out their weapons.

"I'm sorry." I blinked in confusion. "What are we doing?"

Zuri's eyes locked on to mine. "Sin, stay behind us. It's fixin' to get rowdy."

My eyes widened. "Rowdy?" I swallowed hard. "Holy shit! Please don't tell me they're going to try to get inside the van," I squeaked, heart racing like a rabbit as the panic started to take hold of me.

Zuri gripped my shoulders. "Take a deep breath," she ordered in a calm voice.

I nodded and did what I had been told.

Zuri spoke plainly. "Now get yourself together because shit's about to get real chaotic up in here."

What. The. Hell?

My limbs started shaking.

I'm going to die. In a van... out in Nowhereland. Fuck my life!

Kevin yelled into his handheld intercom, "Sniper A and B. Bigsby's goons are at our location. We're compromised and under attack." He stormed over to the solid metal partition erected behind the front seats of the van, locking the fixed door in the center and sealing us inside the cargo area.

"We're on our way," Rocco answered.

Kevin shrugged off his armored vest, handing it to me. "Sin, put this on," he spoke in an even tone once again.

There was a sour taste in my mouth when I asked, "But what about you?"

"Don't worry about me or Zuri. Our job is to protect you."

Zuri took a position in the rear, as if guarding the back door.

Scared out of my damn mind, I followed direction, putting on his vest.

"Sin," Zuri hissed, "brace yourself. They're going to try to get inside the cargo area to kill us."

"What?" I chewed my inner cheek so hard I tasted blood. "How do you even know that?" Sweat trickled between my breasts.

Kevin's face looked grim when he responded calmly, "Because that's what we would do."

My pulse raced as I tried to keep from peeing myself. I was so terrified that bladder control was almost nonexistent.

I marveled at how unruffled Kevin looked when he explained, "Sin, we have two choices. Stay where we are and possibly get blown up in the van by more explosives or shoot our way out of this clusterfuck. We choose the last option. So let's surprise the fuckers."

"Shoot our way out?" I sputtered. "Are you kidding me? I've never touched a gun in my life."

"You want to live, right?" Zuri asked, her voice just as tight as mine.

"Hell yes!" I clipped out with hands on my hips.

"You want to see Core again, right?" Zuri barked.

I screamed, "Fuck yes!" The thought of dying, of losing him, made my heart race with fear.

"Good," Kevin answered. "This is an automatic weapon." He handed me the gun. "All you have to do is point at the bad guys and pull the trigger, and don't stop fucking squeezing until the weapon has no more ammo."

My hands trembled while holding it. I took a deep, calming breath.

Sin, you have to do this.

I steadied the gun.

Kevin picked up another weapon and readied himself beside me. "Zuri? You ready to rock and roll?" he roared.

My head got a little lighter from holding my breath.

"I stay ready," Zuri shouted before grabbing the handle of the back door and swinging it open, which surprised the bad guys, dressed in all black, who were getting ready to place the explosive clutched in one of the men's hands on the back door.

Shit. Shit. Shit.

I heard Core's commanding voice through the two-way radio receiver. "Kevin. Status?" There was a slight pause. "Zuri?" Core hissed.

Shots rang out from inside the van. Kevin and Zuri were unloading their weapons in rapid succession, and all I could remember was Kevin's instruction to point at the bad guys and pull the trigger.

Sin, do it... or you'll die. You'll never see Core again.

I aimed the weapon at the bad guys and squeezed the trigger... surprisingly hitting the guy holding the explosive, which exploded in his hand.

"Damn, Sin!" Kevin yelled. "Boom shakalaka!"

I didn't stop shooting until my weapon clicked. It was out of bullets. Glancing over, I saw Kevin laid out on the floor, covered with blood. I went into reaction mode, picking up his weapon, and I continued to squeeze the trigger along with Zuri, who was holding her own.

I have to protect Kevin as he protected me.

Perspiration rolled down my forehead as I fired at the hostiles, taking out one.

Then, *blam!* The burst of bullets killed two more men. Then there was another burst, and two more went down.

Then there was silence.

I couldn't believe I could kill so effortlessly.

It is all surreal.

I killed at least five men.

Not in a million years had I thought I was remotely capable of doing something like taking a life. No, several people's lives. But I had. And I felt no remorse, just relief and gratefulness that I was here, alive.

Now I truly understood the primal survival drive that coursed through Core and his team. When it came down to it, if the only thing that stood between life and death was the will to survive, who wouldn't fight until their last breath?

My thoughts snapped back to the present when I heard wheels squealing outside and the sound of guns blazing. I wondered if someone was shooting at the bad guys.

And then there was utter silence again.

I crawled over to Kevin. His chest area was a bloody mess, but he was breathing. "Are you going to live?" I asked, cradling his head on my lap.

"Sin." Kevin glanced up at me with a grimace of pain. "You can be on our team anytime." He looked like he'd been through hell, but he still grinned at me.

Frantically, I glanced around for Zuri. She seemed fine. Her weapon was still pointed, at the ready.

"Sin!" I heard Core yell from outside the van.

"Shit!" Zuri's body relaxed. "About damn time. The cavalry is here."

It's over.

My shoulders sagged with relief.

Core's alive... and here.

Core appeared at the back of the van... and I'd never been so relieved to see his face.

In a rush of adrenaline, I scrambled to my feet to meet him. There was a soft thump behind me.

Kevin yelled, "Dammit, Sin!"

Looking over my shoulder, I saw that my sudden movement had caused Kevin's head to hit the van's floor. "Oops! My bad," I offered before hopping out of the van.

Leaping into Core's waiting arms, I wrapped my arms and legs around him. The man felt so good under my hands.

"Thank God," I whispered. "I didn't want to kill anyone else. Five is enough," I finished, burying my face against his beefy neck, inhaling his familiar masculine scent.

Core protectively wrapped his arms around me. "I'm sorry it took me so long to get here."

I slightly leaned back, feeling secure with his grip under my ass, pinning me to him. "But you're here. Alive. And that's all that matters."

His lips quickly took mine, claiming me. His tongue curled around mine, coaxing it to join in. We both groaned at the contact, and my eyes slid closed as his grip tightened, pulling me closer. He pulled his mouth away from me, allowing me to get to my feet but keeping me pinned to his side.

Core asked, "Zuri? Is everyone okay?"

Zuri shakily breathed out. "Yes. Kevin took a bullet, but it looks like it went in and out. He'll live," she finished with eyes assessing the dead bodies littering the ground outside the van.

Ram patted Zuri on the back before hopping into the van.

"Watch it, Ram," Kevin yelled from inside. "Bro! I'm fucking injured. Handle with damn care." There was a slight pause. "Zuri!" Kevin shouted. "Get in here. I need protection from this asshole."

"Jesus." Zuri rolled her eyes. "He's such a big baby." She moved out of sight and farther into the van.

Core and I watched as both Ram and Zuri got out of the van

with Kevin in tow. He was walking between Ram and Zuri—one arm over Ram's shoulders and the other over Zuri's.

"He's good," Ram stated. "The bullet went straight through," he muttered while they carried Kevin toward the waiting vehicle.

Then they leaned him against the hood while they caught their breath. Kevin was a big man.

"I need a fucking drink," Zuri grumbled, bent over with hands on her knees. "No, several drinks," she tiredly huffed out. "And you"—she shot Kevin a dirty look—"weigh a ton. How many times do I have to warn you about the perils of using muscle-enhancing drugs?"

Kevin, who was slumped against the vehicle's hood, grunting as if in pain, abruptly popped straight up. "This is all natural," he growled while stripping off his T-shirt and then pointing to his six-pack abs. "It's called excellent DNA." His entire body was one sheet of pure, rippling muscle.

"Sure it is," Zuri grumped.

"Woman..." Kevin warned.

Core shook his head. "This is like kindergarten."

I laughed, enjoying the fun, sibling vibe. Frankly, it eased any tension that lingered from the danger we'd just lived through. "Give her hell, Kevin," I urged playfully.

Core pinched my ass. "Don't encourage them."

"Bro?" Ram shot Kevin an irritated glare. "Will you shut it?" Ram snatched Kevin's shirt out of his hand. "And no one wants to see this shit." He sneered at Kevin's bare chest while balling up the material in his hand and then slapping it against Kevin's wound.

Kevin yelped. "You fucker!" he yelled. "That hurts!"

Ram scowled. "Press it against your wound to stop the bleeding... and zip it, bro."

Max and Rocco pulled up and then got out of their vehicle.

"I took a bullet," Kevin directed at Max and Rocco.

"So what?" Max frowned. "You want a fucking medal for that shit?"

"Where's the fucking appreciation on this damn team?" Kevin grumbled.

"Kevin," I called, "I appreciate the hell out of you." And that was an understatement. I was damn grateful because both he and Zuri had saved my ass... big time.

"Ditto," Kevin grunted. "Because you're a badass. Shit. I can't believe you took out four men without blinking an eye. Damn, I like your style."

"Four? Oh, hell no," I sputtered, slightly stepping out of Core's embrace, eyeing Kevin. "I got five men in total."

"That's my woman," Core declared, pulling me closer and kissing the top of my head.

Wrapping an arm around his waist, I tenderly squeezed him.

"Well, you don't have to brag about it, Amazon warrior princess." Kevin grinned at me.

"I'm just saying. Do the math," I finished.

"But here's what I can't figure out," Kevin interjected. "Why were your eyes closed while shooting?"

"Oh, be quiet," I scolded and then burst out in laughter.

"Sin, the designer gunslinger," Ram retorted.

"That shit has a nice ring to it," Kevin quipped.

"Kevin!" Zuri snapped. "Will you shut the hell up? You're bleeding like a stuck pig, and we need to get you patched up."

They loaded him into the back of the SUV, and both Ram and Zuri hopped in and pulled away.

Core touched my cheek before saying, "Give me a minute. I need to make this call."

I nodded.

Core pulled out his cell and voice-dialed, "Doctor." There was a slight pause before the person answered, and Core said, "You need to get over to the penthouse. Kevin. No. Flesh wound. Yes. They're on the way. Yes. See you there." He ended the call.

I eyed Core. "You have a private doctor on call?"

"Yep. I keep him on payroll to take care of my team and me

in case of emergency. He even has a private medical office in my building."

I blinked. "Your building?"

"I own the whole building where my penthouse is located. It just makes it easier to maintain our privacy. Ram, Max, Rocco, and Kevin have their own luxury apartments in the building. We call it Command Central because we all live there. Well, everyone except Zuri."

"So it's like a fraternity house?"

"Without the fucking parties," he returned. "The single security code elevator gives us unlimited access to each other's space." He frowned. "That means don't be surprised to see them hanging out in my penthouse or going through my refrigerator like I'm their personal grocery store." He touched my cheek. "Since you're going to be spending a lot of time at my place..."

"Am I now?" I grabbed his shirt, leaning into him.

He reached down, clutching my face. "You are." He kissed me, saying against my lips, "Every night, I want to go to sleep with you in my arms and wake up every morning with my face between your gorgeous legs."

I shivered deliciously. "Damn. That sounds like a plan, McKay."

I sensually licked his bottom lip. He roughly growled before kissing me.

Breaking off the kiss, he explained, "Seriously, there's no privacy. Is that going to be a problem?"

I cupped his cheek. "Core, I don't mind. I like your team. They're your family, so they're mine, too."

I already respected the hell out of Zuri, Ram, Kevin, Rocco, and Max because of their skills but more importantly because of how much they obviously loved, respected, and protected Core. And just that devotion was enough for me to hope they'd someday feel the same way about me.

He gave me an honest-to-goodness bad-boy smile that made my heart thump with joy. "Damn, I'm one lucky man."

"And don't you forget it, McKay." I smiled gently.

My attention was diverted when I heard Rocco mutter, "Fuck! Too many bodies."

Core grabbed my hand as he strode over to Max, taking me with him. My eyes panned over the open field. Rocco was right; there were a lot of dead bodies. I shivered at the reality of this faceoff. So many lives had been lost.

"Text the cleaner," Core directed at Max.

Max pulled out his cell and barked into the phone, "Cleanup requested," and then he clipped out the address to the warehouse and our current location.

Rocco walked up to us. "How are we going to handle Bigsby's body?" he asked Core. "Are we going to leave it for the authorities to find?"

Core nodded. "Yes. We'll have the cleaner dump his body in the Hudson so when it floats to the top in a couple of days, someone will find it, and the authorities will assume one of his rivals did him in."

Core's plan was cold and calculating but bloody smart.

"Got it," Rocco replied before he and Max moved over to the side and started talking in low voices.

Core turned me to face him. "Are you sure you're okay?"

I glanced up at him. His face was relaxed. He looked at peace. It had to have been hell for him, waiting all these years to finally put the past behind him. Now his mother could rest in peace, and he could move on... finally. And so could I. Now all was right in our world.

"Yes," I started and then bit my lower lip, fighting the urge to cry—both sad and happy tears.

It was finally over. Bigsby was dead. His death didn't fill the empty hole from the loss of my dad, but it was a start.

"But let's not do this shit again. Being a commando is not my style. I'd rather stick to designing clothes."

"You've got it, darling," he remarked before hungrily kissing my mouth, tilting my head back and deepening his kiss. He repeatedly swept his tongue through my mouth, pausing only to nibble at my lips before sinking into me again, the passion and heat in his kiss bringing every erogenous zone to life. He lightly kissed my lips before saying, "I'll ravish you later. Now it's time to finish business." He gestured toward the dead bodies.

 19

SINTHIA

EXHAUSTION CONSUMED me as I sat in the passenger seat while Core drove.

We had stayed just long enough to see the cleaner and his crew pull up to the scene in large black vehicles with tinted windows. Then Core had ushered me into his vehicle, leaving Max and Rocco behind to ensure that everything was taken care of, and we had taken off.

"Forget what you just saw, okay, darling?" Core asked me.

I nodded because there was no way in hell I was built for going to jail, ending up as Big Bertha's prison yard bitch.

But now that the adrenaline had worn off, my mind slipped to thoughts of Dad—Ian. I hadn't visited his grave in years. Partly because I'd felt so guilty I had caused his death—though now I knew better—and partly because, frankly, I believed the body was just a shell for the soul, and upon death, it was freed.

Even though it was late at night, I longed to visit his grave at least one more time. So I asked Core to take me there before going back to his place.

"Are you sure?" he asked.

I stared at the skyline through the window and nodded. "Yes. It's time to say good-bye."

"Okay, darling," he responded simply.

After that, I was grateful that he respected my need for space, leaving me alone with my thoughts. Completely calm, I felt my eyelids slide closed even as I fought the need for sleep.

Core's cell echoed throughout the vehicle, startling me awake.

"Shit. Sorry, darling," he said in my direction before grabbing his earpiece and answering the call with, "McKay."

I couldn't hear the person on the other end, only Core's response.

"Hey, Mitch," he greeted. "Look, I'm kind of busy. Can we talk business tomorrow?"

The business conversation lost my interest. Mitch Fillion was Core's lawyer and Erika's husband.

"Now?" Core asked. There was a pause. "Why?" There was another beat of silence. "Okay, if you insist. I'm heading to a cemetery in New Jersey. The address is..." His hands tightened around the steering wheel. "How do you know the location?" He scowled. "Mitch, what the fuck is going on? Okay... but only because you've earned my trust. Don't make me regret this. See you there." He ended the call.

Glancing over at him, I asked, "What's wrong?"

Core frowned as he raced through traffic. "Mitch wants to meet me at the cemetery. He says it's important."

He looked worried.

"What's the problem?" I inquired.

"Maybe nothing. It's just..." He shrugged.

"Relax." I squeezed his leg. "While I'm visiting Ian's gravesite, you can wait for Mitch by the car and take care of whatever he wants from you."

"But that's just it." His eyes slipped to me and then back to the road. "He asked me to make sure you were there, too."

I raised my eyebrows.

What does Mitch want with me?

☙ 20 ❧

SINTHIA

LEAVING Core behind to wait for Mitch, I walked across the grass, not remembering the gravesite being this serene and beautiful. It had been so long since I was there that I fumbled along until I found Dad's plot.

There were fresh flowers lying on top, which was strange because Grace was dead so she couldn't have put the arrangement there. But truthfully, even if she were alive, I couldn't imagine her ever bringing flowers. She had just been too much of a selfish person to give a shit about doing something so sentimental, even for a man she'd shared years of her life with.

With my arms hanging slack at my sides, I stood, staring at his headstone, as the crisp fall air whirled around me. There was a tightness in my chest when I thought about his remains locked in a coffin in the stone-cold earth.

"Hi, Dad. I know it's been..." I croaked and then bit my bottom lip, fighting back the tears that prickled my eyelids. "Way too long. I'm so sorry about that."

Reaching down, I placed the flowers on his grave that I'd purchased after Core and I made a quick stop at a twenty-four-hour grocery store on the way to the cemetery. "I was a coward."

My chin trembled. "I couldn't face the guilt I felt for getting you killed... but now I know the truth."

A tear slipped down my cheek. I dashed it away.

"I know now what you did to give me a place to call home and to make me happy." I swallowed around the lump of emotions clogging my throat. "And I want to thank you for that and for loving me as hard as you did." My voice broke. "And it doesn't matter that you're my uncle. You will always be the man I consider my dad."

Sniffing, I wiped at my nose before taking a seat on the cold grass, facing his headstone. Drawing my limbs close to my body, I whispered, "I love you." A long stretch of silence passed. The only sound was a jet in the distance. "And I want you to know that you can rest in peace because Bigsby's dead." I inhaled deeply, taking in a lungful of air and mentally shaking myself.

"Now we can both breathe easier because Bigsby's no longer in our lives," I heard Erika's husky voice say.

Startled, I looked over my shoulder to find her standing right behind me. I'd been so lost in my thoughts that I somehow tuned out the sound of her footsteps.

"Erika?" I stood up, wiping my hands against my legs. "What are you doing here?" I regarded her for a moment, noticing her face with no makeup, hollowed cheeks, and eyes red and puffy, like she'd been crying.

"Sin"—Erika's eyes locked with mine—"Core told me you know about the ledger and what happened to your dad—to Greer."

"Why would he tell you—"

"Sin." She interrupted me. She moved closer, her eyes searching my face. "It's time for closure for both of us. I'm Aubrey... your mother."

I blinked while teetering on the edge of losing my shit.

My lips parted because, for once, I was at a loss for words. After minutes of silence ticked by, I finally shouted, "This is bullshit,

Erika!" I spit. "Or is it Jemma Kane?" I narrowed my eyes. "No. It's Aubrey Cruickshank, right?" I laughed without humor because my life had officially become some fucked-up reality show, starring me.

Erika frowned. "All of the above."

My heart hammered hard as her response sank in. "I guess that solves that mystery," I muttered.

"Sin." Erika reached for me.

I swatted her hand away.

Her hand dropped to her side. "You're not planning on making this easy for me, are you?"

I stared at her like she'd lost her ever-loving mind. "What do you think?" Heat flushed through my body.

Erika sighed heavily. "I get it. Not telling you sooner was wrong. I messed up." A look of regret crossed her face.

My nostrils flared as my anger began to boil. "No. More like fucked up," I retorted. My entire world felt ripped apart. Up was down, and down was up.

"You're angry with me," Erika accused before running a hand down her face. "I don't blame you." Taking a deep, pained breath, she briefly closed her eyes.

Erika is my mother? How did I not see this coming? But how could I have?

Nothing could have prepared me for this news. Nothing.

But it did explain Erika's interest in me.

"Why didn't you tell me? We've known each other forever." My heart thudded in my chest. I wanted to walk away from her, but I didn't—I couldn't—because I was done running away from the truth. Now I just wanted damn answers.

Erika clenched and unclenched her hands. "If Bigsby found out you were my daughter, he would have killed us both right then and there."

Given what I now know about Bigsby, that is true... but still...

"But Bigsby did find out," I snapped. "That's why he went after my business."

Erika's eyebrows drew together. "And that's why I had my husband, Mitch, get so close to Bigsby."

I arched my brows high. "Mitch knows everything?"

"Yes." She nodded. "Mitch knows about my past, and he also knows about you. We've both been keeping tabs on Bigsby while ensuring you were safe. We've even been feeding the Feds information about Bigsby's shady dealings, including the sex trafficking ring."

I snorted. "Ensuring I was safe?" I pursed my lips. "Well, that was an epic fail because he was plotting to kill me and Core. And the only person who stepped up to the plate to save my ass was Core."

Erika opened her mouth to say something and then stopped short and pinched her lips together.

My breaths quickened when something horrible occurred to me. "Wait. Is that why you hired Jade?" I narrowed my eyes. "To get close to me?" There was a knot in my belly.

Erika crossed her arms. "You know better than that shit." She countered with a sharp tone. "I hired Jade because she's a talented actor."

"You're damn right she is," I defended. "What about Ariana? Did you seek her out because of me?"

Erika didn't seem that cold and calculating.

But shit, what do I really know about her?

"Contrary to your belief, Jade and Ariana didn't have shit to do with you and me. It was fate that brought them both into my same social circle. Nothing more, nothing less. Six degrees of separation is damn real."

I eyed her, really wanting to believe her. "That'd better be the truth, Erika." Stepping forward, I jabbed a finger in her face. "Because they're my family. And no one fucks with my family. No one," I hissed.

Her eyes softened. "I love both of them, Sin. They mean the world to me." She paused. "You know that. Shit, you know me."

I arched a brow. "Do I?"

"You do."

I silently stared at her because the truth of the matter was I didn't know her at all.

"I know finding out that I'm your mother is shocking." Her voice was soft and measured.

I rolled my eyes skyward. "That's putting it mildly." Rubbing my brow to ward off a headache, I replied, "Maybe this is a bad idea. It's been a long damn day, and frankly, I can't deal with more drama right now."

"Please," Erika pleaded, "just let me say my piece. And if you still don't want anything to do with me..." Her voice broke. She cleared her throat. "I won't push it, okay? I'll leave you the hell alone if that's what you really want."

I hesitated but then let out a long and tired sigh. "Fine." My head barely moved into a nod, and I controlled the frown that was threatening to form. "Let's get this talk over with."

Erika's eyes darted around. "Don't you want to go someplace else to talk?"

"No." Irritation stormed through me, and I fisted my hands by my sides. "Right here. Right now."

The confident Erika that I knew fidgeted uncomfortably. "My real name is Erika Aubrey Watson. I never liked my first name, so my mother just called me either Aubrey or Brey."

She bit her bottom lip, and the familiar gesture—something I did when I was anxious—made me relax slightly because it proved that this conversation was important to her.

To ease the tension a little, I asked, "Is your mother still alive?"

She shook her head. "No. I was fourteen years old when she died from cancer. And since I didn't have any family, I bounced around from foster home to foster home until I was done being used by foster parents that were more interested in the monthly check they got for taking me in than giving a shit about me, the little girl who needed stability, love, and protection."

I arched a brow. "And your father?"

"He left my mother when she got pregnant with me." Her eyes hardened. "And he never looked back."

"Oh... I see." And I did.

The pieces to the puzzle of who Erika had been before becoming one of the most powerful women in television slowly started to come together.

She's a broken crayon just like me.

Feeling completely drained, especially after Erika had dropped a big bucket of emotion and a lot of expectations in a matter of minutes, I plopped down on the grass to sit.

Erika followed, crossing her legs, facing me.

"What about Greer?" I asked, uncomfortably shifting on the grass.

She studied me for a few minutes before she spoke. "I was involved with Greer way before I went into business with him and Bigsby."

"By 'involved'"—I made air quotes—"you mean having sex with him." It was a statement, not a question.

"Yes," Erika replied, and I nodded for her to continue. "I knew who Bigsby was, even before Greer gave me the lowdown about him. I'd heard the rumors on the streets that Bigsby was a backstabbing asshole who would cut a person down in a heart-beat, but my business deal with him and Greer was too good to pass up."

I snorted. "It was all about the money, huh?"

"Yes, it was. I'm not going to lie about it." She shrugged. "I was young, ambitious, and yes, greedy." She pursed her lips. "I wasn't thrilled about working with Bigsby, nor did I trust him, so I had Greer be the middleman between us, making sure Bigsby never saw my face. For that matter, none of my clients or girls ever saw my face. I was the puppet master behind the curtain."

I arched a brow. "That was cunningly smart."

She nodded. "I'd started out as an escort and worked for a woman who took me under her wing before she got busted. She ultimately pleaded guilty to arranging an encounter between two prostitutes and a man who turned out to be an undercover police officer. Her downfall was her clients and escorts who snitched her out to the police. I never wanted to be that vulnerable. So when I had taken over her business, I'd made sure never to reveal my identity to anyone.

"Anyway, I wasn't thrilled about working with Bigsby, but he had the right connections to get me the upscale clients I needed, and I had the women to make the engine work."

A big gust of wind blew, and I briefly stared up at the sky.

Erika sighed, an exhale that was one of the weariest sounds in the world. "Business was booming for a good while, but I was smart enough to know that our escort business wasn't my final destination in life. I wanted out, but the escort business was Bigsby's cash cow. He would never let me just walk away. And then there was this little issue. Greer and I had fallen in love, and I got pregnant. With you," Erika confessed, eyes still watching my expression.

Pulling my legs up, wrapping my arms around them, I rested my chin on my knees. "So your little black book was the ledger?" I asked.

"Yes. Greer and I got married secretly, and we needed a little insurance against Bigsby when we demanded release from our business arrangement." Her jaw tightened. "Bigsby was pissed that we wanted out, and that's when everything blew up between us. It was lucky that we'd given the ledger to Ian before..." Her voice broke, and she cleared her throat. "Once Greer was dead, Bigsby came after me. He snitched me out to the authorities as the ringleader of the escort business."

"But he didn't know your identity. How did the police even connect you to the ring?"

"My ex-boss." Her nostrils flared as she took a deep breath in through her nose. "She was the only person who knew my real identity. You see, when she was convicted of pandering, tax evasion, and money laundering, she got three years in prison. When she got out, she wanted her business back. I said hell no.

So she got her revenge by hooking up with Bigsby to take me down."

"Wow." My eyes locked with hers. "Why didn't you just tell the authorities about Bigsby? You had enough evidence in the ledger."

Erika let out a sigh. "I was scared he'd come after me and you. I couldn't risk that. The best way to throw him off our trail was to let him believe that his plan to get rid of Greer and me had worked." She ran a shaky hand through her hair. "Anyway, I wasn't worried about serving time because I had a plan. I threatened to reveal the names of dozens of powerful, high-profile politicians, top law enforcement, influential lawyers, bankers, entertainment execs, and Fortune 500 businessmen listed in my little black book—the ledger. And I had every intention of doing that by splashing their names on the front page of every paper in New York." She jutted her chin out. "So the Manhattan prosecutors—who were also my clients—decided to make a secret deal with me. The arrangement allowed me to avoid jail time, but not before seizing all my assets, along with Greer's and Bigsby's."

I shook my head. "Well, I guess that explains what Bigsby was doing for all those years following my dad's death. He was broke and rebuilding his assets."

Erika cocked her head at my words. "Yes... and also plotting to wipe away any remnants of his sleazy pimp past." Her eyes hardened. "Anyway, after my secret deal with the prosecutors, they wanted me to just quietly go away—which, frankly, I had no problem doing. I wanted to get away from Bigsby. So after I had you, I got out of New York, pronto."

I whispered, "You mean you got out of town without me." My voice swam with emotion, the words spilling out around a rock-hard lump in my throat.

"Sin, I was young with no money," Erika whispered as tears began to pour from her eyes. "I couldn't take care of you. Besides, I was always on the run, and that was no type of life for a baby."

Disappointment churned through me even though I knew she was right.

"I wanted more for you. And I knew Ian would take care of you like his own," she replied, clasping her hands together in her lap. "I"—her voice croaked—"bounced around the country for a while before landing in California, but I've always been around, looking over you."

All my breath and defiance whooshed from my throat in a violent exhale as I sat silently, digesting all of this information.

Everything Erika had explained made sense. She had been young back then and made some fucked-up mistakes. Who knows? If I were in her shoes, I probably would have done the same. All in all, people weren't perfect. But still, I needed time to process everything and come to terms with the truth of Erika being my mother.

I took a deep breath, filling my lungs with air, and exhaled slowly. I wasn't sure if I'd ever have a mother-daughter relationship with Erika, but at least the door was now open.

🙢 21 🙠

SINTHIA

THREE YEARS LATER

IT WAS FALL NYFW—NEW York Fashion Week—one of the busiest, most stressful, and most exciting times of the year for me and my team as we got ready to present my spring/summer collection.

I took a deep breath, glancing around backstage. *Damn! This is the calm before the storm.*

There was nothing but steamers, coffee, and loud music.

The Zen moment was gone fifteen minutes later when the swarm of people—dressed all in black, armed with shears, blow-dryers, and hair spray, ready to bring my vision to life—started to flood backstage. The area became a packed house with models running around and the hair and makeup team covered in the tools of their trade.

Shit. This is finally happening. I'm about to lose my NYFW virginity in three hours.

This was my first Sin Michaels fashion show, and it was happening today, coinciding with the opening of my fashion line's Manhattan flagship store on Madison Avenue.

I smoothed my hand across my stomach to calm my nerves. All of the pieces of my life's work were finally coming together, but I was nervous as hell.

Leading up to today's fashion show, my publicist wouldn't even tell me too much about who was attending because I was so busy with styling and getting everything ready. Plus, I hadn't wanted to have to deal with the possibly horrible news that no one was going to show up.

Because why would they? I'm a designer that only my Sin Michaels A-list following understands.

No fear, Sin! You've worked way too damn hard to get here.

I kept busy, finishing the last-minute details, methodically checking over my collection that was sectioned off on hangers along with snapshots of each model who would be wearing each outfit.

Despite the looks of disapproval and frowns I'd gotten when I announced during an interview that I was staying true to my design sensibilities and heritage by infusing diversity into my show with plus-size and non-white models walking my runway, I was sticking to my position. It was very important to me to pave the way and push acceptance of a more diverse assortment of races, ages, and body types to be represented in fashion.

So fuck anyone who thinks otherwise.

This was my business, and these were my designs. I wasn't going to compromise my ethics or myself for anyone.

And to push the *it's simply not done* envelope further, I had been steadfast in my quest to pay homage to everyone who had supported me along my fashion journey. I'd decided to change the game by opening the show to the general public, and I'd set aside free passes for fans, fashion students, and faculty at FIT, Parsons, Pratt Institute, and The High School of Fashion Industries on a first-come, first-serve basis. Ticket holders would sit separately from industry members and celebrities, who would be positioned in a raised viewing area.

After that, I'd picked an incredible riverside location in Tribeca that allowed for an unobstructed view of the One World Trade Center from every seat. The setting was perfect for my collection—grand but still intimate and the ideal platform to tell the story of my spring/summer collection.

Now just two hours before the show was set to begin, I was obsessively steaming my wrinkled pieces and fixing final details, jostling with hair and makeup teams as well as models and trying not to stress over the press that had started arriving backstage, clamoring to interview me.

I watched as one of the hairstylists, holding several tools in each hand, talked to a reporter while trying not to burn herself or the model. In the crush, everyone was fighting for space in the small backstage area that was our studio for the evening.

I beckoned Giselle, my right hand and creative director. "Status?" I asked.

"Everything's good," she stated with a forced smile.

I gave her a look, lifted an eyebrow, and waited. She knew better than to sugarcoat things for me.

Giselle's resolve faltered beneath my steady, authoritative regard. She sighed heavily. "Okay. Yes, there are a few hiccups with models arriving late, but we're on it."

I eyed the models making the most of their short prep time —eating sandwiches from the buffet, getting their hair, nails, and makeup done, being interviewed, practicing their poses, and looking good for candid backstage photos.

I blew out a breath. "Then why do I feel so damn nervous?" I was a hot mess of knotted nerves.

"Stop worrying, Sin. Everything is going great." A smile curved Giselle's lips.

I nodded because I trusted Giselle. She was a whiz at helping me be as organized as possible.

I'd planned everything in great detail. The venue would open just before sundown, and what awaited guests beyond the metal barricades was a well-planned, multisensory experience, beginning with a wooden and scrap-metal set constructed of only recycled materials and performance artists suspended on platforms against the skyline.

"So in other words, I need to chill the fuck out," I replied—a statement, not a question.

Giselle nodded. "Exactly."

"Okay. Got it," I responded, deciding to use my energy for last-minute adjustments when Jade burst onto the scene with a flock of eager reporters trailing behind her.

Jade grinned at me while waving her hand.

The paparazzi screamed questions, coming at her from all directions.

"Jade! Jade!"

"Jade! Can you pose for a photo?"

"Is that outfit you're wearing from the Sin Michaels collection?"

Jade stopped and preened for the cameras. She was beautiful and lithe with shocking apple-green eyes. Jade was undoubtedly one of Hollywood's most beautiful actresses, and the media was obsessed with her glam style and beauty. But I knew she was more than just good looks. She was funny, genuine, and smart.

"Everything that I'm wearing," Jade quipped clearly to the reporters, "is from the Sin Michaels line." She turned strategically, allowing photos to be taken of her outfit—one I'd designed just for her—a black asymmetrical ruffle crepe jacket featuring an exploded asymmetrical ruffle peplum with square, masculine padded shoulders and silk lapels and button fastenings. Her wide-leg black tuxedo trousers had a tonal satin stripe detail on the sides.

Damn. My bestie is the best commercial for my line. I love it.

A reporter shouted, "How do you describe Sin's style?"

Jade chirped, "Daring, fearless, and constantly evolving." She flipped her hair, playing up to the cameras. "Sin has an exuberant take on fashion that combines a willingness to experiment with a strong sense of self. Sin has fun with her clothes... which makes her clothing *everything*." Jade put dramatic emphasis on the last word. "Sin is the coolest, hottest, most talented, most impressive fashion designer today." Without another word, she sauntered away, toward me.

When she reached me, she pulled me into a tight hug, whispering in my ear, "I brought the paparazzi circus. You know, to whip up more social buzz for you."

"Love you, girlie," I whispered back.

I adored that Jade always had my back and was my bestie and my partner in crime. When she needed me, I would be there just like she'd been for me. It'd been that way from the first day we met as freshmen in high school, and it would always be that way.

We turned in unison, facing the rabid paparazzi. Cameras clicked. Microphones pressed forward.

Jade playfully batted her eyes and whispered, "Relax."

Despite the whirlwind of media coverage I'd gotten over my collection, I still wasn't comfortable in front of the paparazzi's cameras. It was sensory overload. The bright side of this current fiasco was the attention I would get from Jade wearing my couture design.

It had been quite a year for Jade. She was still on fire from starring in a smoking-hot television series. Not to mention she'd finally finished production on her first directorial feature. It had taken so much longer since she did it herself. I was so proud of her.

One reporter asked me, "How do you handle the pressure of being the costume designer for your mother, Erika Watson's, hot new television crime drama series starring Midori Petite?"

Mother... Erika...

Even years later, hearing those two words together... I still couldn't believe it.

Erika is my mother.

I remembered how angry I had been when she revealed she was my biological mother and why she'd left me with Ian. Her path had been complicated, and given what I knew about life now, I understood that sometimes decisions weren't so cut and dry. Life was short, and I didn't want to live it with bitterness and regret. I wanted her in my life... and I'd decided to forgive her, just like I'd forgiven Core.

Simply put, I'd come to terms with the fact that Erika did what she had to do to keep me safe. I had been angry about her decisions, but I hadn't rehashed the past. I'd just moved the fuck on.

Still, it hadn't been a smooth or immediate road to some sort of mother-daughter relationship. Every interaction had felt fraught with meaning. It had been similar to the most difficult dating relationship ever—where both of us were overanalyzing every little thing the other person did. After a few months of this painful tap dance, Erika and I'd decided something had to change. Instead of trying to force an instant bond as mother and daughter, we'd decided to just be friends and let it play out the way it played out.

I cleared my throat before responding. "Easy. Like me, my mother pulls no punches about what she wants. She had a vision, and I made it happen... of course, the Sin Michaels way. When you have a new show, there are so many ways to build it from the ground up," I told them. "Before we did the pilot two winters ago, we discussed the tone of the character, the tone of the clothes, the tone of the show, and what we didn't want the show to be."

Another reporter chimed in, "I've heard you talk about how important it is to have a range of designs for a very diverse group of people. How do you incorporate that mentality into your Sin Michaels line?"

I smiled before answering, "There needs to be inclusivity in the fashion industry. You know, something for a curvy woman and also options for a really petite woman. I want people to appreciate the clothes and not think, *Aw, that's hot, but it only looks good on her*," I told reporters.

Diversity was very important to me, especially given my heritage, and that was why I'd not only chosen the strikingly beautiful buzz-cut, gap-toothed famous black model to parade down the runway tonight, but also another famous hijab-wearing model.

I carried on. "I want to make things for all body types. With the Sin Michaels line, I have so much freedom. I'm curvy, but I don't just design for myself. I use my taste as the muse for everything. I like to play around with silhouettes. I like women to be comfortable in my designs."

Giselle, who was waiting in the wings, dramatically tapped on her watch.

"Okay. Thank you," I said. "I have a show to put on."

Giselle swept in, ushering the reporters away.

Jade bounced up and down. "I'm so fucking excited. My Sin is having her first fashion show," she squealed, pulling me in for a tight hug. "I always knew one day your hot collection would be parading down the runway during Fashion Week."

I hugged her back. "Well, thank you for being my living mannequin."

Since we had been in high school, I'd designed most of my clothes, using her as my sounding board. She was patient, enthusiastic, and always there for me.

She pulled back, beaming with pride. "I'd walk across coals for your ass, and you know it."

She was everything a best friend should be. I gave her a wobbly smile as we dashed away the tears of joy. "Oh hell, now you're getting all emotional on me."

"I can't help it. Look at you." Jade's eyes swept over me. "You're glowing with happiness."

"That ain't nothing but the afterglow from two rounds of sex this morning," I replied, shivering deliciously at the recollection of Core taking me in the shower and then in the kitchen.

"Morning sex..." Jade started. "I haven't had a good, hard pounding in..." She frowned. "Oh Lord, it's been so long I can't even remember."

"And whose fault is that?" I countered. "I can get you some of this if I can only hook you up with—"

"Don't say it." Jade cut me off. "I'm not interested in you hooking me up with Ram, Max, or Rocco."

"Hmm... that's weird." I gave her a mock perplexed stare, tapping my chin. "You didn't mention Kev—"

"Don't even mention that cunt tease's name," Jade warned playfully.

"Kevin!" I burst out laughing when Jade got flustered, and I loved it.

Jade had it bad for Kevin, the high-IQ genius who was the official geek of Core's team.

Jade pointed a finger at me. "You know, ever since you've been getting dick on the regular, you've become a mean woman."

I rolled my eyes. "All I'm saying is don't you think it's fucking funny that every time he sees you, he either hightails it away or stays to give you the mean-mug stare like you're some sort of evil vixen who needs to be doused with holy water to atone for your filthy sins?"

"What damn sins?" She pursed her lips.

"Come on, you know that everyone who watches your television show knows you're a down-for-anything, man-eating tigress." I swiped my hand at her like an animal, making a big cat sound.

Jade burst out laughing. "Don't make me shank you."

"I'm just saying..." I grinned. "Don't kill the messenger." I playfully batted my eyes.

"Well, you have one thing right. I am down for anything with that man. I refuse to chase him... but a bitch like me might power-walk her ass off to get him." She winked while mockingly pumping her arms like she was midstride.

I burst out laughing so hard that tears trickled from my eyes.

Finally catching my breath after doubling over with laughter, I said, "I mean, I love Kevin to death. But seriously, I don't get your weird attraction to him."

Jade could have any man she wanted with a flick of her finger, but she wanted Kevin. Yes, he was supermodel gorgeous. Essentially, he was the way hotter version of Superman's alter ego. But Jade's and Kevin's personalities were polar opposites.

"You're outgoing with a party-over-here vibe... and Kevin, well, he's reserved with an *I'd rather spend my Friday night scouring the Dark Web for intel* thing going on."

She threw her hands up in the air. "Damn if I can explain it. All I know is every time I see that fake Clark Kent, I want to snatch off his glasses and shove my hands down his pants just to see if he becomes"—she waggled her eyebrows—"the Man of Steel."

"Well, you know what they say... Nerds do it better." I grinned.

"Give me some time to snag him... and I'll let you know if that's really true."

I shook my head. "And on that note, I have a show to do." I kissed her on the cheek. "Now scoot your ass to your front row seat and let me dazzle you with my extravaganza of drool-worthy fashion."

"Yes, Queen Sin." Jade bowed dramatically. "See you on the runway, sweetie," she replied before strolling away.

Jade coming backstage was a welcome distraction from my frayed nerves about the debut of my collection.

"Well, back to the grind," I muttered under my breath before turning my focus to the last-minute details that needed my attention.

The final sixty minutes before showtime went by in a blur. In true Sin Michaels style, the hair and makeup teams put the final touches on the models' conceptual beauty looks that included sparkling, tribal facial jewelry, lace masks, floor-length fetish ponytails, and warrior-like metal headbands.

Finally, the group of dressers arrived. Models were outfitted in their looks and lined up backstage, ready for their turn on the runway.

Once the sun had fully set, it was runway time. The formerly deafening hum of workers backstage became so quiet that I could hear a pin drop.

Models lined up, and I double-checked the ensembles as they waited for their cue. The gong signaled the start of the twenty-five-looks show, which would wind around a runway the entire length of the pier.

My stomach fluttered with the excitement that I was about to turn the fashion world sideways.

Three, two, one, go time!

I positioned myself in front of the monitor backstage to watch my collection on the runway. It was equally as important to me to see the women exit the runway as it was to see them walk down the runway. I had to see how the clothes worked and moved from all angles.

Years ago, my life had gone into a tailspin after finding out the truth about my parents and who I really was, and the Bigsby drama had finally been put to rest. I wasn't the same after everything I'd experienced in such a short period of time.

So after much deliberation, I'd decided to take a mini sabbatical to get my head together. Core and I'd traveled the world together to places I'd only dreamed about—Italy, Australia, Singapore, Japan, France, Africa, Morocco, Egypt, to name a few —and I'd immersed myself in the different cultures and their fashion in a way that only heightened my design sensibilities. It didn't hurt that, along the way, I'd collected swatches and bought fabrics during our travels that became the foundation for my new collection.

After our expeditions, I'd come back to the United States refreshed, excited, and ready to take on the fashion world again. I'd scrapped my old designs and started anew by creating a mood board that captured the essence and vibe of my new collection. The process of creating the mood board had allowed the subconscious creative narrative to come out of my head. Then I'd used the swatches and fabrics I'd collected during my travels as inspiration for my sketches, illustrations, and pattern-making. But the creative process was not complete until I'd made patterns and handed it off to my friend and seamstress, Summer.

I liked to keep it local as opposed to sending it to the factories. It was important for me to have the human experience transferred to the garment. The creation process was exhilarating; sometimes I sewed until my fingers bled, and then I began to fit the garments on my foam mannequin that I'd named Jade.

For months, I had created over a hundred samples, but only twenty-five styles had made the show after my editing process. I smiled, remembering the hectic three weeks before the show when it had become intense. During that time, I'd had to firm up the guest list with the show producer I'd hired, which tremendously helped me. She'd not only assisted with producing the show, but she'd also handled the press and sales.

But it was the week leading up to the show that was the worst for many designers, including me. It had been filled with endless days of problem-solving all the things that could and would go wrong. I remembered all of the angst that I'd gone through as my show drew near. It was marathon time with no time to eat or sleep. Shit, I was lucky to get a damn shower in.

I couldn't believe that now it was almost time for curtains up. And after all this work, a typical show only lasted minutes.

But even with all the angst and drama I'd been through just to get here tonight, if anyone asked me, the fashion junkie, if it was worth it, they'd get a resounding, *Hell yes!*

Even despite the fact that, all day, I'd worried if the audience would understand the message—*fashion is for everyone*—of my entire collection based on these selected looks.

As the lights dimmed, the crowd hushed and the show began. I held my breath while self-doubt crept in.

I was scared to death to share my collection with the world even though I knew that my show was courageous.

Eager fashionistas perched in the front row and battled for photos as the models finally made their highly anticipated journey down the runway.

I bit my bottom lip, and I started to wonder if I'd made all the right choices.

The models were on the runway, showcasing the designs I'd worked on for so many months.

The crowd buzzed with anticipation.

The first model strutted down the runway, wearing a black dress featuring an open-knit mesh detail in metallic silver and holding up a black leather purse to her forehead that read *Sin Michaels* in gold letters to let the audience know I was a brand force to be reckoned with.

I could feel the collective sigh from my team. We just loved it so much.

The crowd buzzed with anticipation.

My favorite female R&B vocalist, Infinity, provided the soundtrack, followed by pop hits of the past half century that formed a medley on the Sin Michaels soundtrack—everything from Rihanna's "S&M" to Jay-Z's "Empire State of Mind." The lively sampling was the key to my collection. It was my love letter to diverse women and their individual style.

There was something electric in the room as the next model strutted down the runway with *Who the fuck is Sin Michaels?* etched on the back of an oversize shirt. It was these stolen moments during the show that felt the most special to me because it encapsulated the badass bad-girl DNA of my clothing line.

As the models completed their circuit of the runway and returned backstage, my team of ten dressers quickly changed them into the next look, and off they went again.

The audience pressed forward, applauded, and made sounds of oohing vend aahing. I felt breathless from excitement.

The clothing was a celebration of my life. The models, clad in head wraps with jeweled detailing, represented New York in all of its organized chaos. The collection had beading, sequins, psychedelic prints, tinsel, and more, embodying New York City's essence.

A main focus was lingerie-like lace dresses. Many were draped or tied around the body, which had that edgy Gothic yet romantic feel I was known for. To toughen up the sheer, delicate looks, I incorporated plenty of menswear-inspired suiting pieces —some structured, others done up in fluid silk and heavily adorned with metal hoops and chains, hanging pearls, and textured leather, accessorized with Swarovski crystal lunch bags etched with the letters *SM*.

Palpable excitement buzzed through the charged air.

My team and I'd stitched every single bead, sequin, and rhinestone onto my elaborate clothing by hand.

Along with a selection of menswear, the drama really came out halfway through the show when a series of couture-like looks walked the runway. There were voluminous ballgowns, modern tie-dyed feathers, cascades of fringe, impeccably layered sequins, intricate embroidery, and patchwork—each the result of a painstaking attention to detail.

Jade was among the famous faces on a stylish front row, and she caught the attention of the cameras as she shouted out, leaning forward and cheering with a lot of enthusiasm, as the rest of the audience applauded the designs parading down the catwalk.

Sculptural organza danced around the models like whimsical waves, and then came my va-va-voom blood-red asymmetric halter gown that wrapped around the model's neck in a buckle and slinked down her body with a slit across one hip.

The next model wore a tiara that read *Boss Girl* and a diamond Swarovski crystal suit—silver, slinky, and ultra-sexy with a jacket cut very low to reveal as much cleavage and collarbone as possible.

The last model who took the runway sported a tiara that read *Bossy* as she wore a strapless mini frock that featured a nude underdress covered with embellished, chain-mail-inspired detail. It was sexy and seductive, and it was paired with my favorite fuck-me red-bottomed heels.

And then the show ended all too soon. I could feel the pride in the studio. The looks, the lighting, the hair, the makeup, the nails, the girls, the styling—it all came together to tell the story of female empowerment—love, strength, and inclusion in the world—and I loved it all.

As the models took their final walk, the empowering version of the song "Run the World (Girls)" rang out, allowing the audience to soak up the final moments before it was time for me to go out on the runway to say thank you to everyone for coming and to take my bow.

I swayed over to the mirror to check my appearance. My diamond engagement ring and wedding band glinted while I adjusted my see-through blouse, which was from my collection. It flaunted my very round tummy in all its glory and also showed off a hint of cleavage. I'd teamed the blouse that featured a sheer panel down the front with black jeans and a long silver chain as well as large black-and-silver hoop earrings.

Giselle glanced down at my stilettos. "You know you're going to have to stop wearing those things once you get further along."

I frowned. "Oh, hell no. I'm rocking stilettos until they wheel me into the delivery room, and even then, I'll demand to keep them on." I waggled my eyebrows. "It'll be a very kinky delivery indeed." I blew her an air kiss, swaying past her.

The song, which championed womankind's incredible ability to get shit done, still played as I showed my supermodel prowess, taking to the catwalk, strutting and waving at the crowd while flaunting my huge baby belly in the sheer lace blouse, which left nothing to do with my bump to the imagination.

I was overwhelmed by the thunderous applause and standing ovation from what turned out to be a large group of the most influential names in the New York fashion community. All of these incredible people whom I had so much respect for were there. I hadn't imagined that sort of generosity and support until I experienced it. It was obviously a turning point in my career and definitely a great NYFW moment for me.

But it wasn't until I looked at the front row seats and saw the people who meant everything in the world to me—Cisco, Jade, Ariana, Erika, Mitch, Zuri, and Core—clapping with huge smiles on their faces that the dam of happy tears burst, and they streamed down my cheeks.

There had been a lot of bumps in the road just to get here today, and I couldn't help thinking briefly about Tabitha and if she'd have been here, celebrating my success, had circumstances been different. Not that I missed her or felt any guilt about the way Core had booted Tabitha out of New York with a little cash and a stern warning never to contact me again or come back to the city, or he'd take pleasure in giving the authorities all the evidence he'd collected about her shady dealings with her ex Vargos. And that was enough information to land her in jail for a very long time.

My world was complete now. I had friends—Cisco, Jade, Ariana, and Zuri—who loved me. My mother, Erika—along with my stepdad, Mitch—and I had built a close relationship even though it had taken months of work. And last but not least, Core, the love of my life, who loved and supported me as unconditionally as I did him.

The crowd quieted down when I started talking. "Thank you all for coming tonight. This truly means the world to me. Hugs and Sin Michaels." I blew an air kiss to Cisco, Ariana, Jade, Erika, Mitch, and Zuri and then beckoned my sexy hubby Core over to the stage.

He stood up, kissing the precious bundle in his arms—our baby—before handing him over to Erika with a, "Go to Grandma," order.

Erika clutched her grandson with a wide smile on her face as Core walked over to stand by my side, clutching my hand.

I couldn't believe how much I'd grown emotionally. In the past, I'd decided relationships were too much trouble. It was the easy way out when every relationship had been a certifiable disaster. It was like quitting before I got fired. Up to the point when I'd met Core, however, each one had been too much work for not nearly enough in return. That was never the trouble with my husband, though. Even when it seemed impossible, the end game was always worth it. With Core, every bit of work was worthwhile.

I said to the crowd in a clear, loud voice, "Tonight was a dream come true, one that was made possible by the love and support of my friends, family, and my partner and husband, Core McKay. Together, this sexy man and I have created something strong, beautiful, and precious."

I protectively placed a hand over my belly while looking over at my son cradled in Erika's arms. With Core by my side, now I truly understood what it meant to unconditionally love and be loved. Now my world was complete because he had given me a reason to trust... and love.

I was almost close to tears, just thinking about how much he meant to me. In roughly three years' time, I'd been able to open myself up to him enough to fall for him. I loved him... and that used to scare the shit out of me. Not now.

He turned me around to face him. I stared, mesmerized, as those delicious lips of his came nearer, finally settling across my mouth. He tilted his head to the side and slipped his tongue into my mouth. As soon as his tongue touched mine, I was lost, even right there on the runway. The man had no damn idea what he did to me.

Even after all these years, it was still hard for me to believe the life I now had. Every morning, I woke up by his side, and every night, I went to bed in his arms. Our relationship wasn't perfect. It was perfectly imperfect.

Damn. I've finally found a man who loves me like he means it.

He pulled out of our kiss and drawled huskily, "I love you, Sinful."

"And I love you, Core." And I did with all of my heart because, every day, he showed me with actions and words just how much he loved me.

Even though the process of opening up to Core and love hadn't been easy, I wouldn't change a damn thing. Finding the love I deserved had proven to be the best thing to happen to me in a very long time.

He kissed my fingers before saying, "Now let's go home, Mrs. McKay."

Weaving his fingers through mine, he escorted me along the runway and toward the backstage as the cacophony of the crowd's clapping, cheering, and whistling surrounded us.

~

THANK YOU FOR READING **TWISTED LIES 4!**

More Alpha goodness continues with **SHAMELESS DESIRES!**

If two dirty talking, commanding, alpha heroes stopping at nothing to claim their heroine is not your thing, you probably want to give this book a pass. But if it is your cup of tea?

...well then, buy this bad boy, you're in for a delicious treat.

Click here to read SHAMELESS DESIRES now!>

And sign up for my newsletter to find out about new books...

www.sedonavenez.com/newsletter

ABOUT THE AUTHOR

USA TODAY BESTSELLING AUTHOR SEDONA VENEZ lives in New York City with her hot ex-military hubby—hooah—and their fur babies. She loves writing sizzling, sexy intricate stories about strong but broken characters who push limits, overcome their fears and risk it all for love.

Sedona loves to connect with readers!
www.sedonavenez.com

OTHER TITLES BY SEDONA VENEZ

Aliens!

Galaxy Alien Warriors - The Box Set

Beauty and the Alien Beast

Paranormal Romance
Shifter Alphas Furever Series

Claimed by Her Two Alphas

Claimed by Her Wolf

Claimed by Her Bear

Claimed by Her Dragon

Paranormal Romance
Credence Curse Series

Breaking the Storm

When Lightning Strikes

Taming the Beast

Reason to Love

Taming the Alpha Beast - The Box Set

Werewolves!
Wolf Elite Series

Operation Wolf: Gunner
Operation Wolf: Eli
Operation Wolf: Hunter
Wolf Elite - The Box Set

Bears!
Bear Elite Series
Operation Bear

Dark Romance
Dirty Secrets Series
Twisted Lies
Twisted Lies 2
Twisted Lies 3
Twisted Lies 4
Dirty Secrets - The Box Set

Contemporary Romance (MFM Ménage)
Standalone
Shameless Desires

Billionaire Romance
Standalone
Mr. Billionaire CEO

Urban Fantasy Romance
Magic Fire Collection

EXCERPT: TAMING THE BEAST

Want to sample a new series? Check out my Credence Curse books including this book, <u>Taming the Beast</u>.

I was stark naked—again. With huge ebony breasts swaying, ass jiggling, and designer stiletto-encased feet slapping against the dewy grass, I sauntered over to the center of the clearing.

Perching myself on top of the smooth boulder—or what I now lovingly called my rock of shame—I surveyed my recurring fixation.

My heart seemed to freeze and then pound. "Damn. You're such a beautiful kitty," I whispered.

Water cascaded off the tiger's magnificent reddish-rusty coat with narrow dark-brown stripes as he prowled out of the river toward me with rippling muscles. Its chest, throat, muzzle, and the insides of its limbs were creamy with a milky-colored area above the eyes that spread onto his cheeks.

When I extended my hand, he tilted his large head down, rubbing against it with a chuff-chuff sound.

"Hello, my big kitty. I'm happy to see you again, too," I answered his greeting. My digits trailed up to the white spot present on the back of its ear.

He nudged my hand away before circling me, his fur

caressing my bare legs while I admired the prominent ruff on his head and long tail ringed with noticeable dark bands.

Warmth radiated throughout my body as his fur deliciously tickled me.

"Every dream, you bring me here to watch you swim, and I still don't know why."

My mouth fell open when a deer pranced up to the river and drank from it, completely oblivious to the tiger's presence.

The tiger stilled, waited, and then pounced. The deer didn't even have a chance to run away before the tiger's big-as-saucers paws latched on to its hindquarters, bringing down the deer. The tiger gripped its neck, delivering a crushing bite to its prey. The deer stopped thrashing.

My fingers touched my parted lips before I closed them. "Holy shit."

This was a new addition to my nightly dreams. He'd never killed game before.

Wasting no time, the tiger dragged its dinner toward me, laying the carcass at my feet like an offering.

I gave him a weak half smile, trying desperately not to hurl at the sight of the dead deer. "Thank you, kitty, but it's a little . . . rare for me."

He flicked his tail, making a chuff-chuff sound, before his limbs quivered, shifted, and morphed into a very naked tall, muscular human.

"Elijah?" I stammered.

This couldn't be right. Animals didn't transform into humans, especially not into a man I was crushing on hard in real life.

"Yes, my Hope," he uttered in a dark, masculine voice.

Electricity sparked in my body as my eyes perused his mouthwatering splendor. His short, thick black hair had hints of gold, and his beard was well groomed. But it was his stunning but strange amber eyes with gold flecks that always made my stomach flip-flop, like a fish out of water. His eyes were the windows to his soul. They bored into me with an intensity that made my sex clench.

"Damn. Even in my dream . . . you're fucking splendid," I declared. My eyes trailed down his hard body to his engorged, perfect shaft standing at attention.

He clutched my face between his enormous, calloused hands. "Eyes up here, darling." His face dissolved into an exquisite grin. "Unless you're finally ready to get on all fours for your big kitty?" His hands dropped away and grabbed me around the waist, yanking me against his naked body.

"My, you're such a dirty pussycat, and I love it." I licked his bottom lip.

"So that's a yes." It was a statement, not a question.

"Baby, I'll do whatever you want . . . however you want. But only if you promise to lick all my cream, like a good kitty."

We stared at each other with my legs straddling one of his rock-solid thighs.

"There's nothing good about me, darling, but I can promise to lick you to the very last drop." His voice was thick with emotion. "Just say when, my beautiful mate."

EXCERPT: CLAIMED BY HER TWO ALPHAS

Want to sample a new series? Check out my Shifter Alphas Furever books including this book, <u>Claimed by Her Two Alphas</u>.

In the two weeks since that conversation with Peyton, one snippet of that bizarre conversation kept running through my head. These guys were looking for their perfect *mate*. Not mates, plural. Not one guy wanting one and the other guy wanting... something else. Both guys were looking for the same thing, and according to Alex, that thing was me. But I was only one woman and even if I'd gotten past the weirdness of two guys wanting to share one blind date, I still hadn't wrapped my head around how I could be the perfect mate for both of them.

Yet here I was, trying to figure out how I was going to find not just one, but two blind dates in a crowded bar. I should have backed out.

No. You shouldn't have. It's not going to kill you to do this. If it back-fires, you can tell Peyton "I told you so."

At least I should have figured out some way to recognize these guys, like carrying a rose or wearing a bow in my hair. Or maybe a name tag, so instead of standing in the crowd turning in useless circles, I could find these guys. I made another sweep of the room.

You're overthinking...just take a breath and let go.

I closed my eyes, wavering slightly in my heels, did my best imitation of someone poised and collected, and concentrated on my breathing. Then I opened my eyes. The crowd parted and there he was. Or there *some* guy was, some really handsome guy.

He was sitting at the bar, and he was looking right at me. For a split second I thought I'd made him up, or maybe I'd halluci-nated him out of desperation. Even sitting down, he was big and broad-shouldered, taking up more physical space than anyone around him. Or maybe he just looked like he was. He should have been imposing, scary, but he radiated an all-American boy kind of feel, the hunky guy-next-door who helped you with your groceries or changed the flat on your car. *A nice, safe guy.*

Until I got to his eyes. Blue. Even in the dim light of the bar, I could tell they were blue. The all-American hunk had just turned the tiniest bit dangerous. There was a fire in those eyes that woke up something deep and primal, something I'd thought didn't exist in me. Or at least I'd never experienced it. I wouldn't go as far as calling it love at first sight; lust at first sight, maybe. Whatever it was, it was pretty amazing.

I really wanted to take a step forward, but I was rooted in place. His eyes held mine, never looking away, and it was like a magnet, drawing me closer. Something held me back though.

But wait...what about my date? Just because this guy likes looking at me...and I like looking at him...

I turned away, the act of breaking away from his gaze doing nothing to lessen the heat that had built up inside me. I was supposed to be here looking for my mystery men, not falling for the first guy who caught my eye.

Turn around...what if it's him?

That thought came out of the blue. And for once, I listened to the voice in my head and did a slow turn. The guy was smiling at me, and something inside me simultaneously clenched and loosened up. It was a physical sensation, a thud deep and low, and I took a step back, shocked by my body's reaction.

When he stood, I saw just how tall he was, well over six feet. He cut easily through the crowd toward me with a grace that belied his size. He stopped just in front of me, and I looked up into those piercing blue eyes.

"Hi, Sadie. I'm Dane. Dane Hastings."

I stared. Just plain unattractively, open-mouthed, deer-in-headlights stared at this amazing specimen, who'd just told me he was one half of my blind date. Saints preserve me, maybe I'd gotten lucky. Then it hit me.

Where the hell was the other guy?

www.ingramcontent.com/pod-product-compliance
Lightning Source LLC
Chambersburg PA
CBHW071746190726
48292CB00003B/887